CAPTAIN SKIDMARK

DANCES *with* DESTINY

CAPTAIN SKIDMARK DANCES with DESTINY

JENNIFER A. IRWIN

Charlesbridge

Published by Charlesbridge
9 Galen Street
Watertown, MA 02472
(617) 926-0329
www.charlesbridge.com

Library of Congress Cataloging-in-Publication Data
Names: Irwin, Jennifer A., 1973– author.
Title: Captain Skidmark dances with destiny / by Jennifer A. Irwin.
Description: Watertown, MA: Charlesbridge Publishing, [2023] | Audience:
    Ages 10 and up. | Audience: Grades 4–8. | Summary: "Thirteen-year-
    old Will is generally miserable but finds solace at dance school, and
    then Will's seventeen-year-old hockey-star cousin, Alex, moves in, and
    Will and Alex learn a lot about each other and their relationships with
    their fathers."—Provided by publisher.
Identifiers: LCCN 2021053666 (print) | LCCN 2021053667 (ebook) |
    ISBN 9781623542542 (hardcover) | ISBN 9781632898203 (ebook)
Subjects: LCSH: Cousins—Juvenile fiction. | Fathers and sons—Juvenile
    fiction. | Bullying—Juvenile fiction. | Interpersonal relations—
    Juvenile fiction. | Hockey stories. | Dance—Juvenile fiction. |
    Ontario—Juvenile fiction. | CYAC: Cousins—Fiction. | Fathers and
    sons—Fiction. | Bullying—Fiction. | Interpersonal relations—
    Fiction. | Hockey—Fiction. | Dance—Fiction. | Ontario—Fiction.
Classification: LCC PZ7.1.I787 Cap 2023 (print) | LCC PZ7.1.I787 (ebook) |
    DDC 813.6 [Fic] —dc23/eng/20211130
LC record available at https://lccn.loc.gov/2021053666
LC ebook record available at https://lccn.loc.gov/2021053667

Printed in the United States of America
(hc) 10 9 8 7 6 5 4 3 2 1

Illustrations drawn digitally in iPad Pro with Clip Studio Paint
Text type set in New Century Schoolbook © Adobe Systems Incorporated
Printed by Maple Press in York, Pennsylvania, USA
Production supervision by Jennifer Most Delaney
Designed by Cathleen Schaad

To Richard, my heart.

And to Charlie and Sam, my world.

Find me here.

CHAPTER ONE

It was game two of the bantam double-B regular hockey season, and I was going to murder Artie Kavanaugh. He was sitting next to me on the bench with his big fat face and his baked bean teeth and his single-digit IQ.

"Hey, loser," he said.

I ignored him like I always did, and he slashed the top of my foot with his hockey stick, which hurt like a mother.

"I said, 'Hey, loser!' You hear me?"

"My name's not loser."

How many times had I said that, or something like it, to Artie in the last two months? Fifty times? A hundred?

My name's not loser.

My name's not dork.

My name's not twerp, dweeb, dillhole, or fart-knocker.

"Oh, I'm sorry," Artie said, taking a swig from his water bottle. "I meant freakshow."

Freakshow was new. I was almost impressed.

"What do you want?" I asked, staring out at the

crowd on the other side of the rink. My parents were there in their usual spot, watching the game. Mom was sipping on coffee and chatting with the lady sitting next to her, but when she saw me looking over, she waved excitedly. Dad wasn't talking to anyone. He was frowning and had his arms crossed over his chest.

"What do I want?" Artie asked. He looked up at the rafters as he pondered the question. "I want what I always want. I want to know why you're on this team."

His hockey gear reeked so bad I could almost see black cartoon stink lines coming off him, and I tried to shift over so I could breathe clean air. Unfortunately I was already squashed into the side of the box and there was nowhere to go.

"Seriously," he continued, leaning into me. "You can't skate. You can't shoot. You're built like a six-year-old girl. When was the last time you went into a corner? When was the last time you even scored?"

I had never scored, actually. Not in the nine years I'd been playing hockey. But I wasn't about to tell him that.

When I didn't say anything, he slashed me again.

"Sorry," he said when I cried out. "My stick slipped." Then he smiled at me, and I had to fight the urge to barf, not just from the searing pain in my foot but also from his breath, which smelled like a can of deep-fried buttholes.

"I just don't get it, freakshow," he said. "I mean,

you're such a sad little duster. I can't figure out why you even bother putting on skates."

I glanced over at my father again, who was sitting there looking miserable. It was already the third period, and I hadn't been on the ice yet. For a guy like my dad, having me for a son must have been pure torture.

"I'm sorry," I said quietly.

I wasn't actually talking to Artie, but he leaned closer anyway.

"What?" he asked. "What did you say, you little dork?"

I turned to him. "I said, 'I'm sorry.'"

"Yeah," Artie said, grinning. "You are." Then he took a big swig from his bottle and spit a mouthful of Gatorade in my face.

I ripped off my helmet and started flushing my eyes with water, writhing like someone had thrown a vat of acid at me. It's possible I was overreacting, but you had to know Artie. The dude never brushed his teeth. Plus he was always belching and vurping and hocking up loogies. And once someone dared him to finish off a half-eaten hot dog he'd picked out of the trash, and he totally did it. There was no limit to the diseases that were most likely inhabiting his backwash. I could almost feel them scorching my retinas.

My coach, unfortunately, was not sympathetic.

"Quit fooling around, Stone!" he hollered. But then instead of turning back to the game and ignoring me like he usually did, he looked me over warily.

"All right," he sighed. "We're up by five points. Might as well get out there and see if you can do . . . *something*."

Whoa. Ice time. That was unexpected. And terrifying. I mean, the only reason I was on the team at all was because my dad had pulled strings to get me there. Even so, I'd spent way more time warming the bench than I'd actually spent in games. It's like that when you're the worst player in the entire history of hockey.

But fortune favors the bold, as my mom always says. So I jammed my helmet on my head and crouched down to fumble blindly for my stick, which Artie had managed to kick under the bench.

"Now, Stone!" Coach yelled, while Artie guffawed like an idiot. Even though I hated hockey, at that moment I would have sacrificed my left nut for the chops to score just one goal. Then I could skate to the box, grab Artie by the mask, and shout "Suck it!" right in his big ugly mug.

Coach opened the door and I waddled over, but the second I stepped on the ice, I fell flat on my face.

"For god's sake, Stone! Your skate guards!"

Crap.

I rolled over and looked up at Coach. He was like a rabid pelican with his red face and his beady black eyes and his fat neck that was all puffed out over his collar. He looked close to climbing over the

4

bench and giving me a beatdown, so I ripped off my guards and threw them over the boards as fast as I could.

It took me another minute to climb to my feet, and then I skated in a wobbly circle, trying to figure out where the puck was while Artie and the rest of the guys laughed themselves unconscious on the bench.

And then, all of a sudden, there it was. Someone on the other team missed the pass, and the puck came sliding down the ice toward me. It actually almost hit my stick. It was the closest I'd come to touching a game puck in my life, and I don't know whether it was because of Artie or because I was sick of Coach and his angry pelican neck, but for once I didn't even think about what I was doing. I just put my head down and went for it.

I was flying. I couldn't see anything but the puck. I couldn't hear anything but the sound of my heart beating in my ears. I was tearing up the ice, weaving in and out between players who were practically throwing themselves in the way to stop me. But it didn't matter because this time, I was on fire. This time, the fartknocker was Too. Darn. Fast.

Even the goalie was intimidated. When I got to the net, I could see his eyes were wide behind his mask, and I swear I could hear him saying "Will, no! Don't do it! Don't do it!" and I was all like, "Oh, yeah. That's right. Be very afraid."

I deked. I shot. And then it happened.

I scored a goal.

I actually scored a goal.

Suddenly I was overcome with the kind of joy I imagined only taller and more athletically inclined people were able to experience. I threw myself around the ice, pumping my fist like I'd just won the Stanley Cup, and it wasn't until I started looking around for another player to high-five that I realized something was wrong.

I glanced over at the goalie. He'd ripped off his helmet and was pointing at his face, and for a second I thought, "Why the heck is Zak playing for the other team?" But when he screamed, "We're on the same team, you moron!" I realized my mistake.

If I hadn't been so busy flushing Artie's vile sputum from my eyes, I would've noticed the period had ended and the goalies had switched ends. If I hadn't been so amped to actually shoot a puck, I might have realized the players who were all over me on the ice were actually my teammates and that I'd scored the only goal of my entire hockey career on my own net.

I covered my face with my hands and dropped to my knees right there on the blue line. I'm not sure how long I stayed like that—it felt like hours— but when I looked up, I saw that all the people in the stands were laughing at me. All of them, their big mouths wide open, their eyes squinched tight, fingers pointing.

Then I scanned the crowd and my eyes landed on my parents. My mom had both hands clamped over her mouth like she'd witnessed a heinous train wreck. Which, let's face it, she basically had. Dad sat there watching me, while spectators clapped him on the shoulder as if congratulating him for having an idiot for a son. The look on his face was a mixture of disappointment and something even worse.

Embarrassment.

I had embarrassed my father.

I pulled myself up and skated to the boards, barely able to lift my head. But instead of moving toward the bench, I left the ice completely, stripping down as I walked. My helmet went bouncing down the rubber walkway; my gloves hit the wall with two thuds and slid to the floor. I stopped at the exit to untie my skates, and I kicked them into a corner. Then I pushed open the door and stepped out into the night.

Freakshow had left the building.

CHAPTER TWO

Okay, so here's some things you should know.

Yes, I suck at hockey. I am, in fact, epically tragic at any activity involving running, jumping, or precision hand-eye coordination. I'm also the shortest kid in my class by at least six inches, and that includes the girls. And every third week, I get this recurring zit on my chin that is so huge it looks like I'm starting to grow another head.

I'm also failing math.

I'm not completely useless, though. In fact, there's a bunch of things most people don't even know about that I actually do quite well. I'm excellent at Scrabble, for example. I can also recite the alphabet in six seconds—*backward*. And if I drink enough apple juice in one sitting, I can write my entire first name in the snow. That's a pretty impressive display of bladder control, if you ask me, especially considering my full name is William. I'm hoping by the time I'm fourteen I'll have what it takes to dot the *i*'s.

So.

Maybe I am a loser.

No one thought so at my old school, though. At my old school I wasn't, like, Mr. Popular, but I was generally accepted by everyone, and even the worst, most socially deviant bullies in my class pretty much left me alone. They didn't trip me or steal my lunch or pin me down so they could dangle a long chain of spit in my face until I almost barfed. And they certainly would have never dreamed of drawing a huge penis on my locker door and then plastering it with an array of feminine hygiene products.

Not at my old school.

But a few short months ago, my dad, who up until that point was just a regular high school English teacher, was offered a position as principal at Boundary Street Middle School. Suddenly, and without warning, we had to move to Evanston, Ontario, or the Armpit of the Universe, as I like to call it. Ever since then, my life has taken a most righteous turn toward the cruel and unusual.

It's hard enough being the new kid. It's way harder being the son of the new principal, especially when said new principal is replacing an older, much-beloved principal who just happened to suffer from a fatal heart attack while locked in an outdoor toilet during Evanston's Fort Town Festival. (And can I just add for the record that biting it while you're taking a crunch in a Port-A-Crapper is like top three on my list of the world's worst ways to die.)

Anyone else coming into that principal job might have understood that given the circumstances, it would be best to keep a low profile, at least at first, but there's never been anything low profile about my dad. He's definitely not your usual principal type with a potbelly and a comb-over, that's for sure. He played hockey for the Montreal Canadiens for one season before he blew out his knee and had to quit. He's super tough and really tall, and even though he's pushing fifty, he's still totally ripped. He's the only guy I know his age who actually has a six-pack.

To match his tough looks, he has a tough motto: No Mercy. Which means the minute he stepped through the doors of the middle school, he started running the place like a military unit. He instituted a demerit system, and in addition to the major offenses—like talking back to a teacher or skipping school—people started getting infractions for little things like walking around with their shirts untucked or having their phones out. All of a sudden, students were getting regular detentions and suspensions, and sometimes *expulsions*. They started referring to my father as "Mad Dog Stone."

And that was fine for him, I suppose, since he had all the muscle. It's not so great, though, if you're someone like me and are forced to spend your days surrounded by angry teenagers who are nursing serious revenge fantasies and begging for someone to take them out on.

From the first day of class, it was like every student in the school grew a set of infrared Terminator eyeballs—you know, the ones that generate computer stats down one side about whatever you happen to be looking at.

As soon as they scoped me out, I'm sure this is what they saw:

Object: Will Stone
Origin: son of Mad Dog Stone, the most hated man at Boundary Street Middle School
Age: 13
Height: five-foot-nothing
Weight: 100 lbs
Risk: object is of no threat; he is powerless, pathetic, and couldn't play hockey if he was paid good money to do it
Mission: KILL! KILL! KILL!

You might be thinking that with my father as principal, most bullies would make a point to avoid me, but you couldn't be more wrong about that. Once they realized there was nothing they could do to me that would make me tell on them, I was totally fair game.

And I wouldn't tell, no matter what. Not even under direct examination by my father, which happened from time to time.

Like the Tuesday following the game that ruined my already crappy life, for example.

My dad sent a message to one of my teachers that I was to see him the minute school ended. He didn't come to tell me himself, most likely because he'd barely spoken to me since the night of the game except to say on the drive home, "That equipment is expensive. You shouldn't leave it lying around."

He came into his office, where I'd been waiting, and shut the door, which was never a good sign.

"Good afternoon," he said.

"Good afternoon," I said, swallowing.

He sat down at his desk and shuffled some papers around, and then he cleared his throat.

"So Jeff and Carl said they found you in the cleaning supply cupboard again this morning," he said. He didn't look directly at me while he talked. Instead he seemed to be focusing on the area just above my head. "Anything you want to tell me about that?"

"No," I said. Except yes, I actually did. I wanted to tell him that Jeff and Carl were a couple of turd burglars for ratting me out. I mean, if you can't trust two middle-aged school janitors to keep your secrets for you, then who can you trust?

Dad sighed through his nose, and then he picked up a folder off his desk and held it in his gigantic hands—hands that could crush my tiny skull like a walnut.

"You've been late for a lot of your classes this month," he said, looking down at what I presumed was my file. Nice to know I was only four months into grade eight, and I already had a "file."

I nodded. "Yes, that's true."

"And according to Mr. Proctor, you are, at this present time, flunking math."

At this present time, yes, I was sure I was. If the 12 percent I'd recently received on a factoring test was any indication. I nodded again.

He put the file down and folded his hands on top of it. "This isn't like you, Will. You've always done well academically. So I'm going to ask you again. Is there something going on here I should know about?"

Yes, I thought. *But if I tell you I don't fit in at this stupid school, you'll decide I'm an even bigger loser than I already am. Or worse, you'll try to help me somehow. Either way, I'm not interested.*

I tried to look at him, but it was like staring at the sun, so I glanced down at my lap instead.

"I'm still adjusting? I think? To school? And, uh, classes?"

He sighed again. Silence. And then finally he said, "Will, if you need help, you have to tell me."

"No, sir. I'm good. It's all under control." I smiled weakly at him.

But he didn't smile back. He regarded me a second longer, and then he shook his head and turned away. "All right, have it your way," he said.

Look. I know what you're thinking. Clearly what was going on between me and my dad was

13

less like a father/son interaction and more like an exasperated-bank-manager-dealing-with-an-unruly-client kind of thing. And aside from the bank part, you would mostly be right. Which is why, when he plunked his briefcase down on his desk and began filling it with files, I figured I was dismissed and got up to leave.

"Just a second, Will," he said, without looking over. "The other reason I called you down this afternoon is to let you know we have a guest coming to stay for a while. He might even be there when we get home."

I sank back in my seat. "Is it Poppy?" I asked, cringing.

Poppy was my dad's dad. He lived in a seniors' residence across town, and I didn't like him very much. He smoked a lot and had creepy long fingernails that were orange from nicotine. He was always criticizing my dad, and when my parents weren't around, he called me a peckerhead.

"No, not Poppy," Dad said. "Your cousin, Alex, from Montreal. Uncle Eric's son."

Uncle Eric, my dad's younger brother, was a lawyer, and he lived with my aunt and my cousin in a big house in Montreal we'd never been invited to. According to my mom, there was some kind of falling out between Dad and Poppy and Uncle Eric years ago before I was born, which was probably why the only time we heard from them was when they sent us a card at Christmas.

"Alex is seventeen now," Dad continued. "I enrolled him up at the high school."

"But—why is he coming?"

Dad sighed impatiently. "It's not important," he said. "What's important is that you make him feel comfortable and help out your mom when she asks."

Then he stopped and gave me a stern look, like he was expecting me to argue with him. Which was ridiculous because the only thing more enjoyable or productive than arguing with my dad would be to, like, slam a car door on my hand or poke my eyes out with a radioactive toilet brush.

But mostly I didn't argue with him because I was absolutely overjoyed.

Alex was coming to live with us! For an indefinite period of time! Even though I didn't have the first clue who he was, it was still the best news of my life, for two really big reasons.

Reason number one: The cool factor. Alex was from Montreal, which, compared to Evanston, was about as exotic as you could get without actually boarding a plane. It was the home of poutine and jazz festivals, and from what I'd heard, beautiful Quebecois women who smoked cigarettes in long holders and didn't wear bras. And Alex had lived there his whole life! With his rich parents, in a great big house that probably had servants and everything! Once everyone found out about that, he would literally be the most popular guy in Evanston. And maybe, since I was his cousin, people would consider me awesome by association, and they'd stop looking at me like I was a turd stuck to the bottom of their shoe.

Reason number two: Defense. The chances that Alex would have a strong sense of family loyalty and would be willing to kick ass on my behalf were slim. Still, just knowing I had a seventeen-year-old cousin hanging around might make Artie and his buddy Wayne think twice before they messed with me. A guy could hope, anyway.

Dad cleared his throat.

"Did you hear what I said, Will?" he asked. "I'm expecting your full cooperation. I mean it."

"Of course," I said.

Dad's face relaxed, and he nodded.

"All right then," he said.

He cleared his throat again. Then he reached out and gave me a pat on my head that was so awkward, I was embarrassed for both of us.

It didn't really matter, though. Alex was on his way, and that meant that maybe things were finally looking up. Maybe, just maybe, my days of hiding out in the cleaning-supply closet before class were finally coming to an end.

CHAPTER THREE

The minute I stepped through the front door, my mom pushed a pair of rubber gloves and a toilet brush into my hands.

"You have to help me," she said. "Alex is coming, and I haven't cleaned the bathrooms since Sunday!"

Seeing as it was only Tuesday, I didn't feel particularly concerned, especially since even on her worst week, my mom kept the bathrooms so clean you could eat off the floor if you were into that kind of thing. Still, I humored her—not only because I was suddenly in the best mood I'd been in in months but also because, when it comes to my mom, it's hard to say no, even when she's recruiting me for toilet duty.

You have to understand, I have the best mother in the world. She's a kindergarten teacher, which right away gives you an idea of the super gentle, let's-make-a-craft-and-then-take-a-nap-on-our-mats vibe she rocks. Honestly, she's so sweet and warm that if you opened her up, you wouldn't find regular human parts—you'd find stuff like toasted marshmallows and freshly baked bread.

That's why, instead of complaining, I took the toilet brush out of her hand.

"It's taken care of, Mom," I said.

"Thank you," she said. She kissed me on my forehead and then stepped back to look at me. I cringed, waiting for it.

"You look pale," she said. "Are you feeling okay?"

I sighed. "I'm fine."

She frowned at me. "Did you sleep well last night? You've got black circles under your eyes."

"I got my usual eight hours, Mom. No worries."

She stepped a little closer and glanced over her shoulder like someone else might be listening.

"Did you poop today?" she asked in a low voice.

"God, Mom!"

Like I said, my mother is an amazing woman, but she tends to hover a little more than she should. I suspect a lot of her worrying comes from what she went through with my brother. He was born three years before me, but he died when he was six months old from something called crib death, which apparently happens when healthy babies go to sleep and just never wake up. No one knows why it happens, and there's no way of telling if or when it's going to happen either. It just does, and it's what happened to my big brother.

It pretty much devastated my parents, so they never talk about him. And I mean never. I'm not sure I would have found out about him at all except that one day when I was eight or so, I walked into my parents' bedroom and found my mom sitting on the edge of the bed crying. But not just crying. Sobbing.

Man, I think it would have been easier to watch someone punch a puppy than to see my mom that upset. It totally freaked me out. But instead of comforting her like a good son would, I stepped back into the hallway and shut the door until I could see her through a small crack.

She was holding something to her face that looked like a little blue hat, the kind babies wear when they come home from the hospital. I figured it was one of my old ones and that she was upset I was growing up and wasn't a baby anymore. She gets like that sometimes.

But then my dad came out of the bathroom. He must have had a shower, because he was in a towel, and I prayed he wouldn't start getting dressed in front of me, because that would have totally put me over the edge. The last thing I needed was to see my mom cry *and* to get a shot of my dad's naked butt while he was bent over putting on underwear.

I didn't have to worry, though, because when he saw her crying, he stopped in his tracks.

"What's wrong?" he asked.

She looked up at him. "I can't see his face anymore, Paul," she said. She was crying so hard she could barely get the words out. "I can't remember what he smelled like."

And I was like, *What the eff? I'm right here!*

My dad put his arms around her and rocked her.

"I know," he said. "Even after all this time, I still can't believe he's gone."

He didn't cry, but his face looked more grim than usual. He murmured something else to her I couldn't make out, and she was holding on to him so tightly I could see her white knuckles even from where I was standing.

They stayed like that forever, and I didn't know what to do. Plus I was still really worried about that towel. So I went to my room, lay down on my bed, and tried to forget about it.

A few weeks later, Poppy was over for a visit. He and I were sitting on the front porch while my mom was inside fixing lunch. Dad had disappeared into the garage, no doubt hiding so he could avoid listening to Poppy lecture him for the kajillionth time about how he blew it in the NHL.

As I sat there with Poppy, it occurred to me that even though he was the last person on earth I'd want to ask about family secrets, he was, like, the only person I *could* ask who might know what was going on. So against my better judgment, I took a deep breath and turned to him.

"Ah, Poppy?" I said in a low voice. "I was wondering if I could ask you about something? Something kind of confidential?"

Poppy was a small man, way smaller than my dad, and his face was tanned and shrunken, like those dried-up apple dolls you can buy at craft fairs. He was so thin, he looked like he was made out of leather and sawdust. Plus he had tufts of hair the size of cotton balls growing out of his ears. I didn't even know you could grow hair in your ears, but it most likely explained why he hollered everything he said.

"Poppy?" I repeated.

He turned and regarded me for a moment. Then he took a slow drag off his cigarette and blew a cloud of smoke in my face.

"Jesus, that's an ugly haircut," he growled. "Did your mom put a bowl on your head and just cut around it?"

I was still hacking on his secondhand smoke, so it took me a second to answer.

"Mom doesn't cut my hair." I coughed. "She takes me to her hairdresser."

"Her *hairdresser*? What are you? A girl?"

"Ah, no—"

"You know, it doesn't take a genius to cut hair. I'm pretty sure you could spend your childhood eating paint chips and still manage to give someone a decent cut. Still, the last time I went to Supercuts, they damn near scalped me."

He took another drag from his cigarette and pointed an orange-stained finger at me.

"Which only proves that when real men want a good haircut, they go to the *barber*," he said. "Stanley's down on King Street. Those are my kind of guys. The rest are a bunch of peckerheads."

While I made a mental note to never step foot in Stanley's barbershop if my life depended on it,

Poppy picked up his glass of whiskey, muttered something about how only pansies drink single malt, and took a sip. It didn't seem to bother him that it was only ten thirty in the morning.

Now if I had been smart, I would have ended the conversation right then and there. I would have jumped off the porch and run as fast as my legs would carry me. But like the idiot I was, I stuck around and tried again.

"Anyhoo," I said, "I was wondering if I could, you know, ask you about something. Something important."

"Well, spit it out!" he growled at me. "I'm tired of watching you squirm around like you've got a platoon of army ants marching up your butt."

"Uh, okay," I said. "I, uh, was just wondering if Mom had another baby?" I looked over my shoulder in case Mom or Dad had decided to return. "One that's not, you know, with us currently?"

Poppy squinted at me. "Who? Gordie? What about him?"

It felt like someone had poured ice water down my spine. My arms broke out in goose bumps. I cleared my throat again, but my voice still came out wobbly and high.

"Well, my parents don't talk much about him, and I—"

"Why would they? It broke their hearts when he died. Especially your father's. The kid looked just like him."

For the record, I do not look like my father. He is tall and handsome, with dark hair and brown eyes. I am short and blond and blue-eyed like my mom, and at least according to Poppy, I have "quite the honker" on me.

But this baby, Gordie, had looked like my dad. Just hearing that made me feel like someone had reached into my chest and squeezed my heart until it popped.

"Do you know anything else about him? About Gordie, I mean?" I asked once I'd gotten myself together.

"What do you mean, do I know anything else? I was the kid's grandfather, for Christ's sake. I know everything there is to know."

And then, right there on the porch, Poppy told me the whole story: I'd had a big brother. He was born three years before me, and he died when he was six months old.

A brother.

I'd had a *brother*.

I imagine most people would feel sad to hear that kind of news, but I wasn't sad. I was angry. Life would have been better in a thousand different ways if I'd had a big brother. You know, someone to teach me all the things big brothers are supposed to teach little brothers, like how to ride a bike or how to skip stones across a lake or how to adjust your nuts in public without anyone noticing.

Maybe if my brother had lived, I would have turned out to be cooler or more athletic or just a radically improved version of myself. Because I would have had someone to talk to who could help me figure things out.

Maybe if my brother had lived, I would have had someone who understood what it felt like to grow up in my house and be my father's son.

In the end, that's probably the real reason I was happy Alex was coming. Because he could have been a total dork, or a geek, or even, like, some scrawny dude with zits and poor self-esteem. It wouldn't have really mattered much to me. I just needed someone to be on *my* team for a change.

CHAPTER FOUR

Alex showed up at six-fifteen that night on the dot.

And he wasn't scrawny.

He had shoulders like roof beams, and he practically had to duck when he came through our front door. Like, forget seventeen—he had the body of a twenty-year-old, at least. He had the face of someone older too—a square-cut jaw that had actual stubble on it and dark, manly eyebrows that cut across his face in a severe way. He looked like a freaking movie star, or he would have if he had smiled.

He didn't, though, not even when my dad greeted him. He just nodded and then looked past us down the hall while he ground his fist into the palm of his other hand. Truly, there was something a little Old West about him; he had that flinty, gritted-teeth look of someone who's been living so tough they're completely unfamiliar with the finer aspects of social courtesy. If he had spit on our floor and asked me for a chaw of tobaccy, I would not have been at all surprised.

Mom came down the hall to greet him, wiping her hands on her apron. She had just baked a pie, and now she had a roast in the oven, so our house basically smelled like every happy memory of my childhood.

"My goodness, Alex," she said, smiling up at him. "I haven't seen you since you were a baby! You've gotten so handsome!"

Alex didn't say anything, but his lips twitched into what I supposed was a smile. Mom held her arms up to hug him, but since she's roughly the size and shape of a hobbit, he had to oblige her by stooping down so she could make contact.

When she finally let go of him, she turned to smile at me.

"And this is your cousin, Will," she said.

Alex shifted his eyes in my direction and lifted his chin at me.

"It's nice to meet you," I said. I would have offered him my hand to shake, but I was a little worried he'd rip my arm off at the shoulder.

"Alex is going to play hockey with the triple-A team for the rest of the season," Dad said.

"Oh," I said weakly. "That's great."

Aw, man. Someone, at some time, must have mentioned that Alex was a hockey player, but I'd completely forgotten about it. My best-friend daydream was starting to circle the bowl.

We stood there, the four of us, looking at each other. Finally Mom turned to me.

"Why don't you give your cousin a hand taking his things up to his new room," she said.

"Sure," I said.

I smiled at Alex, but he looked away. So I grabbed his knapsack and one of the smaller suitcases, and he took two bags roughly the size of our dining room table, and we started hauling them up the stairs.

When we got to his door, we set his stuff down. He saw the sign I'd made with blue marker that said ALEX'S ROOM! I'd tacked it on the door in an admittedly lame kind of welcome-to-the-neighborhood-slash-please-like-me-please gesture of friendship and goodwill.

"I made that," I said, smiling feebly at him. "You know, so you'd know which room was yours and everything."

"Oh yeah?" he said gruffly. "Thanks."

Something told me he was not at all thankful, especially when he ripped it off the door and crumpled it up into a ball. Then he tossed it on the floor and put his hands on his hips.

"So what's there to do in this craphole town, anyway?" Except he didn't say *crap*, if you know what I mean.

I scrambled. There is literally nothing to do in Evanston. Like, nothing. There's no movie theater or bowling alley, and if you want to play tennis or basketball, there's no YMCA or anything. I was pretty sure Alex wouldn't be interested in sitting on the couch and watching PBS with my mom, which is what I generally did on Saturday nights, so I racked my brain for other activities that might be of interest.

"Uh," I stuttered, "there's a curling club."

Alex didn't say anything. He just narrowed his eyes and looked at me like I'd spoken to him in Klingon. I could feel myself starting to sweat.

"You could join 4-H," I tried. "I imagine a guy like you probably has all kinds of experience with livestock—ha, ha."

Alex's expression turned into full-fledged stink eye. He picked up his suitcases and started kicking the stuff he couldn't carry into his room.

I was desperate.

"I heard they have a teen dance in the basement of the Our Lady of Guadalupe Church every once in a while," I called after him. "It's free! All you have to do to get in is bring a can of food for the poor and sign a purity contract."

He yanked his knapsack out of my hands and threw it on the bed. He looked ready to kill me. He even made a fist.

"Dancing is for losers, twerp," he growled, and he slammed the door in my face.

And just like that, the bromance was over.

CHAPTER FIVE

"So what's the deal with your cousin?" Safi asked.

It was the following Tuesday, and Safi and I were eating our lunches in the photo-developing lab. It was a five-foot-by-five-foot space next to the boiler room that had been empty since Mr. Mazzella, the photography club supervisor, had his nervous breakdown the year before. Safi had managed to jimmy the lock, and we were cramped together on the floor, surrounded by gallon jugs of stop bath and about a million dust bunnies.

"I hate him," I said. "Deeply and profoundly."

"Homicidally?" Safi asked.

"Almost," I said. "Like, I wouldn't mind killing him, but I'd never do it because I'm too afraid of going to prison."

"Speaking of prison," Safi said. "Did you know that the Corcoran State Prison in California has its own dairy farm? The inmates work on it, and they supply milk to every prisoner in the state! How awesome is that?"

"So cool." I sighed.

Mike Safi was what you'd call a friend of

necessity, which is to say that, given better circumstances, I probably wouldn't have chosen him as my regular hang. He lived on a dairy farm on the outskirts of town, which wasn't a big deal— Evanston was part of the agricultural belt, and basically one out of every six kids at our school was a farm kid. The problem was, Safi took it to a whole other level. Like, if John Deere had a baby with a dairy princess, and that baby was raised in a barn by a tractor and a herd of cows, it still wouldn't have been as amped to be a farmer as Safi was.

He wore plaid shirts and vests and cowboy boots to school every day, as well as a belt buckle with a picture of a Holstein cow on it that said HANGING WITH MY HEIFERS. For a while he even wore a ten-gallon hat he claimed once belonged to a descendant of Wild Bill Hickok, until Artie ripped it off his head and showed everybody its MADE IN CHINA tag. Then he filled it to the brim with gravel and dog crap, and Safi had to throw it out.

Between being the smallest kid in the grade (next to me) and coming to school every day dressed like Woody from *Toy Story*, Safi had experienced some serious blowback from Artie and his friends. In fact, the last four months had turned him into a nervous wreck, and I was willing to bet that if someone farted loud enough, poor Safi would have jumped ten feet in the air— he was wound that tight.

"Well, if I ever murder my cousin," I said, "I'll make sure to do it in California."

"Is he really that bad?"

"Yes!" I said.

"What's so bad about him?"

"Well for one thing, he's, like, a total slob."

He was beyond a slob, actually. It had only been a week since he'd arrived at our house, and already Alex had left his clothes and books all over every available surface and covered our previously spotless bathroom vanity with his contacts container and contacts solution and razors and deodorants and aftershaves and brushes. He filled our sink with teeny tiny black beard hair that got stuck on the soap, which was not only disgusting but also a daily reminder that I still didn't have anything worth shaving yet. And in the morning, while Mom was downstairs making breakfast, he thought nothing of strutting naked out of the bathroom and into his bedroom, totally flaunting his man tackle and giving me a mental image I would have paid good money to have scrubbed from my memory with a big wire brush.

"Plus he eats constantly," I said. "Like, I've never seen anyone consume so much food in one sitting."

"For real?" Safi asked. He'd barely touched his lunch and was gnawing on his fingernails. They were all sore and bleedy looking.

"Seriously," I said. "My mom can barely keep up with him. And he'll eat anything. I watched him eat an entire loaf of bread yesterday. Just the bread. Slice after slice. He didn't even toast it or put peanut butter on it or anything."

"Lena's seen him around school," Safi said. Safi's sister, Lena, was in the tenth grade. "She said he acts like he's all that because his folks have a buttwad of money."

"Well, I don't know if money has anything to do with it," I said. "But the last conversation we had was when I offered to show him around town, and he told me to, and I quote, 'Stay the eff away from me.'"

Suddenly the warning bell rang, and Safi groaned.

"Oh man. I've got gym."

I understood his pain. For guys like us, school was bad, but gym was torture.

"Just tell them you can't play volleyball for religious reasons."

"I tried that last week."

Safi stood up and flattened himself against the wall. Then he cracked the door open a slice.

"I've got chores after school," he whispered, as he peered into the hallway. "Do you want to hang out after?"

"I can't," I said. "I've got hockey practice."

Safi turned back to me with his eyebrow lifted.

"After you pooped the bed in the last game, I figured you were done."

"Apparently not," I sighed. "Although I doubt I'll get any more ice time for the rest of the season."

When he was sure the coast was clear, Safi opened the door. Then he tucked in his shirt and straightened his bolo tie.

"You've got to look on the bright side," he said, as we started walking.

"The bright side?"

He shrugged. "At least hockey practice is two more hours you don't have to spend with your cousin."

"Yeah," I said sarcastically, "things must be looking up."

But then, as if the universe were listening, some random kid stepped out of the bathroom. Safi flattened himself up against the wall like he was trying to make himself invisible, but it was too late for me. The dude knocked my books out of my hands, and they scattered across the hall. My binder exploded in a plume of loose leaf.

"Get a life, buttwipe," he called over his shoulder as he sauntered away.

If only it were that easy.

After school, I went immediately to practice, which meant I was forty-five minutes early. I wasn't keen to start playing, but if I didn't get dressed before the other guys arrived—specifically Artie—I'd have to listen to them yell things at me, like "You suck!" or "Go home, bender!" And if I stashed my stuff in the janitor's closet around the corner, they wouldn't have the opportunity to throw my clothes into the urinal or squeeze Rub-A535 into my jock-strap, which they'd done twice, and it made my wiener so cold and numb I literally thought it was going to shrivel up and fall off.

After I got dressed, I would usually leave the locker room and hunker down in the penalty box until Coach and the rest of the guys showed up. Sometimes I hung out with Mr. Wells, the Zamboni guy, in his little office, or I helped him shovel snow off the rink when he was done flooding it. Sometimes he paid me with Twinkies from the canteen, which was definitely worth the effort.

Today though, Mr. Wells was nowhere to be seen. Instead someone else was on the ice, skating around the blue line in workout clothes and a ball cap.

My heart sank.

It was Alex.

If there was one person I didn't need hanging around while I dragged my sorry butt through practice, it was that turdnugget. I considered getting back into my street clothes and skipping practice altogether, but if I did that, my dad would find out, and then all kinds of crap would hit the fan.

No, I needed to get Alex out of there, and there wasn't any time to waste. So I took a deep breath, walked over to the boards and yelled out, "Hey!"

He glanced up at me and then, without saying anything, went back to practicing. He had scattered a bunch of gates and what looked like an entire bucket of pucks on the ice and was click-clacking a puck effortlessly around—over the gates, under the gates, around the other pucks, off the back of his skates. On and on he went, until his forearms must have been on fire. But it didn't seem to bother him. The dude had dangles for days.

I watched him for a moment longer, and then I rapped on the glass with my fist.

"Hey!" I called again. "What are you doing here?"

"What's it look like, Einstein?" he said, without even glancing up. He drifted away from where I was standing, but I followed him, running awkwardly in my skates along the rubber mats.

"No," I called again. "I mean, *why* are you here?"

He stopped for a moment and looked up at the rafters. I could see his shoulders rise and fall in a sigh. Then he put his head down and kept on clacking.

"Don't you have your own practice? With the triple-A team?"

Clack. Clack. Clack.

"Because the bantam double-B's have their practice here in like twenty minutes."

Clack. Clack. Clack.

"I'm not even sure you're allowed to be on the ice without Mr. Wells's permission. He's the Zamboni guy, but, like, I wouldn't call him that to his face. He prefers the term 'ice technician.' Anyway, he's not going to like it if you mess up the ice before a—"

"Oh my god!" Alex roared suddenly. "Do you ever *shut up*?!"

That hurt. I mean, it's one thing to be called out for being short or for being the new guy or for being totally useless at a sport everyone else worships. But it's yet another to be treated like you're some kind of babbling idiot when all you're trying to do is protect yourself from being humiliated by yet another hostile family member.

"Fine!" I said. "I was just trying to help. But if you want to get into trouble, then that's your problem. I mean, I was just trying to warn—"

CRACK!

Alex reared back and took a slap shot. The puck hit the glass directly in front of my face, and the sound of it echoed through the empty arena like gunfire. I shrieked like an old lady and jumped about a foot in the air.

"Very funny, you jerk!" I yelled at him. "What do you think you're do—"

CRACK! He did it again. If I hadn't been standing on the other side of the glass, the puck would have hit me right between the eyes.

For a moment, no one said anything—we just glared at each other. Then one side of his mouth lifted in an evil grin, and I knew I was in for it.

"Don't do it!"

CRACK!

"Stop!"

CRACK!

"You're a being a total di—"

CRACK! CRACK! CRACK! CRACK! CRACK! CRACK! CRACK!!!

Pucks were flying left and right, and even though I knew they couldn't reach me, I still shielded my head with my arms and ran for cover. That's hard to do, though, when you're wearing skates and equipment, and as I turned the corner by the locker room, I tripped over my own feet and did a face-plant right onto the mat.

That's when Coach came up behind me.

"For god's sake, Stone!" he hollered. "What are you doing on the ground?"

I sighed and rolled over. He was looking down at me over his enormous beer belly, and his pelican neck was red and trembling. For someone who spent as much time as he did working with children, he was doing a really sucky job of hiding his disgust.

"I tripped, sir."

"Well, get up." He scowled. "Practice is starting."

"You should tell my cousin to get off the ice then," I said, struggling to get to my feet.

"Why would I tell him that?" Coach asked. "He's our new assistant."

CHAPTER SIX

Practice was a waking nightmare. Even more than usual. Alex ran all the standard drills, along with a couple new ones I'd never seen before, and every time I made a mistake or missed a pass or fell down when I tried to stop, he looked at me like I had a big hairy booger stuck to the end of my nose.

He was surly.

And miserable.

And he rolled his eyes so much, it's a wonder they didn't fall right out of his head.

About the only thing I could take comfort in was that he was being a universal butthead to just about everyone except Coach, and maybe even a little bit to him too.

What was surprising, though, was that none of the guys on the team seemed to mind. They were too busy gaping at him, slack-jawed, like he was god's gift to creation. They loved his car, which was a dark-blue BMW he made sure to park right in front of the arena; and his skates, which were Bauer Supreme 1S; and his stick, which was a CCM Super Tacks with a retail price of over three hundred dollars.

Big deal.

Then Alex started to actually show us some of his moves on the ice, and I swear, every guy on the team was inches away from falling down and foaming at the mouth.

Oooh, look at Alex's rocket slap shots. They're wicked sick.

Oooh, look at Alex's dirty dangles. He's such a savage.

Oooh, look at the way Alex spits water out of his mouth all the time instead of actually just drinking it like any normal person would do. He has the most epic saliva.

It didn't matter what he did or how hostile he was, they still followed him around like a bunch of puppies without tails. I was sure any second they were going to start crawling all over him and maybe even try to hump his leg a little.

When the miserable two hours were over, I hung back like I usually did, putting away cones and pucks, and making small talk with Mr. Wells while he got ready to flood the ice. All of which took longer than you'd think, because Mr. Wells was a serial oversharer, and by the time he'd filled me in on the status of his arthritis, his chronic hemorrhoids, and the fact that just the night before he'd had to get out of bed eight times to pee, most of the guys had already started for home.

As I made my way to the locker room, Alex appeared out of nowhere in street clothes with his hockey bag slung over his shoulder. I almost walked into him.

"Where the hell have you been?" he said. He looked like he was ready to choke the life out of me.

"I was just helping out Mr.—"

"Hurry up and get dressed," he grunted, ignoring me. "I'm not waiting for you forever."

"What do you mean?"

He rolled his eyes. Again.

"Your dad's working late. Aunt Marion asked me to drive you home."

Just hearing him say my mom's name made me want to drive my hockey stick up his left nostril.

"Just tell her I've got some things to do," I said, glaring at him. "I'll be home before supper."

"Suit yourself," he said. Then he turned and headed for the door.

Passing up a ride with Alex was not a wise move. The walk to my house was at least twenty-five minutes, and it was so cold outside, the minute I stepped out the door and took a breath, my nose hair froze instantly. Still, instead of beating it home as quickly as possible, I made a detour and headed down Main Street. Before I knew it, I was standing in front of Valenta's Czech bakery, where, if I was lucky, I'd get to see Claudia working away in the window, just like she did every Tuesday afternoon from four to six.

Claudia Valenta. I love her more than any woman I've ever loved in my entire life. I would do anything for her, and I'm not kidding about that. Like, if she came up to me one day and said, in her heavy Czech accent, "Vill. Pleez. You cut off leg and give to me," I would literally start scrambling for a sharp knife and a crutch.

She's a year older than me and goes to high school, which seriously limits my chances of ever getting together with her in a boyfriend/girlfriend kind of way. Even so, the first time I laid eyes on her, I knew she was the woman of my dreams.

She's got to be at least five foot seven, and she's sturdy too, with wide shoulders and large hands— sort of reminiscent of those Eastern European women wrestlers who dominate the Olympics, except less manly and hopefully less likely to incapacitate me with a suplex.

And what a face. She's got big blue Bambi eyes and a rosebud mouth. Her hair is blond and silky looking, and she keeps it in braids that she pins to either side of her head, like an old-fashioned milkmaid. She wears dresses with little flowers on them, even in the dead of winter, and she smells like cinnamon and sugar.

I adore her.

Plus she has the most amazing breasts I have ever seen. They are full and round and soft looking, and the first and only time I saw her in a white T-shirt, the fabric stretched across them in a way

I can only describe as magical. Awe inspiring. Hemorrhage inducing, you might even say, since when I saw them, my nose actually started to bleed. I don't think it was a coincidence either. When I looked at her in that shirt, it was like I went into spontaneous combustion.

Normally I would stick around for an hour or so and watch her work from a bench across the street, which I swear is way less stalky than it sounds. Unfortunately she must have been sick or something because she never showed up in the window. Even worse, just as I was getting ready to leave, Artie and his gang of snot rockets came around the corner. They were pretty far away, but they still saw me, and when I saw them see me, I went into immediate panic mode.

"Yo, Stone!" Artie called out.

I couldn't breathe, let alone move. All I could do was put my head down and pray for the sidewalk to open.

"Stone!" Artie called again. He was actually smiling. "Wait up! We want to talk to you!" He looked at his friends when he said that, and I knew their idea of talking to me would probably involve squashing my head into the pavement and forcing me to eat a cigarette butt, which is what they did the last time they "talked" to me.

It took a minute for my fight or flight instinct to kick in, and when it did, I bolted. I knew if I could just get around the corner, I might be able to lose them down an alley. Unfortunately, once I was around the corner, I realized my problem. The entire next block was one big row of attached buildings. There were no alleys and no place to hide.

In a panic, I flung myself onto a lamppost thinking I might be able to shinny up like a monkey, but no luck. So I jumped down, ran a little farther, and leaped dramatically over a garbage can someone had left lying on the sidewalk. Then I spun from entranceway to entranceway, yanking on doors and praying someone would open up and save me.

Lucky for me, someone did.

"Hey!" a voice called out. I turned to see a guy standing in a doorway on the other side of the street. He was smiling and pointing at me.

"You got some moves, man!" he said in a thick Spanish accent. "Why not join us! It's only five dollars!"

I didn't know what "it" was, and I didn't care. All I knew was that if I didn't find a place to hide soon, I was going to have the treads from Artie's boots permanently tattooed on my butt. So I ran across the street and darted past the guy into the entryway of the building.

"Close the door!" I hollered.

"Okay, okay!" he said, following me. "Jeez! Calm down."

He shut the door and turned the lock. Then the two of us watched from behind a curtain as

Artie and his friends went screaming by. Another moment of silence passed, and he spoke up.

"You got some troubles, man?"

"Nothing I can't handle," I said, leaning against the wall and panting.

"Looks to me like you need to lie low for a while."

"That might be a good idea."

"Come with me," he said.

I turned and finally got a good look at him. He was wearing a black-sparkly leotard that was cut to his bellybutton, and his hair was slicked back on his head so that it resembled a shiny black helmet. I was almost sure he was wearing eyeliner, and it looked like he plucked his eyebrows, too, since they were pencil thin and rose up from his forehead like he was in a constant state of surprise.

Considering this might be one of those "stranger danger" situations my mom was always warning me about, I stopped and put my hands up.

"Wait," I said. "What is this place?"

He looked at me like he couldn't believe I'd ask such a stupid question.

"This is the Jesús Rodriguez School of Dance," he said (pronounced *hey-soos*, for those not in the know). "And *I* am Jesús."

"What do you mean, school of dance?" I asked him. "Do you mean, like, break dancing?"

He looked even more disgusted.

"Not break dance!" he said, pretending to spit out of the corner of his mouth. "Ballroom dance!

Like rhumba. Or cha-cha. Or the waltz."

He grabbed my arm and started pulling me.

"Why don't you come? The first lesson is only five dollars!"

"Oh, no, no," I said, laughing a little. I took a step backward. "I don't think so."

Jesús frowned at me.

"Why not? You don't think it's cool? It's not manly enough for you?" He stood up straight and banged his chest with his fist. "Well, *I* dance! And I am the most manly of men!"

I didn't know about manly, but he did have a fair amount of hair on his chest. In fact, it looked like he was wearing a mohair sweater under his dance outfit. I knew I needed to stay off Artie's radar for a little longer, so I nodded at him and tried to smile.

"Tell you what," I said. "I'll come along to watch. But I'm not making any promises about the dancing part."

He took my hand and just about crushed it.

"It's a deal," he said. "I know you're gonna love it!"

I thought to myself, *Jesús, you freaky-looking dude, you are so dead wrong.*

CHAPTER SEVEN

Jesús led me into what looked like a ballroom, with lavender walls and floor-to-ceiling windows and a big chandelier. The lights were soft, and there were a few plush couches pushed against the walls. For a room that was so large it was almost cavernous, it was surprisingly warm and cozy. It even had a nice smell to it, like coffee with a hint of perfume and aftershave. Compared to the rink, which was cold and dark and reeked of BO and desperation, the dance studio was heaven.

Unfortunately, it was immediately clear from the handful of people milling about that Jesús's clientele consisted mostly of middle-aged women wearing some form of skin-tight leopard-print clothing, embarrassed husbands I assumed were dragged to the studio against their will, and a lot of really, really old people. Like, Crypt-Keeper old.

In a panic, I started to back up, but before I could run, Jesús stopped me.

"What's wrong?"

"I don't belong here!" I whispered furiously.

"Don't be silly," he said. He was trying to pull me

into the room, but I was clinging to the doorframe. "Of course you belong here! You're gonna love it."

"But these people are ancient!"

"That's not true!" He held on to my arm so I couldn't get away.

"Just wait," he said. Then he stood up on his tiptoes and began calling "Tessie! Tessie!" in a big, booming voice.

Suddenly everybody in the room stopped what they were doing and turned to stare at us, and my nuts literally climbed back up inside my body.

"What are you doing?"

"You'll see," he said, smiling at me.

That's when the door to the bathroom opened, and the hottest girl I had ever seen—next to Claudia Valenta—came walking over.

It was Tessa Harper. She was way older than me and went to high school, but she also worked at the library, so I saw her every time I went in there with my mom. I'd even talked to her a couple of times. If choking on my own spit and then grunting monosyllabically when she asked me a question could be considered conversation.

Did I mention she was majestically hot?

Did I also mention that as she walked toward us it was like someone had turned on an invisible wind machine and her dark hair was literally blowing back from her face because of her incredible smoking hotness? I could actually hear a random Marvin Gaye tune playing in my mind, as well as a deep, rich voice that was not my own, but was maybe God's, telling me, *Be cool, young William. Just. Be. Cool.* That's honestly what was happening.

"Tessie," Jesús said as she got close. "I finally found a new partner for you!"

Tessa's eyes widened in surprise when she spotted me.

"Really?" she asked. "Are you taking dance lessons, Will?"

"Uh," I said. I was too stunned to speak. Tessa Harper actually remembered my name!

"Of course he is!" Jesús said, giving me a slap on the back.

I expected Tessa to groan or roll her eyes at the prospect of having to spend any amount of time with a fartknocker, but instead her face broke out into a huge smile.

"That's so great!" she said, and I had to drop my head and stare at my shoes because it felt like my entire body was going to explode from happiness.

Then Jesús turned around and clapped his hands.

"Okay, everybody! We're gonna start with the rhumba today!" he called, and before I knew what was happening, he grabbed my hand and Tessa's and pulled us to the floor.

My heart was beating so hard I could feel it in my earlobes. It was difficult to know what freaked me out more: the fact that I was standing next to Tessa Harper and she was wearing an oversized V-neck T-shirt, which meant I could see one of her bra straps, or the fact that I didn't have a clue how to dance and was about to do it in front of the second-hottest girl I'd ever met, as well as a bunch of random strangers.

I stood there in the middle of the floor sweating like a swamp creature, and I attempted to follow Jesús while he showed us something called the rhumba box step. Luckily it wasn't hard. Technically speaking, it consisted of dancing in a square and shifting weight from one foot to the other, with a dash of jazzy Latin hip swinging mixed in. Not cool, but definitely not rocket science either.

The music was rock solid, though. Jesús had on this old-timey Latin stuff by some drummer named Tito Puente, and, like, I'd never heard of him before, but the dude could lay down a beat. I mean, it was practically impossible *not* to move.

Once Jesús finished his demonstration, he grabbed Tessa and me and pulled us together.

"Okay," he said, maneuvering me around like I was a puppet. "Now you take her left hand in yours, and put your right hand on her shoulder blade."

He pushed and lifted and adjusted, and before I even knew what had happened, I was standing there holding Tessa Harper *in my arms*. This was both a good thing, for obvious reasons, and a bad thing, because Tessa was very close, and her hair smelled like strawberries and coconut, and I could no longer be entirely certain things were going to behave themselves down below.

Before I could worry any more about it, Jesús turned on the music, and we started to dance.

As we moved along, Tessa whispered helpfully under her breath, "Left foot forward, together. Right to the side, together. Right foot back, together. Left to the side, together."

After a while, though, she stopped whispering and beamed at me.

"You're really good at this, Will!"

I don't think I'd ever heard that phrase in my entire life, but it got me feeling kind of masterful, so I decided to throw some game in her direction.

"You're the best dancer I've ever seen," I said. "You're better than, like, Beyoncé, or something."

Tessa cocked an eyebrow at me, and then she laughed out loud.

"You're quite a charmer, Will," she said. Then she laughed again and kind of ruffled my hair a little, and I was so overjoyed she could have stashed a hand grenade in my undershorts, and I still would have died with a smile on my face.

Next, Jesús taught us an underarm turn, which was also easy. A couple of moves later, Tessa and I were way ahead of the rest of the folks, who were still working on the basic combinations.

Jesús watched the two of us carefully, and when the music stopped, he clapped his hands.

"Okay," he called. "Everybody look at Will!"

The last person to yell something like that was Artie when he caught me with an involuntary boner in gym class. Even though I was pretty sure I had everything under control, I dropped Tessa's hands as fast as I could and pulled my sweater down over my groinal region.

"Keep your eyes on Jefe here," he said, pronouncing it *heff-ay*. "He is a real man! He knows how to hold a woman! Show them, Jefe!"

I considered bolting, but I knew it would involve knocking down at least one senior citizen, and I didn't want to be rude. Plus Tessa was smiling at me and nodding like she thought it was a great idea. So when the music picked up again, I took a deep breath and started dancing.

"Do a turn!" Tessa whispered. Which I did. And when I followed it with a Cuban walk, all the old people *oohed* like they just got a free card at bingo. Then Tessa was like, "Crossover break!" and we did that too, and the crowd *aaahed* like someone offered them a discount on the early-bird special at IHOP.

Once the song was over, everyone gathered around us clapping like crazy, and it was the first time since I'd moved to Evanston that I'd been surrounded by a group of people who weren't laughing or pointing or flinging cold french fries at me.

Tessa smiled at me, and her big green eyes were all shiny and happy.

"You're a natural, Will!" she said, as the crowd started to disperse.

"Aw, come on."

"No, really," she said. "You should think about signing up for lessons."

I shrugged. "Maybe I will," I lied.

"You should," she said. "You've got a lot of potential. Jesús doesn't call just anyone *jefe*."

"What does that mean, anyway?"

"I think it means 'boss.' Like the man in charge."

"You're kidding."

Tessa shrugged. "It sounds about right to me," she said, and winked.

I straightened up immediately.

"Sign me up," I said.

CHAPTER EIGHT

"All right, take a knee, gentlemen," Coach shouted. "Time for a new flow drill!"

Ugh.

God, I hated flow drills.

They were these complicated sequences where everyone lined up at different parts of the rink and then weaved in and around each other systematically, passing at different points, shooting on the net and picking up rebounds, like a vicious, soul-sucking nightmare.

Speaking of nightmares, Alex was still helping out at practice, and by helping, I mean blowing his whistle at ear-splitting volumes and glaring at us while he mumbled swear words under his breath. Today though, instead of standing there looking cool while Coach did the talking, he grabbed a whiteboard and a marker from behind the bench, and all the guys gathered around him and took a knee.

"Okay, listen up," he said. He had one of those dull jock voices that made him sound like his brains were made of Play-Doh. "I'm going to teach you the Avalanche."

Everyone quivered and stared at Alex, like he was a hockey god about to impart some kind of ancient tribal wisdom. Which was totally ironic because when he was away from the rink, Alex seemed to have about as much interest in hockey as I did. He almost never touched a stick and instead spent all his free time lying on the couch, reading everything he could get his hands on, including Dad's collection of country and western biographies and my mom's Jodi Picoult novels. And he hardly ever watched hockey on TV, but he got his underpants in a total wad if someone interrupted him while he was watching *60 Minutes*. He also wore *glasses*—dorky-looking things with thick black frames that made him look like a total geek.

The fact was, Alex was a full-blown nerd. All he was missing were white socks and a plastic pocket protector. But if any of the guys had known the real story, they probably wouldn't even have cared. In fact, I'd bet good money they would have probably started wearing dork glasses too, and would have spent their time following Alex around with copies of *The Great Gatsby* in their back pocket. Meanwhile, I'd been sneaking out to dance class for a month, knowing full well that if word got out, it'd be total social annihilation. Like, where you don't just die—you get stabbed, shot, blown up, set on fire, and then, even after you're dead, people still come around to pee on your grave.

Alex drew a diagram of a hockey rink on the board and covered it with a bunch of carefully positioned *X*s and *O*s. Then he started talking.

"So," he said. "Vic, Murph, and Dima, you're gonna line up here. And then Charlie, Sam, and Rich, you're over on this side. The rest of you are gonna line up here and here. Vic's gonna take a shot and pick up a puck behind the net, and then the next two guys in line are gonna skate down to the face-off dot and cross each other . . ."

Blah, blah, blah. I knew I should have been paying attention, but I was so confused and excruciatingly bored, and my mind kept drifting, as it usually did these days, to dance class.

I originally had no intention of going back. For one thing, after the first five-dollar lesson, the price to join the studio was super steep, and I definitely couldn't afford to do it without draining all the money in my savings account. But for some reason, when Tuesday came around, instead of catching a lift home with Alex the Wonder Turd, I found myself stashing my gear in Mr. Wells's office and taking off down the street.

I'll just poke my head in, I told myself as I walked to the studio. *Just to say hi and let them know I changed my mind, and I'm not interested. It's the polite thing to do.*

But the second I stepped through the door, Jesús was so excited, he practically leaped across the vestibule to greet me. Before I knew what was happening, he pulled me into the ballroom.

"Everybody! Guess who's here?" he shouted. "It's *Jefe!*"

He threw my arm up over my head, like I was a prizefighter who'd just won in a knockout round, and the whole room erupted in applause. No kidding, I practically got a standing ovation from a roomful of strangers, and all I had to do was walk through the door.

Of course, it's easy to feel like a winner when you're surrounded by a group of dancing weirdos, most of whom are beyond ancient. There was Annie, who was at least a hundred and fifty years old and had one of those old-lady humps on her back. And PJ, who was a little shrunken Quebecois dude who always had crusts of dried spit on either side of his mouth. And Italia, who wore glasses with a chain on them and black nylon stockings that kept sliding down to her ankles and who kept reaching into her bamboo purse to give me hard candies I didn't ask for. I mean, next to that crew, I was a rock star. But it did feel nice to be in a place where people actually wanted me around, which was definitely not something I could say about my experience at hockey practice.

Coach blew his whistle, and I jumped. Everybody was up and skating past me, getting ready for the drill. I'd missed the entire explanation.

"Get the lead out, Stone! Now!" Coach hollered,

blowing his whistle several times. "We haven't got all day!"

He pointed to where a bunch of the guys were waiting on the face-off circle, and I sighed and skated over.

Whenever Coach called a flow drill, I always let the rest of the team go ahead of me. That way, I'd only have to go through the drill once or twice, and if I was lucky and no one noticed, I might not have to skate it at all. Unfortunately, when Artie pulled up behind me, I knew I wasn't going anywhere.

"Hey, butt-munch," he said. "You gonna skate today or are you going to wimp out, like usual?"

I turned around to face him, not because I was brave or anything but because Artie's favorite thing to do at practice was to hook me in the nuts from behind with his stick.

"I'm going to skate," I said, trying to sound as indignant as possible.

Artie belched and stared at me like a moron.

"Why do you bother?" he said finally. "You know all you're going to do is screw it up for the rest of us."

It was pointless to try and defend myself, partly because he had already turned around to talk to the guy behind him, but also because he was right. Flow drills were all about timing. If you started too soon or too late, or if you made a bad pass or missed the one coming your way, everything would fall apart. You'd be the drill buster, and trust me, *nobody* wants to be the drill buster.

I was *always* the drill buster.

So big deal, I thought suddenly. Last week, Jesús taught me how to do a triple cha-cha lockstep into a cucaracha break, neither of which particularly easy, and I totally nailed it almost on the first try. And I knew not one of these Neanderthals would be able to pull that off. Not in a million years.

"Wake up, loser!" Artie hollered, whacking my legs with his stick. "Your turn's coming!"

"I know!"

"Just remember, you're going right. Don't mess it up!"

"What do you mean, right?" I said. "Everyone else is going left!"

Artie sighed. "Weren't you listening?" he said. "Every fifth guy has to go right. You're fifth. You go right."

Obviously I didn't trust him. He was a criminal who would have pushed his own mother down a flight of stairs if he thought it would get him a laugh. However, I knew I'd been daydreaming while Alex was showing us the drill, so it was entirely possible Artie was telling the truth.

I didn't have time to think twice about it, anyway. Murph was streaking down the blue line, curling around the face-off dot, which meant it was almost my time to go. So I took a deep breath and started skating.

To my right.

A decision that, I quickly found out, was very, very wrong.

Coach blew the whistle, and everyone stopped and groaned.

"For god's sake, Stone!" he hollered. "Where are you going?"

"I'm not sure, sir!"

"Come here!"

I skated over as fast as I could, and when I tried to stop, I wiped out.

Some of the guys laughed while I pulled myself to my feet, but a lot of them glared at me and shook their heads, which was way worse. Coach nodded at me silently with his hands on his hips.

Finally he took a deep breath and spoke. "I'm not a young man, Stone," he said in a hoarse voice.

He looked so depressed, I almost felt a little sorry for him.

"If I have one dream before I leave this world someday," he continued, "it would be to run a drill for longer than a minute without you messing it up."

"I understand, sir."

He looked like he was trying to keep himself from throttling me. He threw up his hands in disgust.

"Get to the bench," he said, shaking his head. "You're sitting this one out."

I had no problem sitting on the bench. I'd sat on

the bench for practically every game of the season, and it was way better than actually skating. What I hated was how humiliating it was to screw up in front of everyone for probably the kajillionth time. What I hated was having to listen to the other guys razz me while I hung my head and skated off the ice.

The humiliation didn't end there. I had just kicked the door shut and flopped down on the bench when Alex skated up to the boards and executed a perfect hockey stop. Then he stood there looking at me with squinty-eyed disgust, like I was a human cockroach who'd somehow managed to pull on a pair of skates.

"So what's your problem, kid?" he said.

I crossed my arms over my chest and turned away from him. I even gave the door another kick to let him know I was supremely disinterested in discussing the matter with him.

"Hey! I'm talking to you!" he said.

"I heard you!"

"So what's your problem?"

I shifted a little on the bench, but I still didn't look at him.

"I don't have a problem," I said finally.

"Oh, I think you do," he said, super sarcastic. "For starters, you can't follow a set of simple instructions. And apparently, you still don't know your left from your right, which is totally pathetic. *And* you can't seem to stop in a pair of skates without falling on your ass. So I'd say you definitely have a problem. Are you, like, mental or something?"

I turned to glare at him. "I'm not *mental*," I said. "Just because I have a little trouble with—"

"Whatever," he said, cutting me off. "Your coach sent me over here to go through the drill again because apparently twice wasn't enough. So let's go."

He reached over the boards with one long arm, grabbed the whiteboard, and held it up for me.

"Now pay attention," he said. "*This is a hockey rink*. Do you know what that is?" He jabbed at the diagram with his finger and talked super slow, like I was a two-year-old with a head injury.

I turned away from him. My insides were boiling. It was hard to breathe.

"You're a jerk," I muttered.

He half laughed, half snorted. "And you're the *worst* hockey player I've *ever* seen."

"Thanks."

"No, seriously," he said. "You don't listen, you never know where you're supposed to be, you couldn't skate if your life depend—"

"Okay, I got it!"

"—never met anyone with his head so completely up his own ass. Are you on drugs or something?"

"I am *not* on drugs!"

"Oh yeah?" he said, snorting again. "Tell that to your mom."

The whole world stopped.

"What do you mean?" I asked in a low voice.

He gave me the squint again.

"You've been running around after practice, telling her you're at the library. Well, guess what, Einstein? She called there last week looking for you, and they told her they hadn't seen you in a month."

"What?" I whispered.

"I couldn't care less what you're up to, personally," Alex said. "But you've got her pretty worried about it, and I don't know why you'd do that. She's a nice la—"

Hot rage flashed through my body.

"Don't you talk to me about my mom! She's *my* mom, not yours, and you'd better remember that!"

He glared at me. "And you'd better get your act together, buddy," he said. "You can start by telling your mom what you're up to."

"I'm not up to anyth—"

"After that, you can stop wasting everyone's time and start pulling your weight on the ice. We can find another fourth-line grinder, easy. If you're gonna be on this team, you need to be on it and do your job."

He glared at me. I glared at him. Just as I was about to tell him where he could cram his hockey stick, the whistle blew. Practice was over.

CHAPTER NINE

Dad drove us home in Mom's van, and as usual, Alex sat in the front. I had to sit in the back next to his hockey gear, which smelled like cat pee and the rotting corpse of a deep-sea fisherman.

I barely noticed, though. All I could think about was my mom.

Of course she noticed I'd been showing up late for supper twice weekly for the last month. It's not like I had a raging social life or was a super brain who studied twenty-four seven. It was asking way too much for her to accept, without suspicion, that I had three hours of unaccounted personal time per week.

But what really got me—what really chapped my butt—was the fact that she confided all her fears and worries to *Alex*.

I shouldn't have been surprised. Lately he'd been spending a lot of time hanging out in the kitchen with her, watching her cook and getting things down from high cupboards when she needed them. And whenever he helped her, she'd reach up and pat his face with both hands or ruffle his hair with her fingers, and he'd smile at her with his dimples and his perfect white teeth and bend down a little so she could reach him, like a dog leaning in for a scratch.

I'm not going to say I was jealous or that every time I saw him around her I wanted to take something hard and smash his face in. I would never say something like that, because I am a gentleman and violence of any kind is beneath me.

Still, I fumed the whole ride home. My mother was a traitor. She was talking about *me*, her son, behind my back, to *Alex*, the douche canoe, which was absolutely the worst kind of betrayal. And I was ready to tell her *exactly* what I thought—I was really going to let her have it.

That is until she met the three of us at the door. When I saw the worried look on her face, I forgot all about being mad.

"What's wrong?" Dad said.

Mom sighed and put her hand on Dad's chest.

"Your father's here," she said in a hushed voice.

Dad's face fell. I groaned.

"He came over to meet Alex, and I invited him to stay for supper."

She gave Dad a look like she was expecting him to object, but he just took a deep breath and nodded grimly at her.

Alex looked back and forth between my parents.

"What's the big deal?" he said.

I could already hear Poppy getting closer. He was grumbling to himself, but because he couldn't hear very well, his grumbling was way louder than it should have been.

Mom turned to Alex and gave him an anxious smile. "It's just—your grandfather," she said quickly. "He can be a bit—I mean—the best way to describe him would be to say he's like a—"

"Buncha peckerheads!" Poppy hollered in his gravelly old man voice. "What are all of you doing standing in the doorway?"

Dad sighed and shut the door behind us.

"There's no need for that language, James," Mom said. She always talked to Poppy the same way—kind of slow and loud—like he was a tourist from a foreign country who didn't speak English.

She put her hand on Alex's arm and smiled.

"James, this is your grandson Alex."

Poppy didn't smile. Instead he stepped up to Alex and kind of poked him in the chest.

"So you're the hockey player," he said.

"Guess so," Alex said. He was looking down at Poppy, who was at least a foot and a half shorter than he was, with a bemused smile on his face. He didn't seem at all scared, which was shocking since on his best day, Poppy was freaking terrifying.

Poppy stepped back and patted himself, looking for his cigarettes, which he found and pulled out of his pocket. "I'd probably be able to recognize you better if your dad had ever brought you around for a visit."

"Well, he's a busy man."

"He's a peckerhead, is what he is," Poppy said. He pulled a cigarette from the pack and put it between his lips. It bobbed up and down while he spoke. "What kind of son doesn't take the time to visit his own father? Got a light?"

"There's no smoking in the house, James," Mom said.

Dad was busy hanging everybody's coats up in the closet. He didn't even look in Poppy's direction.

Poppy glared at Mom, and then he turned back to Alex and took a drag off the unlit cigarette. "Does your father still work at that big fancy law firm in Montreal?"

"My father *owns* that big fancy law firm in Montreal," Alex said.

"Ha!" Poppy snorted. "He got his act together, did he? Well, that's good to know. Christ, when he was a kid, he was so backward he couldn't have found his ass with both hands if he was looking for it." He laughed like he'd made the best joke ever. Then he stopped, and his face grew grim.

"But he always had the smarts," he said. He tapped his head with one crooked orange finger. "I always knew Eric would make something important of himself. God knows, nobody else in this family has."

Dad pressed his lips together and shut the closet door. Then he breathed out a long breath through his nostrils.

"Don't start, Dad," he said.

Poppy squinted and pointed at him. "You could've been a star in the NHL, *Paul*," he said. "And instead you decided to be a principal at a *middle school*." He wrinkled his nose like someone had cut a bad fart.

"James!" my mom said. "You know why Paul had to stop playing. It wasn't his fault."

Poppy opened his mouth to say something, but before he could, Dad cleared his throat.

"Why don't you make yourself comfortable in the living room, Dad?" he said. "I'm going to change my clothes, and then I've got some work to do outside before dinner."

He strode past Poppy to the stairs.

"I can help you, Dad," I said.

Dad stopped halfway up the stairs and turned back to look at me.

"No," he said. "Alex can give me a hand. You stay here and help out your mom."

"Okay." I sighed.

So while Mom got Poppy a drink and found a sports channel on TV for him, I stayed in the kitchen and watched Dad and Alex out the window.

I don't want to sound like a chauvinist or anything, but it's kind of obvious where you rank on the male food chain when you're in the house peeling carrots, not to mention wearing the apron your mother absolutely insisted you put on, while the real men are outside swinging axes and stacking wood.

There they were, though. Working together with their strong arms and their broad shoulders and their 6 percent body fat. Alex hauled the big logs to the stump, my dad split them, and Alex collected the pieces and stacked them against the shed. It was all very systematic and efficient. They were a great team.

It used to be *my* job to stack the wood. Even when I was very little. I'd button up my flannel jacket—the one I'd begged my mom to buy me because it looked just like my dad's—and put on the mini work gloves Dad bought me from the hardware store. I'd stand off to the side and watch while he raised the axe over his head and brought it down in one strong blow. Sometimes the split wood would teeter on the block before it tipped over onto the ground. Sometimes though, he'd hit the logs so hard the pieces would go ricocheting across the lawn, and I'd go running for them. I'd pick them up in my arms and stagger back to pile them, one by one, against the shed. Even though it was hard work, and I was exhausted by the end of it, I always felt like I was having the time of my life.

Truthfully though, I wasn't very good at it. For some reason, no matter what I did, the stack was always a mess. There were big gaps where the odd-shaped wood didn't fit together properly, and I could never seem to get the bottom row straight. Once the pile got high enough, it would lean dangerously to one side or the other, and sometimes it would fall over.

My dad never seemed to mind.

"It's all right, champ," he'd say, crouching next to me, surveying the mess with his hands on his knees. Back then he almost never called me Will unless he was mad at me for something. He always called me champ.

He'd move fast, and in ten minutes he would rebuild what had taken me two hours to stack. Then he'd put his arm across my shoulder and rub my head with his work glove, and I'd lean into him, loving him so much it would feel like my heart was going to burst right through my jacket.

"Don't worry, champ," he'd say. "One of these days you'll get it."

He said that about hockey too. When I fell down, which I did a lot, or when I couldn't skate backward, or when the other kids on the team razzed me because I kept dropping my stick or my gloves, or when I couldn't seem to find the puck no matter how hard I tried.

And I'd feel better almost instantly, because if my dad said it, then of course it was true. I *would* get it someday. It was only a matter of time.

Except I didn't get it.

After years of practice, that stack of wood never did turn out right. If it didn't topple right away, it was sure to the minute the ground shifted and froze, and I'd watch from the window while my dad put it back together again. I was embarrassed because I knew I was too old to be making the same mistakes.

After years of practice, I was still an ankle skater who dropped his stick and could barely skate backward. While the other boys practiced crossovers and wrist shots, I was still trying to stop without falling down or running splat into the boards.

After a while, my father started giving me "the look," which if you've never seen it, is hard to describe. It's angry, even though it doesn't want to be; and frustrated, even though it knows it probably shouldn't be; and embarrassed, although it would never admit it in a million years. It's the kind of look you give to someone when they've disappointed you in every way possible, but you're still legally obligated to take care of them.

You can't look at someone like that and have things stay the same. As time went on, my dad stopped calling me champ, which made sense since there was nothing particularly champion-like about me. He also quit making a rink in the backyard like he used to every winter, which was almost a relief, since after a while even the idea of putting on skates at home made me so anxious I would literally get the runs.

He stopped asking me to help with the wood too, and even though I wanted to help him, I couldn't bring myself to ask him if he needed me.

And now it was obvious. He didn't need me. He had Alex.

It was fine with me. It really was. I was of no use to my father, and I knew it. In fact, even though I wanted to be mad at Alex and to hate him for replacing me at that woodpile, I knew I couldn't be. Not really.

I was smart enough to know Alex hadn't taken anything from me I hadn't already lost a long time ago.

CHAPTER TEN

Safi met me at my locker after French class on Monday. He was sporting a shiner that was an ugly shade of yellowish green.

"Artie?" I asked, pointing at it.

He shrugged. "Wayne," he said.

"Fist?"

"Nerf football."

I nodded. Wayne Dorsey was Artie's best friend, and like Artie, he was dumber than a bag of hair. However, he did possess the uncanny ability to beat the crap out of people while still making it look like an accident. He never hit anyone in the head with a football, baseball, basketball, dodgeball, Coke can, meatball, pencil, or shoe on purpose, because apparently you can be a starting pitcher on the baseball team and still have the world's worst aim.

"What'd your dad say when he saw it?"

Safi stared at a piece of gum that was fused to the floor. "I told him one of the cows kicked me while I was mucking out the stalls."

"Did he believe that?"

He shrugged again. "I guess so," he said, and then he blinked.

I grabbed my lunch out of my locker, and we headed to the photography lab.

"Oh, hey," Safi said. "I almost forgot! Did you hear about what happened with your cousin and Duke Baynam's girlfriend on Friday night?"

"No! What?"

"Lena told me they hooked up at Zipper's cabin party." He waggled his eyebrows at me.

"Wow!" I said, and not sarcastically either. Duke Baynam was the captain and highest-scoring player on the triple-A team—that is, he *was* until Alex showed up. He also had a bad temper and was known to be a seriously dirty fighter. Rumor had it Duke was slashed by another player at an away game, and before the refs could get to them, he went into a frenzy and actually *bit the dude's ear off.* Which probably wasn't true, but still. They didn't call him the Pit Bull for nothing.

Safi grinned at me. "I heard Duke's looking to bust him one, and he's waiting until the game on Saturday night so the whole town can watch it go down!"

I was suddenly very, very happy.

Mr. Big Shot Man had finally gotten himself into a little trouble. In town only a month and already he'd messed around with another guy's girlfriend and was about to have his butt handed to him. And it was all going to go down at the game, in front of the entire population of Evanston. I was so thrilled I practically cha-chaed down the hall.

When Safi and I passed the cafeteria, the roar of students was deafening, but instead of rushing by like we usually did, we stopped in the doorway and peeked in.

"Sure would be nice to eat in a room with windows," Safi said.

"Yeah," I said.

Safi gazed at the hot-lunch counter like it was draped with supermodels.

"They sell french fries," he said mournfully.

"And pizza," I said.

"God, I love pizza," he whispered. We were both drooling.

"Look over there," I said. I pointed my chin at a table where Evan and Kole were sitting.

Evan Flinker and Kole Beaudet were pretty much the most popular guys in school. This was probably due to the fact that they were tall, and of course they played hockey. But unlike Artie and his loser crew, Evan and Kole played for the bantam triple-A team. They also had girlfriends and, like, knew what deodorant was and how to use it. So they were pretty golden.

They had never messed with me or Safi personally, but I suspected that was probably because they were too busy playing hockey or talking about hockey or shooing away the flock of girls who constantly surrounded them.

At that moment they were sitting with the rest of their friends, talking and laughing and throwing french fries at each other with the blissful confidence that came with not having to worry every second about getting their butts kicked.

We watched them a moment longer, and then Safi turned and looked at me. His eye was puffy and painful looking where Wayne had clocked him. He touched it gingerly with one hand.

"Did you ever wish—" he said, wincing. "Did you ever wish you could be someone else?"

"Every day, buddy," I said. Then I patted him on the shoulder. "Come on. Let's go."

We had a home game that afternoon, which meant I could sit on the bench and watch the other guys play while I ran through dance routines in my head. I'd already lied to my parents and told them I was going for dinner at Safi's after the game, so when it was over, I said a quick goodbye and sprinted to dance class.

Annie was the first person to greet me. She was wearing bright-red lipstick that went well beyond the edges of her lips, and when she smiled, I noticed it was all over her teeth. She also sported a sparkly pink headband spiked with big peacock feathers. Finally, as a finishing touch, she had on a shiny purple skirt, but she was wearing it *over* her pants.

I'm no doctor, but it was obvious she was having some kind of senior-citizen meltdown. Before I could call for backup, though, she said, "What do you think of my outfit?" Then she did a little twirl that took way longer than it should have.

"Wow," I said. "It's, uh, something. What's the occasion?"

"Jesús opened the costume closet!" She raised her arms and shook her fists like she was holding a pair of maracas. "We're all dressing up!"

Oh man.

I glanced around the room. All the women were decked out in sparkly dresses with ruffles and beads and feathers and fringes. The guys were wearing suits with rhinestones and flashy ties. Everyone looked pretty good. Sort of glamorous in an old-fashioned kind of way. Except for Mike, the middle-aged accountant. He had on a toreador jacket and skin-tight spandex pants and did not look happy about it. And PJ must have opted for the Aladdin look, because he was wearing a fez, shiny-looking red harem pants, and a vest to match. Even though the vest was buttoned up, I could still see a hint of his potbelly and droopy man boobies.

I took a step backward.

"I just remembered," I said. "I have to get home. I promised my mom I'd help her debone a chicken."

"But it's cha-cha night!" Annie said, shaking her maraca fists again.

I zipped up my coat. "I know, and I was really looking forward to it."

I'd just about made it out the door when Tessa showed up.

She was wearing a super-short sleeveless black dress that was covered in strands of sparkly silver beads. Her hair was out of its usual ponytail and floated in waves and curls around her shoulders. She was also wearing makeup, but unlike Annie, who looked like she'd drawn hers on with a crayon in the dark, Tessa was wearing just enough to look spectacular. In fact, she was so hot my mouth literally fell open.

"Will!" she called. "You're here!"

I let the door swing shut with a bang.

"Yes, yes, I am," I said thickly.

"Great," she said. "Jesús opened the costume closet. He said he found something for you that's perfect."

The next thing I knew, I was following Jesús into the wardrobe room. He was wearing another black leotard, but this one had a picture of Elvis bedazzled on the back. He was also wearing a pair of sparkly leather wristbands.

"That's quite a costume, Jesús," I said.

He smiled. "Thank you! I made it myself," he said. "I call it my Sixty-Eight Comeback Especial. Long live the king, eh, Jefe?"

"I'll tell you the truth, Jesús," I said, looking back over my shoulder to make sure Tessa wasn't listening. "I don't think I'm really into dressing up today."

"Oh, come on," he said, fake spitting. "It's just for fun."

"No, seriously, I—"

But he'd already pulled out a pair of black dress pants and a black button-down shirt.

"Here," he said, pushing them at me and pointing to the back of the room, where a curtain was strung up for privacy. "Try this on."

On first glance the clothes didn't look too outrageous. I didn't realize until I'd put them on, though, that he'd actually given me some kind of 1970s disco outfit. The pants had big bell-bottom legs, and the shirt was covered in black sequins and had a super-wide collar.

I stepped out from behind the curtain, and Jesús looked me over.

"It's a little big," he said. "But not so bad. I can fix it."

"I think the shirt's missing a couple of buttons too," I said, while he crouched at my feet and pinned up my pants. Actually, there were more than a couple buttons missing. The shirt was done up at my bellybutton, but above that everything was hanging open.

Jesús looked up and shook his head. "No," he said. "It's supposed to be that way. Very sexy."

I looked down at my blinding-white pigeon chest.

"I don't really think I have the body to pull it off."

Jesús tapped his lips with his finger and thought about it for a moment. Then he reached into a drawer and pulled out a lace scarf that he tied around my neck with a flourish.

"It's perfect!" he said. He clapped his hands together and then shook them in front of my face.

"You look so good!" he said triumphantly.

"Really?" I asked, while he began pinning my other leg. "You don't think maybe the scarf is a tad girly?"

"Girly?" he said. He screwed his face up like the question was ridiculous. "It's not girly! You look great! You are a manly man, just like me!"

He stood up and thumped himself with his fist and smiled at me proudly. I couldn't be sure, but it looked as though he'd sprayed his chest hair with glitter.

"Okay?" he said.

"Okay," I said.

He patted me on the head.

I suppose I could have taken off. Just grabbed my stuff and run home as fast as I could before anyone saw me. But when I came through the door, Tessa was waiting for me.

She looked me over, and her eyes grew wide. Then she smiled, but it was one of those aw-you're-cute-but-also-incredibly-pathetic-and-hopefully-someone-will-put-you-out-of-your-misery-soon sort of smiles. Like the kind you'd give a three-legged dog dressed up in human clothing.

"You look good," she said.

"I look like a disco pirate," I said miserably.

She laughed and then put her arm around my shoulder and gave me a squeeze. Even though I knew she was just being nice, all the usual alarms started going off in my brain.

AWOOOGAH! AWOOGAH! SOME FEMALE CONTACT HAS BEEN MADE! MAN THE DECKS BELOW!

"You know," she said, leaning her head toward mine, "Jesús was telling me before you got here what a great dance couple he thinks we make."

AWOOGAH! SHE REFERRED TO US AS A COUPLE!

"And he also said that in a couple of months, we will most definitely be able to consider ourselves intermediate dancers."

HER ARM IS STILL AROUND ME, AND HER LIPS ARE VERY SHINY AND KISSABLE LOOKING! AWOOGAH!

"And," she continued, "he said there's a chance we might be able to dance in the professional show at the Spencerville Fair."

The alarms went silent. Tessa looked at me, expecting some kind of answer, but I was speechless.

"So," she said, giving me a dazzling smile. "What do you think?"

I finally found my voice.

"Not in a million years would I ever consider doing that," I said.

Tessa laughed until she realized I wasn't kidding. "You're kidding, right?"

"I have never been more serious about anything in my life."

"But why? Don't you think we're good enough?"

"Sure, we're good enough," I said. "I just don't want to do it."

She crinkled up her forehead like she couldn't understand what I was saying.

"But this could be a great opportunity!"

"Opportunity for what? To be totally humiliated?"

Tessa frowned and took a step backward. "We wouldn't be humiliated!"

"Oh no?" I gestured to my shirt and bellbottoms.

"Well, obviously you wouldn't wear *that*," she said. "You could wear whatever you want!"

I shook my head. "No way. Absolutely not. Never to infinity."

"Will, I saw the show last year, and it was phenomenal. Jesús brought in dancers from all over," she said. "This could be our chance to dance on the same stage as real professionals."

I was about to tell her that I didn't care if Mikhail freaking Baryshnikov showed up onstage to dance with us when Jesús came into the room and clapped his hands.

"Okay, people!" he called. "Get ready!"

We got into position, and I made a face like I was so super concentrated on dancing I couldn't possibly engage in any more conversation. That didn't stop Tessa, though. She just kept on talking.

"I don't understand you," she whispered. "I thought you loved dancing!"

I sighed. "I do. Here. In this room. And that's it!"

"But what's the point of doing it if no one ever gets to see?"

I sighed again. Clearly she wasn't getting it.

"Look, Tessa," I said. "The fact is, I've used up almost all my savings to pay for these lessons. In about a month or so, I won't have any money left. So it doesn't really make a difference anyway."

Tessa's mouth fell open. "Are you saying you're going to quit?"

"I don't want to." I shrugged. "But I'm tapped out."

"Can't you ask your parents to loan you the money, at least?"

"No way," I said. "That's never going to happen."

"But why not? I'm sure they would. Maybe we could get Jesús to call them and tell them how much potential you have and what a shame it would be if you stopped—"

I put my hands on Tessa's shoulders and stood up on my tiptoes so I could look her straight in the eye.

"Listen to me," I said in a low voice. "There is no way anyone can find out I take these classes. Like, ever."

Tessa's big green eyes got even bigger. "What?"

"I mean it," I said. "No one. Not my parents, not the people at school, and *definitely* not my cousin."

Tessa looked at me for a moment, mystified, and then thankfully the music started.

Even though we were really good at the cha-cha, we still had to concentrate on the moves, which saved me from having to explain myself more. Just to be sure, though, I packed everything I could think of into the dance—spins and turns, whisks and walks, syncopated Cuban breaks and cha-cha chases. Before long, the thing happened that always happens to me when I dance. All of a sudden, I wasn't Will Stone, the thirteen-year-old freakshow who walked around school for half a day with a sign on his back that said MY ASS STINKS. I was Jefe, the big man in the barrio, dancing on a sun-baked street, surrounded by beautiful sweaty girls in tight pants and tube tops. Tessa was my woman, and I was her man, and my only job was to take her in my arms and show her what I was made of.

As the song ended, I spun Tessa one last time and dipped her low. Everyone around us clapped, and I couldn't help thinking a thought that had never once occurred to me in my lifetime: *Damn. I'm. Good.*

Jesús must have been thinking the same thing, because he crossed the room to where Tessa and I were standing.

"Will and Tessa, everybody!" he said, putting his arms around our shoulders. "They are such especial dancers. So beautiful!"

Everybody clapped again. Jesús's eyes were all teary, and he looked like he was about to say more when something caught his eye at the back of the room. Suddenly he stopped and put his hand over his heart.

"¡Oh, dios mío!"

"What is it, Jesús?" Tessa said, frowning at him. "What's wrong?"

"¡Oh, dios mío!" he said again. His eyes were huge. "¡Es el fantasma del joven rey!"

"What?"

"It's the *king*, Jefe!" he said in an awed voice. "It's Elvis!"

Tessa shot me a look, and then she said in a gentle voice, "Elvis is dead, Jesús. He died years ago, like, in nineteen—"

"No!" Jesús said. "He's not dead! He's young and alive and standing right there!"

We all turned to look at the door, and that's when my heart stopped beating and fell out of my butt.

I groaned. "That's not Elvis," I said. "It's my cousin. Alex."

CHAPTER ELEVEN

He was leaning in the doorway with his arms crossed, grinning at us. Before I even knew what I was doing, I raced across the room and put both hands on his chest and pushed him through the door.

"Why are you here?" I whispered furiously.

"I wanted to see what you were up to," he said as he stumbled backward. "Nice scarf, by the way."

I pushed him across the vestibule and out the front door. He was too busy laughing to get mad at me for touching him—otherwise I'm sure he would have pounded me.

"So let me get this straight," he said, as we faced each other on the sidewalk. "You've been sneaking away after hockey practice to go to *dance class*?"

He started to laugh again, and if I could have, I would have pulled the parking meter I was standing next to out of the ground and impaled him with it.

"It's not dance class!" I said. "It's—it's an—aerobic movement workout set to music. That I take lessons for. It's for my physical fitness, if you must know."

"So dance class, in other words."

"Shut up!" I hissed. "Why are you here, anyway? Did my mom send you?"

"No," he said. "I was just curious."

"Well, it's none of your business! Don't you have anything better to do with your time than to follow me around town and make a fool out of me?"

"I don't think I need to follow you around to make a fool out of you," he said. "You do just fine on your own. Are those *disco* pants?"

"Oh, that's right," I said. "I forgot. You *never* do anything stupid or embarrassing."

He leaned back against his Beemer and smirked at me. "Unlike you, I've mastered the art of not making an ass out of myself on a daily basis."

I wanted to karate kick him right in his smug face, but before I could even think about how to do it, Tessa opened the door.

"Is everything fine out here, Will?" she asked.

She'd thrown her coat around her shoulders, but I could still see most of her outfit, including her legs, which looked like they went on for about a mile. When Alex saw her, his eyebrows shot up, and he pushed himself off his car.

"Hey," he said, in a voice that was two octaves lower than usual.

Tessa didn't say anything. She just looked at me.

"Are you all right, Will?" she asked again.

I sighed. "I'm fine," I said. "I'm just having a conversation with my—"

"I think you're in my chem class," Alex said, cutting me off, which was totally rude.

Tessa must have thought so too, because she stared bullets at him.

"I'm Alex," he said.

"I know who you are," she said.

"Oh yeah?" he asked, all white teeth and dimples.

Then at that very moment, the most amazing thing happened. A car screeched into the parking lot. We turned to look as a girl jumped out of the driver's side and started marching in our direction. I didn't know who she was, but I could tell just by looking that she was a puck bunny. She totally fit the profile: tight clothes, lots of makeup. A group of girls followed in her wake, like a school of angry, big-haired fish.

I heard Alex mutter a swear word as they approached. His eyes were darting back and forth too, like he was trying to figure out which way he could run.

It was too late, though. She planted herself in front of him and crossed her arms. The rest of her friends did the same.

"So where were you this weekend?" she asked, jawing on her gum like a waitress at a truck stop.

"What?" Alex was trying to look confused.

"I texted you like twenty times, and you never answered."

Alex cleared his throat. "Sorry, Sheri," he said. "I was really busy this weekend."

Of course. The mystery woman was Sheri, Duke Baynam's girlfriend.

She glared at him, and the rest of her friends did too.

"Busy, huh?" she said. "Doing what?"

Alex didn't say anything. He just looked at her for a long moment, and then he shrugged.

When Sheri saw that, she wilted a little. Then she pulled herself up, took a deep breath, and started beating the crap out of him with her purse. Once she started, her squadron of girlfriends followed the leader and began hitting him with whatever they had in their hands—purses, backpacks, and in the case of one girl, three quarters of a raspberry donut she managed to squash into Alex's neck.

They beat on him for a good minute while he tried to shield his head with his arms. When she'd had enough, Sheri stopped. She held up her hand to the others, and they stopped too. Alex peeked his head out when he realized the coast was clear.

He turned to look at Sheri and said, "What is your prob—"

And *BAM*! She slapped him right across the face.

"Go back to Montreal, rich boy." Sheri sneered.

Then she saw Tessa standing off to the side, and her eyes widened.

"And stay away from my sister!" she screeched, grabbing Tessa by the arm and dragging her back into the studio.

CHAPTER TWELVE

I was lucky Mr. Wells was willing to open up the DJ booth at the far end of the ice. It meant I was able to watch Alex play that night in relative comfort and safety. I didn't go to many games, because in addition to hating playing hockey, I also wasn't particularly keen on watching it. But you couldn't have paid me good money to miss what was gearing up to be the grudge match of the century between Duke and Alex, the hookup king.

Unbelievably, Safi had skipped a 4-H meeting to watch the game with me, and even though we were in the booth and no one could really see us, he was still holding a little sign he'd made that said Go Bruins! He'd also painted two horizontal slashes across his cheeks in blue and green. It was surprising how supportive Safi was of the team, considering the fact that most of the players wouldn't have thought twice about kicking the crap out of him as a fun way to pass the time.

"So is your cousin as good as everyone says he is?" Safi asked, as we watched the warm-up.

"I don't know," I said. "I've never seen him in an

actual game. He can't be *that* good, though. If he were, he'd be in the major juniors by now."

"Lena said he's phenomenal. Like the next Connor McDavid."

"No way." I snorted. "It's all hype."

Except it wasn't.

Because Alex wasn't just good.

He was phenomenal.

The whistle blew, and the second his blades touched the ice, Alex exploded. He seemed able to hit his top speed with one stride even if he'd been barely moving only seconds before. And even though he was probably the biggest guy on the team, he could get really low on the puck, so it was almost impossible to knock him off it.

And they tried, believe me. The other team did everything they could think of to take him down, but they couldn't, mostly because they could barely keep up with him, but also because he was immune to pain. They slashed and cross-checked, and he kept on, brushing them off like they weren't even there, like he was some kind of machine.

"Wow," Safi breathed. "He's a monster."

Unfortunately for Alex, Duke was a monster too, and he was dedicating all his energy not to playing the game but to messing with Alex in every way imaginable.

Like two minutes into the play, for example. Duke took four or five strides past the blue line and rifled a slap shot that caught Alex in the face.

"Yikes!" Safi said. "Alex is lucky he's wearing a visor."

"He just got a puck in the face," I said. "That's still going to rattle him."

"It didn't seem to. Think it was an accident?"

"No way," I said.

It wasn't an accident in the second period either, when Alex had the puck pinned against the board and Duke ran into him while he was supposed to be digging it out. Twice. It was clear that either Duke was having his most uncoordinated night of the season, or he had taken a page from the how-can-you-blame-me-when-it's-an-accident playbook.

The big moment, however, happened during third period. The other team dumped the puck into the corner, and Duke, on defense, grabbed it from behind the net and started skating up the ice. By the time he got to the top of the face-off circle, Alex was at the red line, curling up the ice and looking backward for the pass.

There was no way Duke could have missed the defenseman bearing down on Alex, but he shot anyway. The minute the puck touched Alex's stick, the guy hit him so hard that Alex actually left the ground for a second before he slammed into the ice.

"Suicide pass!" Safi yelled out. He leaned back in his chair, covering his face with his hands like he couldn't bear to look.

The hit was low and hard, and I would have been very surprised if Alex didn't have at least a couple of cracked ribs. I know the wind was knocked out of him, because when he hit the ice, he just lay there for a minute or so before curling his knees up underneath himself.

I have to give him credit, though. He shook it off. The coach was there beside him, ready to walk him to the box, but Alex got to his feet on his own and skated off the ice. And although he must have known Duke set him up, he didn't even look his way. He just sat down on the bench with his stick between his knees and watched the play, and when the whistle blew, he was back on the ice again as if nothing had happened.

"Man," Safi said, shaking his head in wonder. "Your cousin may be a butthead, but he's super tough."

I had to agree, and thanks to Alex and his five goals and two assists, our team ended up winning its best game of the season.

Safi and I sat and watched the whole thing, waiting for something else to happen, but nothing did. But that didn't mean the feud was over. Call me sadistic, but I was really interested in seeing what kind of shape Alex and Duke were going to be in by the time they hit the parking lot. That's why, instead of catching a ride home with Safi like I'd told my parents I would, I hung around waiting for Alex to leave the locker room.

I should have gone home. I was stupid not to. I was even more stupid to assume that because the place had cleared out, it was okay to come out of hiding. In fact, I was such an idiot, I was actually whistling a tune to myself as I walked into the canteen. When I dropped a couple of coins in the drink machine, it was like I'd completely forgotten where I was. And who I was.

The paper cup had just fallen into place when I heard voices behind me.

"Hey, freakshow," one of them said.

I took a deep breath, grabbed my cup with a hand I willed to stay steady, and turned around. Artie and Wayne were standing there, gaping at me like the boneheads they were.

I thought of throwing my hot chocolate in their faces and running, but at the last minute logic kicked in. I'd locked the door of the DJ booth behind me when I left. There was nowhere to run to.

I was trapped.

"Whatcha whistling, dork?" Artie said.

I didn't bother saying anything to him or even acting like I didn't already know I was about to be the victim of some serious ass-kickery. So instead I just shrugged. Then Artie snatched the cup from my hand.

"Didn't you hear me, loser?" he said, with a tight smile. "I *said*, whatcha whistling?"

I didn't have time to answer before he poured the hot chocolate directly over my head.

It was super hot, and I shook my head back and forth in surprise like a dog shaking off water. When

I did that, Artie blinked and took a step backward.

"Did you see what he just did?" he asked Wayne.

"What?" Wayne said.

Artie shook his head at me, his eyes glittering with malice.

"He just got hot chocolate all over me," he said. Without looking away, he raised a hand slowly and wiped his face. And then he stepped forward and did something that, up until that point, he had never dared to do to the principal's son.

He punched me right in the nuts.

Look, like all guys, I'd had my moments of testicular pain. You know, where a girl runs into you with a low-slung backpack, or you brush against a desk in a weird way or something. But I'd never actually had anyone make contact there deliberately. And although I always guessed it would probably be painful, I had no idea how excruciating it was until it actually happened.

When Artie's fist connected, it was like an atomic bomb went off in my crotch, and the pain radiated through every cell in my body right up to the tips of my hair. Then, once the tidal wave of agony flashed through me and knocked the wind out of my lungs, it settled down deep in my belly and boiled there until I thought I was going to puke out my spleen.

I sank to my knees and keeled over until my cheek was smooshed against the floor, and the only view I had was of Artie's salt-encrusted boots.

After what seemed like an eternity, I felt one of them nudge me with his shoe.

"Is he, like, dead or something?" Wayne asked.

"No," Artie said. "He's still breathing. Plus he's drooling. You don't drool when you're dead."

Had I not been hovering on the verge of unconsciousness, I might have argued with him on that point, but as it was, I let it go.

"Yo, dude," Wayne said. "His cousin's going to come out any second. Are we finishing this or what?"

"Let's go," Artie said.

I shrieked as they caught me under the arms and tried to hoist me to my feet. Instead of standing up on my own, though, I continued to moan and dangle. I was too busy trying to cup my aching nuts to consider walking. Finally they gave up and dragged me through the double doors of the arena, down the steps, and around back to the parking lot. I heard the metal screeching of the dumpster lid opening, but instead of throwing me in like I thought they would, they pushed me up against the side.

"I gotta give you credit, dork," Artie said. "I figured after everything we've done to you at school, you'd for sure tell Mad Dog, and then we'd get expelled. But you haven't, and that impresses me."

He took a step closer. Instinctively, I tried to move backward, but Wayne held me tight.

"In fact, I'm so impressed, I'll make you a deal."

He took another step forward, close enough that

I could see a big zit in the middle of his forehead. It was white and ready to pop, and it made me want to hurl just looking at it.

"When we get to school on Monday, I don't want to see you in the hallways or in the gym or in the cafeteria. And if I catch you in any of the classrooms, you're dead meat. But if you can manage to stay out of my way, I'll leave you alone."

"But the only way I can do that is if I drop out!" I said. "My parents would freak if I did that!"

Because seriously, I would have dropped out of school months ago if I thought they would have let me get away with it.

"Well now, I don't think you're motivated," Artie said with mock disapproval. "Does he sound like he's motivated to you, Wayne?"

"No way, man," Wayne said.

Artie smiled again. He looked delighted. "Let's motivate him," he said.

Wayne tightened his grip on my arms. Artie drew his fist back. I closed my eyes and waited for the inevitable, bone-crunching hit.

"What do you two morons think you're doing?"

I opened my eyes, and Alex was standing there. The coach always made the guys dress for games, so Alex was in an expensive-looking suit and overcoat, which for some reason made him look bigger and more menacing than ever.

I felt Wayne's grip on me loosen, and I sank to the ground still cupping my nuts in my hands.

Artie turned around, and I watched as his eyes traveled up to Alex's face—up, up, up, until his head was practically perpendicular to the rest of his body. If I hadn't been in so much pain, I would have laughed like crazy. Artie was big, but next to Alex, he looked like one of the Seven Dwarfs.

"Oh hey, Alex," Artie said. He tried to smile, but his face was all twitchy. "Nice game."

Alex ignored him. "What the hell do you think you're doing?"

Artie must have decided the best defense was a good offense, because his face got stern. He pulled himself up as tall as he could and said, "That's none of your effing business." Except he didn't say *effing*.

Alex looked at him for a moment, and before I even knew what was happening, he grabbed Artie by the collar and practically lifted him off his feet. Then Alex half carried, half dragged Artie past me and slammed him into the side of the dumpster.

When he did that, Wayne made a strangled sound like a wounded moose and came running at Alex, but Alex didn't even skip a beat. In the time it took for me to blink, he dropped Artie and turned and hit Wayne so hard he went skidding backward on his butt across the icy pavement. After that, Alex turned and picked Artie up again, holding him high against the side of the dumpster while Artie twisted and squirmed and clawed at his hands.

I scrambled backward like a crab to get out of

the way, and I sat there watching. I mean, my jaw was literally hanging from its hinges. I'd never seen anyone take hold of someone like that—it was like something out of an action movie.

"You need to get something straight," Alex said. He was holding Artie high enough that their faces were just inches apart. "From now on, you leave the kid alone. If I even see you *looking* at him"—on the word *looking*, Alex slammed him again—"I'm going to find you" (*bam!*) "and kill you" (*bam!*). "Am I making myself clear? Is that enough *motivation* for you?"

Bam! Alex slammed Artie into the dumpster one more time, and it made a really loud clanging sound. A couple of guys who were getting into their cars on the other side of the lot looked over, but no one did or said anything. I guess fights behind the arena were not an unusual occurrence.

Artie's eyes rolled in his head, but he nodded. "Y-y-yes," he said hoarsely.

"Good," Alex said, dropping him. "Now get out of my sight."

Artie scrambled to his feet and stumbled to where Wayne was waiting for him. It wasn't until they were practically on the sidewalk that he turned back around. Then Alex stomped at the two of them with his fists cocked, and they took off running down the street.

It was so ridiculous, I started to laugh. Then I started to cry.

Then I bent over and threw up.

I could hear Alex sigh above me, but instead of looking at him, I stayed where I was.

After a minute, he cleared his throat. "You all right?"

"I don't know," I said. I wiped my mouth with my sleeve and closed my eyes.

"Come on," he said. "Let's get out of here."

I pulled myself up slowly, and he held on to my elbow until I was steady on my feet.

"Thanks," I said, giving him a small smile.

He looked down at me and nodded slightly.

"If you puke in my car, I will destroy you," he said.

Then he turned on his heel and walked away.

CHAPTER THIRTEEN

Question: What do you do when the one person you swore to hate—who you prayed would die in the most tragic and disgusting way possible, like from an attack of flaming hemorrhoids or in some bizarre mishap involving a toilet, superglue, and a twenty-five-gallon tank of Brazilian piranhas—saves you from probably the worst beating of your life?

Answer: you suck it up and try to be nice.

That was hard to do, though, when that person was Alex, and he was acting like a spoiled, moody poop head.

In the car he said absolutely nothing to me. In fact, the silence stretched so long I was practically coming out of my skin. Finally I turned to him.

"So did you rip Duke a new one for what he did to you in the game?"

Alex glanced at me. "I think we're even," he muttered.

Then he slammed his hand down on the steering wheel and half shouted, "For god's sake, isn't there anywhere in this craphole town to get something to eat after eight o'clock?" (Except he didn't say *crap*.)

"If you take a left, Fong Wings is on the corner of King and Edward."

He didn't even ask me if I wanted to go there. He just grunted and careened in that direction.

He didn't cheer up when we got to the restaurant either. When we sat down at our table and the waitress brought us our menus, he took his from her silently and began flipping through it as if she weren't there. And when she came back with a small teapot and two little cups without handles, he didn't even glance her way. He just tapped the top of his cup, and when she poured him some tea, he didn't thank her. In fact, he was so rude that when she asked if *I* wanted tea, I made a big show of thanking her so she could tell I was super grateful.

The waitress walked back to the kitchen, and I turned to see Alex watching me with a cocked eyebrow.

"Like green tea, do you?" he asked.

"Not really," I said. "Why?"

"Well, you just seemed so thrilled to get it. For a minute there I thought you were going to wet yourself."

I gave him the dirtiest look I could without actually making eye contact.

"I was just trying to be polite," I said. Then I mumbled, "You know, it wouldn't kill you to be nicer to people."

He looked up from his menu. "What did you just say to me?" he asked. There was a noticeable edge to his voice, so I knew he'd heard me the first time. But even though I was afraid of him, I was also getting really tired of the whole tough-guy thing. So I took a deep breath and looked him in the eye.

"I said, it wouldn't kill you to be nicer to people."

He glared at me. I swallowed hard and drummed the tablecloth with my fingers, but I didn't look away.

"I just saved you from getting your ass kicked, you little twerp, and you're telling me I need to be nicer to people?"

I swallowed again. "I appreciate that," I said. "But you know, she's a person like anyone else. She deserves respect too."

"Good for her," he said. "But right now, I'm paying her to serve me. Why should I thank her for something I'm paying her to do?"

I shook my head, stunned by his arrogance.

"I'm stunned by your arrogance," I told him.

To my surprise, he actually laughed.

"Who's arrogant?" he said. "She poured me a cup of tea, Will, she didn't give me a kidney. Am I supposed to fall all over her for that?"

"You don't have to fall all over her," I said. "But a thank-you would have been nice."

"That's what the tip is for."

I shook my head again and stared down at my place mat.

"What's it to you, anyway?" he asked.

"What do you mean?"

"I mean, why are you so worried about being nice to people? No one's nice to you."

It was true. Aside from my family, Safi, and the folks down at the dance school, there wasn't one person in my life I could actually say treated me as if I were a human being and not, like, a flaming bag of dog crap. But for some insane reason, I still held out hope that things would get better.

"I don't know." I shrugged. "I guess I still have faith in humanity."

Alex had actually been smiling, but when I said that, a cloud passed over his face. "Well, that's where we're different," he said. He tipped back in his chair a little and pondered the ceiling. "I gave up on humanity a long time ago."

I was about to respond when the waitress came back to take our order.

"Six spring rolls," he said, "and an order of moo shu pork, shrimp chop suey, vegetable lo mein, and a beef egg foo young." Then he looked at me. "What do you want?"

I blinked. I'd actually thought he was ordering for both of us.

"Oh, uh," I said. "I didn't, you know, bring any money."

"For god's sake." He sighed. "Just give her your order."

So I did.

When he handed the menus back to the waitress, he smiled a little and thanked her. Then he looked at me.

"Happy?" he asked.

"Yes, I am, actually," I said.

The food came fast, which was a relief, because after our discussion about manners, we both ran out of things to talk about. I was enjoying myself, though. Alex didn't order my food for me and didn't argue with me when I told the waitress I wanted five egg rolls and a fortune cookie. He drank tea and ate with chopsticks and was so much like a grown-up, especially sitting there in his suit, that I half expected him to push back from his meal, light up a cigar, and start discussing his stock options.

He didn't, though. Instead, halfway through eating and completely out of the blue, he looked at me and said, "So how come you haven't told your parents about your little after-practice activity?"

The egg roll I'd been chewing suddenly became hard to swallow. I put the rest of it down on my plate and stared at it.

"I just don't want them to know," I said.

"Don't you think they're gonna figure it out eventually?"

I sighed. "My dad—he would not be thrilled," I said, and then I gave him a look. "You know, because dancing's for losers and everything."

One corner of Alex's mouth lifted up into a smile. "Did I say that?"

"Yes, you did," I grumbled.

"Sorry," he said, grinning. "I can be a bit of an ass sometimes."

Then he tipped his head back so he could drop a dangling pile of noodles into his mouth.

I sighed again. "Well, none of it will make a difference in about a month or so, anyway."

Alex chewed and swallowed. "What won't make a difference? What's happening in a month?"

"In a month, I'll have used up all my savings, and I won't be able to afford to go to dance class," I said glumly.

The fact that I was running out of money wasn't something I told Tessa just to get her off my back about the fair. But until that moment, I hadn't considered how bad I'd feel if I had to give up my lessons. That thought, coupled with my nuts, which were still aching, was enough to kill my appetite completely.

Unfortunately Alex wasn't finished with me yet.

"So what's the deal with those idiots out in the parking lot?"

"What do you mean?"

"I mean, why are they trying to kill you?"

"Because they can, I guess," I said.

"Does it have something to do with how useless you are at practice?"

At first I thought he was trying to be a jerk

again, but he was looking at me like he was genuinely interested in hearing my answer.

"No," I sighed while I picked at my egg roll. "They're just evil. I could be Wayne Gretzky, and they'd still find a reason to kick my ass."

Alex nodded, and I slunk down in my seat. Then a thought occurred to me, and I perked back up again.

"Hey," I said as casually as I could, "have you ever considered teaching self-defense? I'd be a great student."

He didn't even look up from his plate. He just snorted and shook his head, as if what I'd said was the most ridiculous thing he'd ever heard.

"No, really," I said. "If I could defend myself, maybe they'd leave me alone."

"Listen, Karate Kid," he said, pointing his chopsticks at me. "You're fourteen pounds soaking wet. Even if I wanted to, which I don't, there's nothing I can teach you that's going to help you in a fight when it's two to one."

I sighed, and he glanced up at me from his plate.

"Look," he said, "you don't need to worry about it now. They know I'll kill them if they touch you. They'll leave you alone. It's cool. It's over. Breathe easy. Are you going to eat that?"

I passed my plate over to him and watched while he inhaled my egg roll in almost one bite.

"Why did you help me, anyway?" I asked him.

He looked at me for a minute while he chewed.

"For one thing, having to watch you get pummeled by a couple of knuckle-draggers kind of bummed me out."

He wiped his mouth with his napkin. Then he crumpled it up and threw it on the plate.

"But also, I need a favor from you."

I *knew* there was something.

"I want to—" he said and stopped. "I want to start studying at the library at night," he said finally. "And I need you to come with me."

"Why?"

"I don't know," he said. "Because it's quiet there, and we can get more done."

"No," I said. "Why would you want me to come with you? What do you need me for?"

"I just don't want to go alone," he said.

That didn't make sense. He did everything alone and seemed to prefer it that way.

Then it occurred to me.

"Are you going there to see Tessa?" I asked.

His mouth opened in surprise, but he shut it quickly and shook his head.

"No," he said, clearing his throat and looking away. "Not at all."

I couldn't help myself. "That's not true," I said. I smirked at him. "You like her."

"Don't be an idiot," he said, sitting back from the table and crossing his arms.

"Yeah, you do," I said. "But I don't blame you. She's great. You'd be stupid if you *didn't* like her."

I didn't think it was possible for a guy like him to blush, but he did, although I wasn't sure if it was because I called him on his crush or because I implied he might be stupid. It must have been the first one, though, because he didn't reach over and punch me in the throat. Instead he motioned for the waitress.

"First of all," he said, leaning forward and pulling his wallet from his back pocket, "I don't *like* her. I'm just tired of doing homework at the dining room table."

He opened his wallet and pulled out a credit card—*a credit card*—and handed it to the waitress, motioning to her that he was picking up both our bills.

"Second," he said, leaning in and keeping his voice low, "if you tell anyone about your little theory—like Tessa, for example—I will pound you."

I swallowed. "I won't," I said. "I wouldn't do that, I swear. Is that *your* credit card?"

"Yeah," he said, and then he shifted in his seat and turned his head to look out the window. "Anyway, even if I did like her, it wouldn't make much of a difference. She hates my guts."

"Oh, I wouldn't say that," I said. "Is it, like, yours? Or is it your parents' and they gave it to you to use?"

"It's mine," he said. "What do you mean, you wouldn't say that?"

"I mean that I don't think she really hates you. Not completely, anyway."

He sat forward in his seat. He was trying to give me his gunslinger glare, but his eyes were too shifty.

"Why?" he asked. "Did she—say something? To you? About me?"

"No," I said. "It's just that Tessa isn't the kind of person who really hates anyone."

"Oh," he said. He slumped in his chair.

"Trust me," I said. "Just give her a little time. She'll get over it. I promise."

I would have never expected a guy of his caliber to look so hopeful and desperate all at the same time. Before he could say anything, though, the waitress came back with his card. She handed him the little plastic plate with the bill on it, and he signed it.

"So do your parents make the payments on that thing, or what?"

"What?" he said.

"I'm just wondering if your parents pay for your credit card."

"Oh." He shook his head, like he'd just woken up. "No. I pay for it."

"How?" I asked, zipping up my coat. "Do you have an allowance or something?"

"No," he said. "I own a mine."

I laughed. "Funny," I said.

"I do," he said, putting his hat on.

"What do you mean, a mine? Like a coal mine?"

"No," he said. "A black granite mine. My grandfather gave it to me on my ninth birthday."

"*Poppy* gave you a black granite mine?" It was a hard thing to believe since every time I saw Poppy, he asked to borrow money from me. Asked is a generous term. What he usually said was something like, "Hey, kid. Give me ten bucks. I ran out of money for smokes." And when I told him I didn't have any, he'd call me a peckerhead.

"Not Poppy, you idiot," Alex said. "My other grandfather—on my mom's side."

"Yeah," I said. "That actually makes more sense."

We walked outside to Alex's Beemer, which was parked at the curb.

"You must make a lot of money from this mine."

"You know," he said, "some might consider hounding a person about his wealth to be in poor taste."

When I didn't respond, he sighed.

"God," he said. "Yeah, okay, I guess I do. I don't really keep track. It just goes into a bank account, and when I need something, I draw from it."

I smiled to myself as I slid into the car. A perfect plan was hatching in my brain.

"So are you gonna help me with Tessa or what?" Alex asked as he turned the key in the ignition.

I looked at him and sighed. Deeply.

"I'd love to help you," I said in a mournful voice.

110

"The problem is, once I run out of money and stop going to dance class, Tessa won't care about anything I have to say."

He shot me a look. "Oh yeah?" he asked.

"I mean, if I had the *money*, I might have the time to foster a deep and meaningful relationship with her. The kind of relationship where I might encourage her to be open to pursuing a romance with someone like yourself."

"Is that right?"

"Yes." I sighed. "But sadly, without the *money* to pay for my lessons, I just don't know how I could possibly make it happen. I mean, it's not like I own a mine or drive an expensive luxury car—"

"All right, you little dipshit," he said. "What's it gonna cost me?"

I grinned at him. "I'm sure we could work something out."

Alex shook his head as he pulled away from the curb.

"And they call *me* a criminal," he muttered under his breath.

CHAPTER FOURTEEN

Okay, so I was wrong when I told Alex that Tessa was too nice to hate anyone.

She totally hated him.

Like I'd-totally-run-you-down-with-my-mom's-Chrysler-except-I-still-only-have-my-learner's-permit-and-I-could-get-into-trouble-but-I'm-totally-willing-to-chance-it-because-I-hate-you-that-much—that kind of hate.

She was sitting at the circulation desk when we walked into the library, and she smiled when she saw me. But when she spotted Alex, she drew back a little and screwed up her face into a frown and looked away.

I heard Alex sigh behind me. I led him over to the reference section, where he sat with his back to Tessa and pulled his bag onto the table.

"So what do we do now?" I asked him.

He shrugged. "We do our homework," he said, and began pulling books out of his bag.

It was a lesson in playing it cool. We sat there for two hours, and he didn't look her way once. He kept his head down and did his work. He had a lot of it too, because he was in all the honors courses—trig, calculus, chemistry, and AP English—which surprised me, since most of the jocks I knew, like Artie and Wayne, were dumber than rocks.

You'd think all that reading might have helped him come up with a better plan for attracting Tessa, but it hadn't. Instead he just sat there working away, completely silent, except for once when he asked me for an eraser, and another time when he helped me with my French homework. That is if you could consider calling me an idiot and telling me I had the handwriting of a twelve-year-old girl helping.

I have to admit, that hurt. Especially the twelve-year-old-girl part.

"I'm not a girl," I whispered furiously. And then, before I could stop myself, I added, "You buttface!"

Alex glanced up from his textbook, but instead of feeding me my teeth, he just rolled his eyes.

"I didn't call you a girl," he said. "I said you had the *handwriting* of a girl. Big difference."

"Well, you have the handwriting of a serial killer," I said, pointing at the chicken scratch on his page.

"At least I don't dot my *i*'s with little hearts."

"They're *circles*."

"They're *stupid*," he said.

"*You're* stupid!"

It was a super-mature comeback.

Alex finally raised his head to look at me. He

pushed his geek glasses up with one finger just as three moony preteen girls walked past our table and smiled dreamily at him. Even when he looked like a dork, he still got more action than I did.

"What exactly is your problem?" he asked with a sigh.

"My problem is I don't appreciate you calling me a girl just because I'm short and like dancing."

"It's funny how I never said any of those things."

"You were thinking them, though."

"I don't know what you're talking about," he said, picking up his pen and turning back to his work. "But if your little dance class is causing you so much stress, why am I shelling out big bucks for you to be there?"

"I didn't say I wanted to quit," I said. "But it would be nice if I could do what I want without people thinking I'm a loser."

Alex lifted one eyebrow. "This is Evanston, kid. Who gives a crap what anyone here thinks about you?"

I cared. A large part of me still held out hope that someday I'd manage to work my way into the general population and wouldn't have to spend my lunch hours in the photo-developing lab with a kid whose idea of fun was flipping through the Burpee seed catalog while discussing the merits of different brands of combine harvesters.

I was ready to tell Alex that and more when he stood up.

"Be right back," he whispered.

He disappeared into the stacks for ten minutes or so, and when he finally reappeared, he looked harried.

"What's with you?" I asked him.

He didn't say anything. He just glanced at his watch, and for the first time the whole night, he looked over at Tessa. Then he began stuffing his schoolbooks back into his bag.

"Time to go," he whispered. He put on his coat while I shoved my things into my knapsack as fast as I could, and then I tripped behind him, struggling into my jacket, while he walked across the room to the circulation desk.

"Your glasses!" I whispered to him as we approached. He fumbled for them and stuffed them into his pocket. Then he cleared his throat.

"Hey," he said quietly. He placed a couple of books in front of Tessa.

Tessa kept her head down, ignoring him, until the librarian sitting next to her looked up and said, "Theresa, can you help the young man? I'm doing an interlibrary loan."

"Sorry, Mrs. Anderson," Tessa said. She looked up at Alex, her mouth a grim line.

"Do you have a card?" she asked.

He didn't seem to notice that she was giving him some serious stink eye. He just shook his head.

"I'm using my cousin's card," he said. "If that's all right."

"Fine," she said.

Without looking my way, he gave me a hard nudge with his elbow, and I scrambled to fish it out of my wallet. When I handed it to her, she snatched it from me and gave me such a dirty look I actually took a step backward.

It wasn't until she pulled the books closer to her that I got a chance to read the titles, and then I realized what Alex was up to.

It was obvious he got the first one from the children's section. It was a thin book that had two teddy bears shaking hands on the front. The title was *Hey, There! Be My Friend!* When Tessa read the cover, she blinked and glanced up at Alex quickly. Then she frowned again as she flipped open the book and scanned the barcode.

"This is due in two weeks," she said. "Will that be enough time for you to read it?"

He grinned at her. "I think I can manage."

She closed the book and slammed it down in front of him. The sound boomed through the almost empty library, and Mrs. Anderson jumped in her seat. She gave Tessa a quizzical glance, adjusted her glasses, and continued with her work.

Tessa picked up the next book. It was another one for little kids called *Everyone Makes Mistakes*. She looked at the title and shook her head, flipping it open.

"I've heard that's a good one," Alex said. "Have you read it?"

Without looking up or saying a word, she pursed her lips and scanned the code. When she was done, she smacked the book on top of the first one, and the sound echoed like a thunderclap. Alex laughed, but the sound scared the heck out of me and Mrs. Anderson, who gave a small yelp of fear.

"For heaven's sake, Theresa!" she said.

Tessa blushed and kind of slunk in her chair.

"Sorry, Mrs. Anderson," she mumbled.

"I'm going to tidy the periodical section," Mrs. Anderson said, getting up and looking grumpily over her glasses at us. "Can you finish up here without me?"

"Of course," Tessa said. She smiled slightly and nodded, while Mrs. Anderson ambled down the basement stairs. No one said a word until she rounded the corner, and then Tessa turned to Alex.

"What are you doing?" she demanded in a hushed voice.

If looks could kill, he would have been on the floor with a spray of blood pumping from his jugular. It didn't seem to bother him, though. He grinned at her like he was having the time of his life.

"What do you mean?" he said.

"I mean, you're not here to check out those stupid books, so what's going on?"

"As a matter of fact," he said, "I came here to study. With my cousin. In an environment amenable to deep thought and quiet contemplation."

She glared at him, and he laughed.

"Okay," he said. "So maybe I dropped by because I was looking for a way to get you to quit ignoring me."

"Well, I'm not interested in talking to you," she said. "And I don't want you coming around here anymore either."

"Why?" he asked. "Because of Sheri?"

"Among other things."

Alex sighed. "Oh, come on," he said. "I had no idea she was your sister."

"That doesn't make it any better."

He sighed again. "Nothing really happened, anyway."

Tessa folded her hands on the desk and gave him the same look my mom always gives me when I forget to put the toilet seat up before I pee, except way more harsh.

"Okay, maybe *something* happened," he said. "But it's not what everyone's saying happened. Where I come from, you don't have to marry a girl just because you kissed her a couple of times."

Tessa didn't say anything, and he held out his hands in a kind of pleading way. "Look, I apologized to her," he said. "I said I was sorry. What more do you want from me?"

Huh. I didn't know he'd apologized to Sheri. Personally, I didn't think he had it in him. It must have been news to Tessa too, because it took her a minute to reply.

"I don't want anything from you," she said finally, and then she swallowed. "Nothing."

He took a step closer and ducked his head a little. His voice was low.

"I thought—" he said, and *he* swallowed. "I thought if we had a chance to talk, you might stop listening to other people for a second and decide for yourself what kind of guy you think I am."

This time it was Tessa's turn to laugh.

"Please," she said, sneering at him. "I know *exactly* what kind of guy you are. And I've got better things to do with my time than to spend it with someone like you."

Yeesh.

Alex's shoulders fell, and he nodded, silent.

He took the books he was holding and laid them gently on the counter in front of her, pushing them forward a little with his fingertips.

"I'm sorry I wasted your time," he said quietly. "You don't have to worry. I won't bother you again."

Then he turned and walked out of the library.

CHAPTER FIFTEEN

The next night, the spectators in the Robert Tipney Arena were disappointed, not only because the Bruins were losing the championship final but also because the star they came to watch every week was completely off his game. The regulars remarked to one another, while they sat in the stands drinking whisky-laced coffee, that Alex Stone seemed more interested in destroying the players on the other team than he did in scoring goals.

For the first time since we'd moved to Evanston, I watched the game by myself from the glass so I was as close as I could be to the action, and I'd never seen anything like it.

Ten minutes into the game, Alex got his first penalty for boarding. Five minutes after that, he slashed a player's forearm and was lucky the ref didn't notice, because just moments later he got a double minor for spearing a guy in the gut. It got so bad at one point that the goon from the opposing side skated past Alex and gave him a warning bump. He must have said something to him too, because Alex flung off his glove and grabbed the guy by the mask, dragging him forward until their helmets banged together. You could see the guy's terrified eyes as he struggled to get free of Alex's grip. Alex let go only when he saw the ref skating over.

The rest of the period went downhill from there.

It might have been fine if he had scored a few goals while he was busy beating the other team to a pulp, but he hadn't. Not one. And by the time first period was over, even the home crowd had stopped cheering for him.

It was clear he was still sore about Tessa. After she'd told him off, he was so mad that he got back in the car and took off before I was even buckled in, squealing tires and everything. Then he drove home like a maniac and practically took the corner of our crescent on two wheels. Even worse, when I'd given him a pat on the back and told him there were plenty of fish in the sea, he told me to "Piss off, twerp."

The second period began, but Alex was last in line when his team took the ice. Clearly his crazy behavior had exhausted him, because as the team skated their laps, he dragged behind. His heart wasn't in it anymore.

Then Tessa appeared beside me.

She was wearing her winter coat. It was white and had a fur collar. She looked awesome.

"What are you doing here?" I asked her.

"What do you think?" she said. "I'm here to see the game. Did I miss much?"

"No," I said. "Just Alex trying to kill every player on the other team."

I pointed at Alex, who was coming down the side of the rink. He was skating with his head down, but he lifted it as he passed us and must have caught a flash of Tessa, because he did a double take and looked again. When Tessa saw that he'd spotted her, she lifted her hand and pressed it against the glass.

Alex's smile was so wide I could see it even behind his mask. He looped around to where we were standing and tapped the glass with his stick as he skated by. Tessa smiled. Then Alex turned and took the corner backward, like he couldn't take his eyes off her, and she dropped her head and bit her lip, as if she was trying to keep her smile from spreading too far across her face.

After that, Alex's game got a whole lot better.

It was as though the puck were attached to his stick with an invisible cord that stretched and pulled but never broke. It didn't matter how lousy the pass was or how many of the other players tried to take it from him, he just kept playing it—off his stick, off his skate. Once he even swatted it out of midair as it flew past him and fired it into the net.

By the start of third period, Alex had managed to tie the score, despite hardly any breaks. The opposition double-teamed him, triple-teamed him, and they tried to anticipate his moves, but they got nowhere and nothing. No puck, no clean hits—they couldn't even lift his stick off the ice. The dude was unstoppable.

Finally it was down to the last ten seconds of the game. Alex brought the puck up the ice along the boards. He deked out the first man as he crossed his own blue line, and defender number two was left in the dust when Alex chipped the puck off the boards to his right and went around on the left.

Then he skated past Duke. It looked like he called something out to him as he went by, but it was impossible to tell, mostly because just about every player on the opposite team was clamoring around him, trying desperately to take him down.

Of course they were. They all knew where he was headed. He was going to wrap around the back of the net, forcing the goalie to hold his position on his left-hand side, and with his long reach, Alex was going to tuck the puck in between the goalie's right pad and the post. He'd done it once before, earlier in the season, and it was magic.

The clock was running out, and everyone in the arena, including me and Tessa, was holding our breath as Alex began to swoop toward the net. No one in the stands could take their eyes off him. Neither could any of the players on the ice. Which is why no one was looking at Duke as he charged up the center with his stick down.

Alex was paying attention, though. Just as the goalie flew across the crease to beat Alex to the other side, Alex flipped a no-look pass behind his back to Duke, and before anyone knew what was happening, Duke dumped the puck into the empty net and scored the winning goal.

The buzzer rang, and everyone went nuts. The people in the crowd were laughing and screaming and jumping up and down. And not just the high school kids either. The grown-ups were going at it too. Parents were throwing themselves into one another's arms. Up in the stands, a trio of middle-aged ladies had pulled off their jerseys and were swinging them around their heads like they were getting ready to rope cattle.

Even before Alex had managed to clamber out from under his teammates, the crowd had already started chanting his name. When he got to his feet and took off his helmet, smiling up at everyone, they went wild again.

There was no denying it. Alex was a superstar.

He didn't seem fazed by any of it, though. He took his place in line, and then someone rolled out the red carpet, and a couple of dudes in ugly suits handed out championship medals. Alex was given the MVP trophy, and he smiled politely and shook everybody's hands. But the whole time, he kept sneaking glances at where Tessa and I were standing, and when the ceremony was over, he was the first one off the ice.

Tessa and I followed the crowd and made our way to the back door. As we passed the girls who were hanging around the entrance to the locker rooms, I noticed Sheri there with her posse. She was talking and laughing really loudly and calling out to anyone who happened to pass by. Every once in a while, she'd look around and then take a sip out of a flask she was hiding in her coat.

"Your sister's over there," I said.

"I know," Tessa said, not looking over.

"Are you waiting for her or for Alex?" I asked her.

"For Alex," she said.

"Why?"

She sighed and then gave a little shrug. "I wanted to—apologize."

"Oh."

"He was a jerk," she said, "but I also know what my sister is like."

She glanced over at Sheri, who had tripped on the rubber mat leading to the locker rooms and was lying on the floor, laughing her head off like a fool.

Tessa turned back to me and shrugged again. "Anyway, I think that maybe I was a little hard on him."

I opened my mouth to say something, when I caught sight of Alex leaving the locker room. He was walking fast and carrying his gear on one shoulder.

Tessa saw him too. She pulled me in front of her and held on to my shoulders, like she was getting ready to push me into him and run away.

"What are you—?" I started to ask.

"Just stay!" she whispered fiercely into my ear.

At that moment Alex caught sight of us, and he flashed another giant grin.

"Hey!" he said to Tessa. He tossed his gear to the side and shoved his hands into the pockets of his dress coat.

Tessa's nails felt like eagle talons on my shoulders. I managed to wrench myself away so I was standing beside her.

"It's great to see you," he said. He smiled down at me. "Hey, kid."

I gave him a wave, and he turned back to Tessa.

The two of them looked at each other in silence for a moment. He must have been nervous, because even though the arena was colder than a well-digger's nuts, as Poppy would say, I could see a bead of sweat trickling down the side of his face. Finally he pulled at his tie a little and cleared his throat.

"So what did you think of the game?" he asked her.

"It was good," she said. "You should watch yourself on the cycle, though. You need to make sure your guys are getting the puck."

Alex smiled and ducked his head a little.

"Are you saying I'm a puck hog?" he asked.

Tessa blushed and tried not to smile back.

"Maybe," she said.

Alex laughed. "Well, I'll definitely keep that in mind for next season," he said.

Another moment of excruciating silence passed before Tessa took a deep breath.

"Anyway," she said. "I just came to say I was sorry. About what happened the other night. I shouldn't have told you not to come around the library anymore."

"Oh yeah?" he said hopefully.

"Yeah," she said, shrugging. "It's a free country. You can go wherever you want."

It was hardly an invitation. Alex's face fell a little. Then he took a deep breath.

"There's a party at Lewin's place tonight," he said. "Do you want to come along?"

She shook her head. "No, no," she said. "That wouldn't be a good idea."

"Okay," he said, nodding quickly. "It's no big deal." I could tell, though, that it most certainly was a big deal.

"It's nothing personal," she said. "But—my sister will be there."

"Right," he said, wincing a little.

"Plus parties aren't really my thing, anyway."

"So what *is* your thing?"

She shrugged again, and Alex nodded again and tried to smile. The situation was tanking fast, and we all knew it.

It was time to start earning my money.

"Alex is taking me to the movies up in Brookville tomorrow night," I said. "You should come with us."

Alex's eyes grew wide. He looked at me, and then he looked at Tessa and nodded quickly.

"Yeah, you should," he said.

"I don't know," she said. "I've got a lot of homework to do. Plus, my sister—"

"Oh, please, Tessa," I said. "It would mean a lot to me." I swallowed. "It's—it's my birthday tomorrow."

"It's your birthday?"

"Yeah," I said weakly.

"Really?"

"I swear to god!" I put my hand over my heart and waited for the lightning bolt. When nothing happened, I continued.

"Anyway, Alex told me he'd take me and my friends out, since he's got his license and everything, but no one else wanted to come." And then I dropped my head dejectedly and scuffed my shoe on the rubber mat.

I can really lay it on thick when I want to.

I guess she must have believed me, because it was like someone flipped a switch and her whole face lit up. "That's nice of you," she said to Alex.

Alex smiled and shrugged, and then he shot me a look like he'd never seen me before.

"So will you come, Tessa?" I asked, giving her my best pathetic look. "Please?"

She thought about it for another moment, and then she nodded.

"Great," Alex said. "I'll pick you up at eight. Where do you live?"

"Uh," Tessa said, glancing in her sister's direction. "It would be better, I think, if you picked me up at the library. Is that okay?"

"Sure," he said. "Of course."

"Fine," she said. "I'll see you then."

She turned and walked away, and Alex stared after her with a dazed look on his face, like someone had hit him with a cartoon shovel. I could practically see a dozen little Tessas chirping around his head.

Once the door closed behind her, he actually smiled down at me and messed up my hair a little, but nicely. Not in an I-horked-into-my-hand-and-now-I'm-rubbing-it-into-your-hair kind of way.

"I think things are looking up, kid," he said.

The funny thing was, right at that moment, I believed him. I mean, I was hanging out with the MVP of the championship game and the coolest guy in Evanston, and for all anyone else knew, the two of us were best buds. Bros. Homies. I was so proud I couldn't help but swivel my head around to see if anyone was left in the building to witness what was, up until that point, the most self-affirming moment of my life.

I felt so happy I could have floated right up to the big steel rafters of the arena, like one of those shiny balloons little kids get on their birthday.

But like it usually does, everything in my life crapped out in a most spectacular way.

CHAPTER SIXTEEN

"Alex!" my dad called. "There you are!"

Dad was walking quickly down the dressing room corridor with one of the scouts who had come to watch Alex play.

The scout looked pretty classy, dressed in a navy-blue suit with a crimson-colored tie that had a university emblem all over it. He had his coat in one hand and a clipboard in the other.

"This is Jim McRae," Dad said. "He'd like to speak with you about next season."

Alex stiffened. A muscle jumped in his jaw, but he managed to nod at the guy and shake his hand.

"Why don't we go to the office and sit down?" Dad suggested.

Without glancing my way, he ushered the two of them down the corridor, while I stayed behind and watched them go.

It was just as well. I didn't need a complete stranger witnessing my inability to follow along; it was bad enough being left out of conversations at home. Since Alex had arrived, dinner table discussion, which used to be mostly between my mom and dad about things I had no interest in, were now replaced by hockey talk, which I also had no interest in.

Alex, keep focusing on your core during dry-land training. It's working for you.

Alex, your snapper is looking really deadly out there.

Alex, be careful. You're always trying to put it upstairs. The goalies will start to pick up on that.

It was like listening to Safi talk about silage. They were so into it, at least my dad was, that I swear I could have dropped my drawers in the middle of the dining room and peed on the ficus, and no one would have noticed.

I had no interest in being invited into their stupid little office so I could listen to them speak gibberish and pat each other on the back. I really didn't. Like, even if they'd asked me to come along, I still wouldn't have.

Instead I found a little space underneath the bleachers by the back door where I was sure no one could see me, and I practiced my footwork drills. Jesús was teaching us the tango, which I'd thought would be simple but was most definitely not. Every time I thought I was getting the moves right, Jesús would say something like, "Pick up your feet, Jefe! No slide slide! Ball of your feet, not your heel! Clean and controlled!" Jesús could be a real taskmaster when he wanted to be.

The space underneath the bleachers was a little

cramped, but there was just enough room to practice the basic pattern. I was starting the ocho cortado when I heard Dad and Alex coming down the corridor. Instead of calling out to them, though, I paused for a minute to listen.

"He's interested," Dad said. "But this is university hockey. And you know the NHL prefers to recruit out of the juniors."

"But I *could* get recruited out of university," Alex said. "It happens."

"Sure, sure," Dad said. "It's just—you'll play way less if you're in school, which means not as much skill development."

Alex looked down at his shoes and mumbled something I couldn't hear. I moved closer so I could peek at them around the corner of the bleachers.

"Hey," my dad said. He bumped Alex on the arm.

Alex raised his head and gave Dad a look like someone had just pooped in his cornflakes.

"You don't have to decide now, Alex," Dad said. "Think it over. Weigh your options. This is a big decision."

Alex shrugged, and my dad gave him another chuck on the arm. I snorted quietly and shook my head. *Everybody cry for Alex*, I thought. *He has so many scouts interested in him, he doesn't know which team to pick. Poor baby.*

Just as I was about to walk over and put an end to the lovefest, my dad reached up and put his hand on Alex's shoulder and gave it a shake.

"You played a great season," he said. "I'm proud of you, champ."

Champ.

I held my breath, while my dad and Alex opened the arena door and walked out into the night. I don't want to be dramatic or anything, but the pain I was feeling at that moment was almost exactly the same as when Artie punched me in the old funsack. Except this time, I was feeling it everywhere. And instead of wanting to cry and also puke, I just wanted to punch someone's face in. Mostly my own.

But doing that would have been psycho, and I knew it, so I zipped up my coat and stepped out to the parking lot.

Which was empty.

They'd left without me.

For a minute I stood there staring, while the rain slooshed inside the collar of my jacket and down my neck. I'm not going to say I cried, but I had that painful kind of throat constriction that generally precedes weeping. That feeling was quickly replaced by a rage that was so sudden and all-consuming I actually kicked over the first thing I saw, which happened to be a Rubbermaid garbage can. Then I tried to stomp on it, but when I couldn't do any damage (because it was made out of rubber, apparently), I picked it up and flung it across the parking lot. Old food trays and red-checkered hot-dog wrappers went flying everywhere. That's when some old guy who lived across the street from the arena opened his front door and told me to "Get the eff home, you little bastard!" and threatened to call the cops, so I took off running.

I couldn't go home, though. Not yet. There was no way I was walking through the front door to see Dad, Mom, and Alex enjoying themselves in Happy Family Land, probably completely oblivious to the fact that I wasn't even there. Like, that would have totally sent me over the edge.

So instead I decided to go to the cemetery to visit my brother.

It's not as weird as it sounds. Poppy told me my parents had buried Gordie in the Sandy Hill Cemetery so he could be in the same place as my grandmother. When we moved to Evanston, I made sure to take a trip to see for myself. I'd already been to my grandmother's grave; she was in the old part of the cemetery, surrounded by a phalanx of Stone relatives. It had taken me a while to find Gordie, though, because he was buried in the new section, under a willow tree, and the branches drooped down so low you almost couldn't see his headstone.

Since then I'd made it a point to visit him when I could. I'd swing by after school, or even on weekends sometimes, and sit on the stone bench next to his grave while I talked about what was going on in my life. I guess the idea that my brother might be out there somewhere listening and caring about the things I told him, especially when no one else did, made me feel better. Plus he was an excellent listener.

Once on what proved to be a very bad day, I showed up to find Dad there. I hid behind the tombstone of Alexandra Lindy, beloved wife and mother, for a half hour—watching while Dad stood looking down at Gordie's grave with his hands stuffed in his pockets. He kept brushing at his eyes with the back of his hand, so I guess that meant he was crying, but I couldn't tell, and either way, I didn't want to think about it. After that, he bent over and kind of rubbed the top of the gravestone a little, like it was a person he was trying to comfort. Then he left.

Look, I don't want to sound like a baby. Obviously I understand it didn't matter how long ago Gordie died or the short time he'd actually lived, Dad was always going to love him, and, like, keep him in his heart and everything. But the irony that my father could make such an effort to actively remember his son who died over fifteen years ago but could still forget his living son who'd been standing right next to him thirty minutes before was definitely not lost on me.

That's what I was thinking as I trudged up the hill to the cemetery. I was almost at the gates when Dad screeched up in his truck and rolled down the window.

"Will!" he basically shouted. "Where the hell have you been!"

I shouldn't have been surprised he was angry, but I still jumped a little.

"I was just—"

"I thought you caught a ride home with Mom! Why didn't you call after Alex and I left?"

"I'm sorry," I said. "I went outside to find you, and the door locked behind me."

I might have pointed out that I could have easily called him if he and Mom let me have a phone, but it didn't feel like the time.

"Just get in!" he said.

I walked around the front of the truck and got in. I hadn't realized how wet I was until I bent my head to buckle my seat belt and water started dripping off my nose.

"You're soaked," Dad said. He shook his head at me like he was personally offended by the concept of water. He leaned over and dug around in the back seat until he found an old mashed-up and slightly stained roll of paper towels.

"Here," he said, tossing them at me. "Dry off."

He put the truck in gear and pulled out into the street. I had to unroll four or five layers of the paper towel until I got to some that looked like they weren't soaked in coffee or some other unknown substance, and then I dabbed at my hair.

Finally, without looking at me, Dad said, "You know, you really scared your mom."

He was speaking pretty calmly and quietly while at the same time giving off an I'm-trying-very-hard-to-contain-my-anger-son-but-one-wrong-move-and-I'm-going-to-go-completely-Old-Testament-on-your-butt-so-you'd-better-tread-very-very-carefully vibe. And even though intellectually I knew that in my entire life my dad had never touched a hair on my head, I was still pretty terrified.

"I know. I'm sorry—"

"She was worried sick. This time of night, and in the rain, it's almost impossible for drivers to see. Someone could have hit you. What were you thinking?"

I was thinking that I was completely forgotten and abandoned by you at the rink and also about how you've never really loved me, but whatevs.

"I was just trying to get home," I said.

"Then what in god's name were you doing all the way out here? It took me twenty minutes to find you!"

"I don't know," I said, shrugging. "I guess I just kind of felt like taking the scenic route."

"At eleven thirty at night? In the rain?"

"When you say it like that, I guess it does sound a little crazy—"

"Crazy!" he said. "It's beyond crazy! Goddammit, Will! Sometimes I wonder if you have any sense at all!"

There was no point saying sorry again, even though I was. Instead I slouched down in my seat, and Dad didn't say another word until he pulled into the driveway. Then he turned off the engine, but instead of getting out, he just sat there for a moment.

"Look, Will," he said. "I know I've been busy lately, but this is a really important time. Alex's got a lot of scouts after him, and there's a lot of pressure about what his future is going to look like. I need to help him deal with it, and I can't be worried that you're putting yourself in danger and scaring your mother half to death."

"O—kay," I said. I was trying hard not to sound like I was on the verge of crying, which I sort of was.

Dad glanced at me and sighed again. "We all have our responsibilities in this family, Will. We all have our roles to play."

"I kn-know," I said. "I un-derstand."

Of course I understood. That's why I was so upset. It didn't matter what happened, and it didn't matter what anyone did. Alex was always going to be a hero, Gordie was an angel, and I was most definitely a ghost.

CHAPTER SEVENTEEN

Earlier in the year, Artie and Wayne had stolen my clothes during gym class and barricaded me in the ladies' locker room, along with a bunch of semiclad girls who were busy getting dressed for class. For three long minutes, I had been trapped while the girls threw hair products at me and screamed, "Pervert!"

Those three minutes—while I banged helplessly on the door and tried to hide my man parts with a handful of discarded yellow pinnies—were less stressful than the first three or so hours I spent with Alex and Tessa on their first date. And just a shade less humiliating.

It started with the car ride. Alex and I were both silent on the way to pick up Tessa. I didn't have much to say, because I was still mad about being left behind at the rink.

We were halfway to the library when Alex glanced my way.

"What are you so quiet about?"

I shrugged. "What do you mean?"

"I mean, you're never quiet about anything.

Ever," he added, which I thought was uncalled for. "So what's your problem?"

I shrugged again and looked out the window.

Alex sighed, and after a moment he cleared his throat.

"Look, I'm sorry your dad and I forgot you. We both thought you went home with your mom."

We.

"Hey," Alex said. "Didn't you hear me? I said I'm sorry!"

"I heard you," I said.

"So?"

"So what?"

"So I never apologize to anyone for anything. You should appreciate that."

"Oh, what an honor," I said, clutching my clasped hands to my chest. "I'm so overwhelmed! Whatever will I do with myself?"

"What is your problem, Will? I'm trying to be nice!"

"I didn't realize it was such a hard thing to do. Especially considering the fact, if it weren't for me, you wouldn't even be going on this date right now."

"And if it weren't for *me*, you'd still be getting your ass kicked by a couple of morons."

"You only helped me because you needed me to get Tessa to like you. The only time you're ever nice to me, which isn't often by the way, is when you want something."

Alex stepped on the brakes. Then he shoved

the gear into neutral and turned toward me. I thought for a second he was going to beat me up, so without taking my eyes off him, I groped for the door handle.

"You really think that?" he asked.

I swallowed. I really did think that, but I didn't want to say it out loud. I shrugged again.

"Well, then you're an idiot." He shifted back into gear and started driving again. "And you can be an idiot all you want tomorrow," he said. "But for tonight, could you just be cool? I'm a little—nervous—and the last thing I need is for you to be acting like a baby."

"Why are you nervous? You're such a perfect, amazing person—haven't you ever been on a date before?"

He ignored my comments and blew out a long breath. "Not like this one," he said.

We pulled up to the library, and Alex turned in his seat again.

"Look," he said, like he was trying hard not to kill me, "I appreciate you're the reason she's going out with me tonight. But if it's all the same to you, I can handle things from here."

"Are you telling me to get out or something?"

"No, but if you could just keep your trap shut for the next few hours, I'd appreciate it."

I put my hands up. "Fine by me," I said.

He got out of the car, and I climbed into the back seat. I watched him walk up the sidewalk to greet Tessa, and it was all tight smiles and crossed arms and hunched shoulders. The whole thing was so awkward I could barely watch.

Then Tessa got in the car and handed me an envelope.

"What's this?" I said.

She gave me a strange look. "It's a birthday card!"

Yikes. I'd forgotten all about that. I felt my stomach give a little twist thanks to the sudden and intense guilt I was feeling for having basically snowed my friend into a date with someone she didn't even like.

"Oh, thanks," I said weakly.

"Open it up!"

"Sure thing."

It was a card with a picture of Swiss cheese on it, and underneath it said, "This is a cheesy birthday card." Inside was a gift certificate to the studio for forty dollars.

"You can put it toward a proper pair of dance shoes," she said.

"Aw, thanks, Tessa," I said weakly. "You didn't have to do this."

"Of course I did!" she said, smiling warmly at me. "You're a great kid!"

Ugh. The guilt.

Alex pulled away from the library while Tessa turned around and buckled herself up. And then no one said a word for the entire ride. Seriously. It was complete and total radio silence. Unless you counted the fifteen times Alex cleared his throat, which I do not, since last time I checked the sound of someone harrumphing into his fist does not qualify as conversation.

It didn't get much better once we got to the theater, either. Tessa totally kept up the silent treatment, and Alex didn't seem to know what to do about it, so he overcompensated by buying a truckload of crap from the concession stand.

All I wanted to do was get the heck out of there. I couldn't, though, because it was too far to walk home. Plus I knew Alex would kill me if I took off. So instead I did what anyone might do if they were stuck in an impossibly tense situation with no escape and enough junk food to feed an army of couch potatoes.

I ate.

I ate and I ate. And then I ate some more.

I started with the nachos, which were covered in jalapeño peppers and cheese the same color and texture as a melted-down traffic cone. Next was the popcorn. I finished my bag, and then I nudged Tessa and asked for hers, which she handed over with a small, distracted smile. Once I was through that, I started on the sour peaches, then the Junior Mints, and then I made my way through two bags of Swedish berries. Finally, in the last five minutes of the movie, I tore open the jumbo-size bag of M&M'S and poured them straight into my mouth. I'm not even sure I took the time to chew. I just gulped them back like Alex did when he was drinking from the milk carton.

Once I was done, I didn't feel better. My stomach, which wasn't feeling great to begin with, started churning, and I felt a white-hot blade of pain shoot through my bowels once. Twice. I knew from past experience it was only a matter of time before I would need to get to a toilet if I was to avoid a potentially devastating public incident.

I could have gone to the bathroom in the theater. However, just as I was about to make a beeline there, I noticed Artie and his dirtbag friends hanging around just outside the door. I thought of asking Alex to accompany me, but there was just no way of doing that without it sounding super sketchy. My only hope was that Alex had given up on Tessa and would drive her straight home and put a blessed end to a disastrous evening.

No such luck. When we got into the car, Alex turned to her.

"Do you want to go somewhere else?" he asked.

She shrugged a little. "I'm pretty tired," she said.

Good. Good! I thought as my guts groaned and creaked like the boards on a sinking ship. *Be tired. Be very tired. Demand to go home. Right now!*

Alex leaned back on the headrest and turned to look at her.

"Come on, Tessa," he said. "It's only nine-thirty."

She shrugged again and sighed.

"We could go get something to eat?" he said.

Oh god. Not more food.

"I don't know," she said. She swallowed and looked out the window.

Alex glanced back at me, and then he shifted a little closer to her.

"Just give me a chance, Tessa," he said in a low voice. "Please?"

I heard her sigh again as my guts twisted up another notch. I could feel pressure building that had nothing to do with what was going on in the front seat.

This is taking too long! Just drive! Drive somewhere! For the love of god!

Just as Tessa turned her head away from the window to look at Alex, it happened.

I didn't poop my pants exactly. I did let out a long, epically loud fart, and even though I knew it wasn't so bad that I would have to change my pants, I was certain it had touched at least one layer of cloth in a significant way.

And oh my gentle lord, did it stink.

At first neither Tessa nor Alex said anything. They just turned slowly and looked at me with wide eyes.

"Did that just happen?" Tessa asked Alex, while he glared at me accusingly.

"I'm sorry!" I yelled. "I think I'm sick!"

Then the stench hit. They covered their noses with their hands and bolted from the car.

When I scrambled out, the two of them were leaning into each other, doubled over. They were laughing so hard they weren't even making any noise. In fact, Alex was so hysterical he was drooling a little, and when Tessa saw that, she nearly keeled over.

I was mortified. I'd never farted in front of a girl in my life, except for maybe my mom, and even then only by accident.

"It's not funny!" I shouted, hating them both.

"We're not laughing at you, Will," Tessa gasped as she wiped at her eyes.

"You're such a liar!" I said. "You're laughing right now!"

"I'm sorry," she said, inhaling deeply, trying to calm down. She looked at me holding my aching stomach, and her eyebrows drew together in real concern. "Seriously, though. Are you okay?"

"No! I'm not!" I said. "I thought it might be cool getting out of the house for once on a Saturday night, but you both wrecked it, and now you're making fun of me!"

"Come on, Will," she said. "Don't be mad. Is there something we can do for you? Do you want to go back in the theater and use the bathroom?"

I felt another wave of pain roll through me, and I knew this time it was the real thing. I didn't even bother to answer her. I just took off running.

CHAPTER EIGHTEEN

I spent twenty white-knuckled minutes evacuating my nervous bowels in the restroom. Thankfully Artie and his friends, as well as the rest of the crowd, had cleared out. Anyone who dared come in left pretty quickly, so at least when I came out of the stall, I could throw my underwear in the garbage without anyone seeing me.

Turns out soiling myself in public was a real icebreaker, though. By the time I got back to the car, Tessa was her old self again, and when Alex suggested we take a drive to Dairy Queen, she didn't object at all.

We sat at a picnic table outside. The air was cool, and Tessa shivered a little and buttoned up her sweater. When Alex saw that, he took his jacket off and put it around her shoulders. It was a classy move.

"But you'll be cold," she said.

"Nah," he said, shoveling an oversized spoonful of ice cream into his mouth. "I'm always hot."

I guess Tessa agreed, because I saw her sneak a glance at Alex's muscles, which bulged through his sweater. When she saw that I caught her checking him out, she blushed and looked at the fields surrounding the parking lot.

"The fireflies will be out soon," she said in a strangled voice.

Alex stared down at his ice cream while he tried unsuccessfully to cut a piece of banana with his spoon.

"I don't think I've ever seen a firefly," he said.

"You've never seen a firefly?" Tessa was incredulous.

He looked up and smiled at her. "No fireflies where I come from."

"I forgot," she said, biting into her ice cream. "You're one of those fancy city boys."

She was teasing him, but I could tell he liked it. His face softened, and he caught her gaze and held it.

"Yeah," he said quietly. "I'm fancy all right."

I began to get the distinct feeling that despite being responsible for making the evening happen, I was definitely entering third-wheel territory.

"Your dad never took you camping?" she asked.

"No," he said, shoveling in another mouthful. "My dad never did anything like that with me. He was always too busy working."

"What about your mom?"

Alex half snorted, half laughed. "My mom? Take me camping? Please." He shook his head like the idea of it was the craziest thing he'd heard all night. "The only thing my parents are interested in when it comes to me is hockey."

"I can relate to that a little," Tessa said. "I come from a long line of hockey players."

"Yeah? Your dad played?" Alex asked.

"No." She grinned. "My *mom*. She won a silver at Nagano. It was actually the first year for women's hockey in the Olympics."

"She was in the Olympics? Are you serious?"

"Yes." Tessa laughed. "Hockey is huge in my house. I think I was on skates before I even knew how to walk."

"So why don't you play now?" I asked.

Tessa shrugged. "Sheri and I both played competitively for a long time. She was insanely good—she actually played on the boys' team until she was thirteen and made the district all-stars every year. But then—" Tessa stopped and sighed. "Then our dad got sick, and Mom needed us, and we just couldn't manage it. After Dad died, I guess our hearts weren't in it anymore."

Alex had been about to take a bite of ice cream, but he stopped and his face fell. He put his spoon down.

"I'm sorry," he said.

"You don't have to say that." She shrugged. "It's not your fault."

"I know," he said. "But I'm still sorry."

Tessa traced the outline of a heart that someone had carved into the table.

"Sheri took it hard," she said, without looking up. "She kind of fell apart."

No one said anything, and Tessa sighed.

"All that drinking and partying? That's not the girl she is." She looked up at Alex. "It's not the girl she used to be, anyway. You should just know that."

Alex's face flushed, and he dropped his eyes. "I'm sorry," he said again.

Everyone was silent for a moment.

"Anyway," she said, shrugging again, "with hockey out of the picture, I've had time to do other things. Speaking of which, Will, I forgot to mention. Jesús officially invited us to dance at the Spencerville Fair, and I told him we'd do it."

She said it so casually it took a moment to sink in. It felt like someone had knocked me in the chest with a two-by-four.

"You did *what*?" I practically shouted. "There is absolutely no way I'm dancing at that fair!"

"You have to," she said. "We're already committed. Plus it's for charity."

"You had no right to sign us up without talking to me first!"

"I did talk to you!"

"Yeah, and I said I wasn't interested!"

Tessa sighed and turned to Alex.

"Alex, can you please tell Will he doesn't need to be embarrassed about dancing in public?"

Alex started to choke on his ice cream. "Sure,"

he said, coughing into his fist. "There's nothing at all weird about that."

She narrowed her eyes at him.

"You think there is?"

I could see Alex was torn between telling the truth and staying on her good side. He coughed a little more and concentrated on stirring what was left of his ice cream with his spoon.

"Look," he said, "I'm all for the kid doing his thing and everything, but you can't deny the fact that, for a guy, ballroom dancing's a little—"

"What?" she asked. Her eyes were like slits.

"Different," he said carefully. Then he looked at me. "No offense."

Offense taken, I thought, even though I knew he was right.

"Why?" Tessa asked. "It's just dancing. Don't you dance?"

Alex laughed out loud. "No," he said, like it was the most ridiculous thing he'd ever heard.

"You're kidding me," Tessa said. "You've never danced in your entire life?"

"Nope," he said. "And I never will."

"What if Tessa asked you to?" I said. "Would you then?"

That stopped him for a second. He screwed up his face like he was thinking about it, and then he looked at Tessa and grinned. He reached out and, with his thumb, he rubbed away a bit of ice cream that had dripped onto her chin.

151

"I'd definitely consider it," he said.

It was almost eleven—Tessa's curfew—so after she excused herself to go to the bathroom, I waited in line with Alex while he ordered fries for the ride home.

The place was still packed, and more people arrived every minute before the doors closed for the night. Alex and I stood wedged between a young couple with a sleeping baby and a middle-aged man and woman who were wearing tennis whites with sweaters tied over their shoulders.

"I can't believe you're still eating," I told him. "I think you have some kind of medical condition."

He slapped a heavy hand down on my shoulder. I practically dropped to my knees with the weight of it.

"Listen," he said. "Thanks for coming along tonight. I mean it."

He had an odd look on his face I'd never seen before. I couldn't be sure, but it almost looked like gratitude. I was practically speechless.

"It's okay," I stammered. "I mean, you're paying me, aren't you? It's all part of the package."

"Well, maybe next time I can get the package that doesn't involve you crapping your pants in the back seat of my car."

I sighed. "Ha. Ha. Ha."

He laughed and started to say something else when a group of girls pushed their way into the restaurant. I turned to watch them pass, and as I did my whole world came to a screeching halt.

It was Claudia Valenta.

And she. Was wearing. A tank top.

She followed another girl who pushed through the lines to get to the far end of the restaurant, where it wasn't quite so crowded. Her friend excused herself to wiggle between me and Alex, and it took me a second to realize that Claudia was going to pass right in front of me too.

In that moment, I swear, everything went into slow motion. It was like I was in a dream state. She looked at me. I looked at her. She smiled slowly. I smiled back, all stretched lips and teeth. *Excuuuuussse meeeeeee*, she said, in one of those deep, slow-motion voices that made her sound a little like Satan. *Nooooo prooooobleeeeemmmmmm*, I said back, sounding the same way.

Then it happened. The guy holding the baby bumped into her, and she stumbled and pressed up against me, her hands on my shoulders, her boobs brushing across my arm as she slid past.

Thwack! The sound of fabric against fabric—of boob against arm—was amplified in my ears until it was all I could hear.

In that second, it was like I touched a live electrical wire. I might have even cried out a little—I don't really remember. All I do know is that a jolt of electricity went through me, traveling across every nerve in my body before gathering farther south and throbbing there like a swarm of bees caught in a jar.

It wouldn't have been a problem if I hadn't been going commando, but I was, and one thing experience taught me was that these moments are a lot easier to contain when you're wearing tight undershorts.

I was actually dizzy, most likely because a large percentage of my blood had relocated from my brain to other regions.

I was just coming back to my senses when Alex said, "What's with you?"

"Nothing," I said quickly. "I wasn't looking at anyone."

The corner of his mouth lifted in a smile.

"You like that girl?" he asked, lifting his chin in Claudia's direction.

"What girl?"

"The one that's got you pitching a tent in your pants right now."

I scrambled to pull my shirt out of my jeans, but it wasn't long enough to cover what I needed it to cover.

Alex rolled his eyes, and he unzipped his sweater and tossed it at me. Now he was down to his T-shirt.

"Get a hold of yourself, kid," he said.

I wrapped his sweater around my waist. No one else had noticed my predicament. All the same, I knew I needed to do something to take care of the situation, and I needed to do it fast, so I squinched my eyes tight and tried to concentrate.

"What are you doing now?" Alex whispered fiercely.

"I'm thinking about dead cats."

"Oh, for god's sake," he said. "Just wait for me outside!"

He pushed me through the crowd, and I hobbled to the door, bent over like an old man with a cane. Even though Alex's sweater was hiding everything, it felt like every person who passed me on my way to the car knew exactly what was going on and was laughing at me because of it. I felt like Quasimodo in that book I had to read for French class, *The Hunchback of Notre Dame*, lurching through jeering crowds on the streets of Paris. Except the disfiguring hump wasn't on my back, if you know what I mean.

Ten minutes later, Tessa and Alex met me at the car.

"What's up, kid?" he said, chuckling to himself while he stuffed fries into his mouth.

I wanted to kill him.

"What's so funny?" Tessa asked, smiling.

"Oh, nothing," Alex said, grinning at me. "It's just interesting to think of Will waiting out here for us. All alone. Standing at attention, so to speak."

He laughed again, and Tessa gave him a quizzical look before she got into the car. I sighed and crawled into the back seat, waiting for death.

Alex parked across the street from Tessa's house. I watched as he walked her up to the door, and the two of them stood talking for what seemed like hours. I was getting pretty bored, when Alex said something to make Tessa laugh. Then he moved in even closer and took one of her hands. I perked right up because I knew he was going to kiss her, and I figured when it came to moments like these, I needed all the instruction I could get.

He had to bend down quite a bit before he could make contact. He put one arm around her, and then he put his other hand kind of on her cheek and up into her hair, and by the time he kissed her, she looked like she was ready to melt into a big puddle on the step.

Man, he was smooth.

And yet, sadly, not quite smooth enough.

They'd made contact for about five seconds when the front door flung open to reveal Sheri. At least, I think it was Sheri. It was hard to tell. She was in her bathrobe, with a towel around her head and what looked like green goop all over her face.

She wagged her finger at Alex, and he jumped away from Tessa with his hands up like he'd just been caught trying to shoplift her. Then Sheri dragged Tessa into the house, and Tessa barely had time to wave goodbye before Sheri slammed the door in Alex's face.

He stood on the stoop for a moment, staring in shock at the closed door. Then it opened, and his jacket came flying out. He shook his head while he picked it up and jogged back to the car. He had a big grin on his face.

"That was awkward," I said as I climbed into the front seat.

"Please," he said. "You crapped in your pants at the movie theater and popped a raging boner in the middle of a crowded Dairy Queen. If there was a prize for awkward this evening, I'd say you won it, Skidmark."

He glanced over at Tessa's house one last time and then pulled away from the curb.

"So who's the girl?" he asked.

"She's no one," I said quickly. "Forget it."

"Are you telling me this happens whenever you make the slightest physical contact with any girl? Do I need to start carrying a bucket of water around with me whenever we're out together?" He looked over at me.

"No! Everything is under control."

"So who is she?"

Her name is Claudia. I'm going to marry her one day, and our children will be in the Olympics.

"She's just a girl," I said. I stared at the dashboard as if my life depended on it. "Just a girl I kind of—like. I wasn't expecting to see her tonight, that's all."

"Does she go to your dance school too?"

I glared at him because I thought he might be making fun of me, but he was looking at me like he expected a real answer.

"No," I said. "She works at the Czech bakery. She doesn't know who I am."

"Well, we'll have to change that," he said. "You can keep the sweater, by the way."

He leaned over and cranked the stereo. Then we rolled our windows down and drove over to Main Street, where we cruised for a while. Unfortunately, because it was Evanston, it only took about five minutes to drive each way, even with the lights. Still, for a while, we were just two cool guys in a cool car out on the town: Alex the Hockey Stud and his sidekick, Captain Skidmark.

It was easily the best night of my life.

CHAPTER NINETEEN

I imagine Tessa thought she was doing us a favor by signing us up to dance at the Spencerville Fair—in front of a packed crowd that would most definitely include many horrendous people from school and, quite possibly, my parents. In reality, all she did was light a fuse on a bomb that was going to blow my entire life to smithereens in a little over a month.

That's why, on Tuesday night, my plan was to convince Tessa to change her mind about the show, no matter what. Unfortunately, by the time I got to the studio, she was already paired off with PJ. This was a bummer for two reasons: it meant I had to wait until break to talk to her, and it also meant I was stuck dancing with Annie, who was one strange little bird.

The good news was it was swing night, which was one of my favorites, and even though I was worried I was going to break Annie in half if I tried to spin her, she turned out to be surprisingly resilient.

She was also freaking brilliant at East Coast swing. She knew all the moves, and unlike with

Tessa, I didn't have to fight to lead her. It was like she knew exactly what I was going to do before I even knew it myself, which basically made her the Wayne Gretzky of swing dancing.

"This is the dance I used to do when I was a girl!" she hollered as we triple-stepped around the room. Annie always hollered, even when music wasn't playing.

"Mr. Johnson, god rest his soul, used to pick me up on Saturday nights, and we'd dance until the sun came up, just like this!"

"Mr. Johnson?"

"My husband!"

"Oh."

"His first name was Chauncey!" she said, making a face. "Chauncey Johnson. Can you imagine?"

It was definitely hard to believe.

"Well, I couldn't *think* about calling him *Chauncey*. So on our wedding night I told him, 'From here on in, I'm calling you Mr. Johnson, and that's the end of it!'"

I couldn't help myself. I had to ask.

"So did you ever call him Chauncey again?"

"Not once in fifty-eight years!" she said.

We did a couple of pivot turns, and then she said, "You know, I didn't like Mr. Johnson much when I first met him. He had big googly eyes on either side of his head. Made him look a little like an iguana."

I literally did not have a response for that.

"But when we danced!" Her eyes misted over. "I couldn't help but fall madly in love with him. He was just so graceful!"

"I wasn't aware that grace was something women looked for in a man," I said, as I spun her into a sweetheart hold.

"Oh, certainly," she said. "If a man knows what he's doing on a dance floor, he pretty much knows what he's doing everywhere else. If you know what I mean."

She looked up at me and waggled her eyebrows. Then she grinned so wide I could see the metal clips that held her dentures in place. I had to fight to keep from clawing out the part of my brain responsible for sight and memory.

"And what about you, Will?"

"What do you mean?" I asked, alarmed.

"Well, a dancer like you? You must have all kinds of girlfriends."

"Uh, no. You'd be surprised at how many girlfriends I do not have."

"That can't be! With those eyes? You're like a young Paul Newman."

"The salad dressing guy?"

"You know, there's a girl who sings in my choir at church. I think she'd be perfect for you. She has a lovely personality."

Oh god. The last thing I needed was Annie setting me up. Plus I knew what "lovely personality" meant. It was code for homely church nerd.

Thankfully, right at that moment, the song ended, and Jesús called for a break. Annie thanked me for the dance while she patted me on the face for long enough to make it uncomfortable. Then she ambled off to talk to her friends.

Just as I was about to look for Tessa, Jesús passed by.

"Oh, Jefe," he said, smiling warmly. "I'm so happy you and Tessie are gonna do the show. This is very especial for me."

"Yeah, about that," I said. "I'm a little worried that I—"

"That you don't have a costume? No need to worry, Jefe," he said. "I got something perfect in mind for you. I already started making it."

I swallowed a lump in my throat that was the size and texture of a kiwi.

"Jeez, Jesús," I said, willing myself to stay calm. "It's not necessary that you go to that kind of trouble for me. I mean, to be honest, I don't really think I'm down for this—"

Jesús gave me a confused look, which was probably hard for him to do considering his eyebrows looked like they were trying to escape from his forehead.

"What's this 'not necessary,' Jefe? This is your first big show, okay? You're gonna be dancing for hundreds of people. Of course, it's *necessary!*"

Oh lord. Kill me now.

At that moment, PJ wandered over. He was still

wearing the fez from his dress-up-day costume. For some reason, he'd embraced it as some kind of weird fashion statement.

"Did you say Will is dancing in the fair?" he asked, in a voice that was way louder than I wanted it to be.

"Yes," Jesús said. "He and Tessie are gonna dance with the pros. They will be great advertising for the studio!"

PJ's face broke out into a huge smile, which did nothing to dislodge the humongous spitballs on either side of his mouth.

"That's great, Will," he said. He held his hand out to me, and I shook it. His fez had begun to slide sideways, and he pushed it back into place and crossed his arms.

"You know, last year a television crew came in from Kingston and recorded parts of the show for the news. If they come this year, you might be famous!"

He smiled triumphantly at me like he'd told me I won the lottery. The tassel from his ridiculous hat was swinging all over the place. I hate to admit it, but it was the first time in my life I ever considered punching out a senior citizen.

"Just think, Will," he said. "In a few weeks, maybe your whole life will change!"

That's what I was afraid of.

CHAPTER TWENTY

"Do you think you'd recognize me if I dyed my hair black?" I asked Safi as we put our books in our lockers Friday after French class.

"Probably." He shrugged. "Why? Are you gonna work on a disguise or something?"

"No," I said. "It's nothing. Forget it."

"I don't know why you'd bother, anyway," Safi continued. "Ever since your cousin put the boots to Artie and Wayne, they haven't looked sideways at you."

It was true. After the incident behind the arena, I barely saw Artie and Wayne in the halls, and when I did, they just put their heads down and kept walking.

They weren't the only ones, though. These days, everybody seemed to be leaving me alone. No one tripped me in gym or knocked my books out of my hands. No one came up to me in the hall and said, "Hey, loser. Your dad just gave me a detention for chewing gum," while they hocked a big, slimy wad of it on my binder.

I shook my head. "I don't know," I said. "I don't

trust the whole thing. Plus Artie's still giving you a hard time."

"Only when I'm not with you, buddy." Safi grinned at me and gave me a playful smack on the back. "So let me know when you're ready for me to move in."

As we passed the cafeteria, Safi stopped and looked through the window.

"It would be a bad idea to go in, right? I mean, even though no one's giving you a hard time anymore? It still might be better to just hide in the lab and eat what we brought, don't you think?"

He stood there waiting for me to answer. Lately he'd stopped wearing his cowboy clothes. Instead he was wearing a Senators cap and a T-shirt that said I ♥ Hip-Hop Music that might have been ironic if anyone else had been wearing it, but on him it was just sad. He had big black circles under his eyes.

All of a sudden, instead of feeling afraid, I felt angry.

"Screw it," I said. "I've got six bucks in my pocket, and I'm sick of tuna. Let's get something."

"Are you sure?" Safi asked.

"Sure, I'm sure," I lied. "We'll be all right."

We grinned at each other and threw our lunches in the garbage. Then we walked into the cafeteria and made our way to the end of the line.

I don't know about Safi, but my heart was doing the merengue in my chest. I made sure to scope out all the exits—both regular and emergency—we could run for if the situation called for it.

We moved down the line and the lunch lady dumped pizza and french fries on our plates like it was no big deal, like being there wasn't the bravest thing we'd probably done in our entire lives. Then I paid the guy at the register, and Safi and I stood together, holding our trays and looking around the room.

"I guess we should sit," I said.

"Yeah," Safi said, "but where? I saw Artie by the back entrance, so definitely not there."

"Over there might be okay," I said, pointing to a table full of girls.

"No way," Safi said, shaking his head. "That's where Becky Sjonger sits. She called me a festering pus hole in gym class yesterday."

"What does that even mean?"

"I don't know," Safi said, shrugging. "But it didn't make me feel good."

Then he nodded in the direction of Evan Flinker and Kole Beaudet and sighed.

"We won't be eating at that table, that's for sure."

Then as we stood there staring like idiots, Evan turned in his seat.

"Yo, Stone!" he called. "C'mere a minute."

We froze. Safi shifted his eyes in my direction.

"What do we do?" he whispered out of the corner of his mouth.

I weighed the options. It wasn't like Evan and

his friends could beat us up right there in the cafeteria. The worst they could do was embarrass us, and even though I didn't want that, it might be even worse if we ran.

"Come on," I sighed, and started walking toward their table. Safi only hesitated for a second before he followed behind.

"Hey," Evan said as we approached. "What's going on?"

"Nothing," I mumbled.

That wasn't exactly true. A waterfall of sweat was flowing from my armpits. It was only a matter of time before my deodorant gave up, if it hadn't already, and then I would not only be a loser, I would be a loser with apocalyptic BO.

I glanced at Safi, and he was shaking so bad the cutlery on his tray was clinking together. Luckily no one else seemed to notice.

Evan tipped back in his chair. "So someone told me Alex Stone is your cousin," he said. "Is that true?"

I blinked. "Oh," I said. "Uh—yeah, he is."

"I heard he's being scouted by the NHL."

"There's been some scouts talking to him, yes," I said.

Evan looked around at his friends, and they all nodded their approval.

"You wanna sit down?" Evan asked.

I looked at Safi, who was shaking his head ever so slightly.

"Sure," I said weakly. And then a little louder: "I'm with my friend, though."

"He can sit too."

Evan gestured to the guys across from him, and they shuffled down to make room for me and Safi. Instead of sitting, though, Safi lowered himself to the bench slowly and then hovered there like the seat was made of lava and he was worried about burning his butt.

"Sit!" I whispered.

He sat.

I sat down next to Todd Berger, a right winger, who thrust an economy-size bag of Cheetos in my face.

"Want one?" he asked. His mouth was full, and he was spitting orange powder in every direction, which was totally gross, but I took a handful.

As I sat there munching my Cheetos, I took a moment to appreciate the significance of the situation. It was twelve thirty-five on a Friday, and Safi and I were in the cafeteria sitting at the cool table with half the starting line of the bantam triple-A hockey team. And they hadn't brought us over so they could make fun of us or squirt ketchup down our pants or force us to drink a glass of congealed french fry gravy. They legitimately wanted us there.

Somehow, after months of being treated like the scum of the earth, Safi and I had hit the big time.

Berger poured the last of his Cheetos in his

mouth, crumpled up the bag, and turned his attention to Evan and Kole, who were now in the middle of a heated argument.

"Pavelski did it," Evan said. "And Nystrom."

"So?" Kole said, squinting up at him scornfully.

"Desjardins and Niedermayer have done it too, and they're hall-of-famers."

"Good for them," Kole said.

I leaned over to Berger. "What are they talking about?"

He answered me through an explosion of Cheetos dust. "They're talking about guys in the NHL who figure skate to improve their technique."

"Oh."

"I'm just saying *I* would never do it," Kole continued.

"Why not?" Evan asked.

Kole blew out an exasperated breath. "Because real guys don't figure skate!"

Evan leaned back in his chair and grinned at Kole. "Since when are *you* the expert on what real guys do?"

Everyone went, "*Oooooooh!*"

Kole didn't get mad, though. He just smiled.

"Well, maybe I'm not an expert," he said calmly. "But I'm almost positive real guys don't help their moms make cupcakes for the bake fair."

All the guys went, "*Whoaaaaaaa!*"

Evan smirked. "You enjoyed those cupcakes, as I recall," he said. "But while we're on the subject,

I bet most real guys don't own a copy of *Taylor Swift—Greatest Hits*."

Everyone busted a gut, including Kyle Stephenson, a chipmunk-cheeked defenseman, who was laughing so hard he almost fell off the bench. Kole gave him the hairy eyeball.

"At least I don't use strawberry body wash, *Kyle*."

Kyle's cheeks turned bright red. "I like how it smells!" he said.

Then he pointed at Dave, who was sitting across from him. "Dave watches *The Bachelor*!"

Dave didn't even flinch. "I'm not ashamed of that," he said. "*The Bachelor* is a quality program."

"That's nothing," Caleb said. "I watch *Project Runway* with my sister all the time. That's way more girly."

"That's not girly," Mason said. "I've got something girly for you."

Something miraculous was happening. Suddenly they were all trying to one-up each other with all the less-than-manly things they did when no one else was around. Mason cried every time he watched *The Lion King*. Evan drank tea with his grandma when he visited her for Shabbat. Nico let his little sister paint his nails. Ethan flossed his teeth.

They were having a great time, laughing and high-fiving each other, and for a second, I thought all my problems were solved.

Before I even knew what I was doing, I yelled out, "I take ballroom dance classes!"

The laughter died.

Everyone was staring at me, including Safi, whose mouth fell open.

Oh, this is bad, I thought. *I have made a horrible, horrible mistake.*

Finally, Evan spoke up. "Dude," he said, "did you just say you take ballroom dance classes?"

"Yeah," I choked.

I glanced over at Safi. He had a toothy smile plastered on his face, but his eyes were wide and petrified. He looked like a wild animal that had been caught in a trap and was seconds away from chewing its own leg off.

"He's just kidding," he said, nodding quickly. "Right, Will?"

I glanced around the table at all of them. What I wanted to say was, *No! I'm not kidding! I take dance classes! And they're cool and fun and completely normal, so stop looking at me with your stupid buggy alien eyes like I just told you I killed a drifter and buried him in my basement!*

I didn't say that, though. Instead, I smiled weakly.

"Of course I'm kidding," I said. I forced a dry, stuttering chuckle. "I don't take *dance* classes. What do you think I am, some kind of loser?"

Everyone looked at each other for one more silent, terrifying moment, and then they all started to laugh.

"Good one, Stone!" Berger said, giving me a whack on the back with his Cheetos-stained hand.

"Yeah," Evan said, "you had me there for a minute."

It was amazing how relieved they all looked.

They laughed about it for a couple minutes more, and I laughed with them. When the bell rang, I followed them out of the cafeteria. But instead of following Safi to math class, I went to my locker, grabbed my bag, and walked home.

CHAPTER TWENTY-ONE

I was going to be in massive amounts of trouble if and when my dad found out I'd skipped the rest of school, but for the first time in my life, I didn't care. When I got home, I slammed the front door behind me, hurled my bag to the floor, and booked it up the stairs to my room without even wiping my feet on the mat. It was all very dramatic. Or it would have been if anyone had been home to witness it.

Usually when I'm feeling depressed, I put on a Tito Puente album and practice dance moves in front of the mirror, which always makes me feel better. Not today, though. I cranked the music as loud as it would go, and I practiced my Cuban slide variations. But every time I looked in the mirror, all I could see was Evan's face when I told him I took dance lessons—it was like I'd hocked a hairball into his french fries. So instead of continuing, I stopped midstep, kicked my dresser, and stormed into the bathroom.

As I stood over the toilet taking a whiz, I surveyed Alex's mess of crap on the counter. He had every type of personal grooming product found in the Western hemisphere, including a bottle of mango-guava shampoo he bought special from a salon in Montreal, which I wasn't allowed to use on threat of death. He also had like eighteen tubes of hair gel. And mousse, whatever that was. But somehow no one called him a girl.

Apparently all you had to do to be left alone in this world was be a tall, good-looking, elite-level hockey player. Then you could do anything you wanted and no one would give you a hard time about it. In fact, I bet Alex could waltz down the street naked with monkeys flying out of his butt, and people would probably give him a standing ovation.

It must be nice, I thought as I picked up a tube of gel, *to be able to just live your life and not have to give a crap what other people think.* I flipped the cap open.

The instructions said to apply a dime-sized amount of gel to wet hair, which I read only after I applied a palm-sized amount to my dry hair. Big mistake. My hair did not look tousled and stylish, like Alex's. Instead it looked like a giant had horked green snot onto my head. Even though I tried to distribute the gel more evenly, there was just too much of it, so eventually I had to give up and comb my hair back from my forehead like Jesús did, until it looked like a shiny cap on my head.

I had to admit, though, I looked kind of cool. Kind of like a badass gangster type. All I needed was a gold tooth and a switchblade and one of those leather jackets with zippers all over it. And maybe a cool car.

Celia Cruz was singing "Quimbara," which was one of my favorites. I danced closer to the sink and gave myself a rakish smile in the mirror.

"Why, Claudia," I said. "Fancy meeting you here. You're looking especially bodacious this evening."

The space between the sink and the tub was limited, but I still managed to execute a pretty impressive cross tap-jazz square combo.

"What's that? You think guys who dance are awesome and manly?" I smiled knowingly. "I assure you, you couldn't be more right."

I shimmied my shoulders and step-tapped until I could feel myself starting to sweat. I spied Alex's shaving cream by the sink.

"Do you know what else is manly?" I asked, picking up the bottle and turning it around in my hand. "*Shaving* is very, very manly. I actually have to do it twice a day because my beard is so thick and masculine."

I had never shaved, actually. I had no real reason to. I didn't even have one of those fuzzy puberty mustaches, like Safi did, which everyone gave him a hard time about.

Still, what Claudia didn't know wouldn't hurt her, so I took off my shirt and pants, and grabbed a towel and hung it around my neck like Alex did when he got out of the shower. After that, I squirted a ball of shaving cream into my palm and rubbed it onto my face and neck. The foam didn't look thick enough, though, so I dabbed on two more handfuls, making soft peaks with it, like my mom did with meringue when she was making a lemon pie.

Celia Cruz was singing away in the background, and I belted out a few of the lyrics with her.

"¡Ay dios mio, pero que lio!"

I did a hook turn, whipping around fast to face myself in the mirror.

"Shaving is something a father is supposed to teach a son," I told Claudia, searching through the mess on the counter for Alex's razor. "But my father was always far too busy for such things. It's like that when you're a judge on the Supreme Court."

I rinsed the razor under the faucet. "Luckily it's always come easy to me," I said. "In fact, I've been told I'm something of a natural."

I tapped the razor on the side of the sink like Alex did, and then positioned it at the top of my cheek, right near my ear. At least, that's where I thought I was putting it—it was hard to see with all the foam on my face.

I gave Claudia a sly wink, and then I pulled the razor down, and in one swift movement *I cut my freaking earlobe off*!

Okay, it was actually a pretty tiny cut, but I must have hit an artery or something, because it wouldn't stop bleeding. I fumbled through the medicine cabinet, but I could only find an industrial-sized Band-Aid for, like, elbows and kneecaps, which was way too big. Plus I was bleeding too much for the adhesive to stick anyway.

Some of the shaving cream leaked into the cut, which stung like fire. When I tried splashing cold water onto it, I somehow managed to soak myself completely along with my underwear, which I took off and flung into the bathtub.

"Not to worry," I assured Claudia. "These things happen when you're a man."

I was doing my best to maintain my composure, but that's hard to do when you're buck naked and bleeding with a face full of shaving cream.

Finally I found the tensor bandage Alex sometimes used on his knee and managed to wrap it over my ear and around the top part of my head a couple of times. I'll admit that it messed with my gangster vibe, but it was still better than bleeding out on the bathroom floor.

Once I fastened the bandage to my head, I picked up the razor again. This time I started with my mustache area, and I managed to cut myself only once in a very minor way just under my left nostril.

"You know, Claudia," I said as I tore a tiny piece of toilet paper from the roll, "you are seriously the most beautiful girl I've ever laid eyes on."

I leaned into the mirror so I could see better. "No, don't argue with me, chica," I said, as I stuck the piece of toilet paper on the cut. "It's true."

I moved even closer and locked eyes with my reflection.

"In fact, you make me wild with desire," I said breathlessly. "I want to kiss you. Right here. Right now."

"Well jeez, kid, it's tempting," Alex said from the doorway. "It'd be weird, though, since we're related and everything."

He scared me so bad I actually shrieked. I tried to cover my man parts with the same hand that held the razor, and I came dangerously close to nicking my wiener, which made me shriek again.

"What are you doing here?" I shouted, grabbing a towel off the rack and wrapping it around my waist.

"Weight training's canceled, so I'm home early. *Chica*," he added. Then he shut the door. I could hear him laughing all the way down the hall.

CHAPTER TWENTY-TWO

I played sick and spent the rest of the night and most of the next morning hiding in my room to avoid Alex. By two thirty the next day, I was so bored I actually considered doing my homework. That's when he showed up at my door.

"Hey," he said, poking his head in. "Let's go for a drive."

"If you just want to get me alone so you can roast me about yesterday, no thank you."

Alex grinned and stepped into the room. "Which yesterday? Do you mean the yesterday when I found you dancing naked in the bathroom with your face covered in shaving cream? That yesterday?"

I sighed. "That would be the one."

He laughed. "I'm not going to roast you," he said. "Let's just get out of here."

"Why?"

"Because it's Saturday, and I've got some time to kill. Now move it!"

I stood up, and Alex looked me over. Then he wrinkled his face up.

"You need to put a different shirt on," he said.

"What's wrong with this one?"

"It's got a picture of Cookie Monster on it. It's for little kids."

"But he's a zombie. He's eating Big Bird."

"I don't care. Take it off," he said. "And we need to do something with your hair."

"Why?" I asked as I pulled my shirt over my head.

"Because you look like you let your mom's kindergarten class cut it. Now shut up and hurry."

He rooted through my closet and found a shirt he considered "decent," and while I put it on, he disappeared into the bathroom and came back with a handful of foam, which he rubbed into my hair. When he was done, he stepped back to take a look at me and sighed.

"It'll have to do," he said.

"What will have to do?"

But he wasn't listening. I chased him down the stairs, and he didn't say a word to me. He cranked the music in the car so loud I could barely hear myself think, let alone have a conversation. He turned it down only when we pulled up in front of the Czech bakery.

"What are we doing here?" I said, in a voice several octaves higher than usual.

Alex pulled the parking brake.

"I'm going to level with you, kid," he said. "I think it's time you got a girlfriend. Like, at this point, I'm thinking it's kind of necessary."

"What are you talking about?" I was gripping my seat with both hands and trying very hard not to become hysterical.

"I'm talking about the fact that you've been spending way too much time alone in the bathroom these days," he said. "You're in desperate need of some action with someone other than, you know, *yourself*."

I put my head in my hands and groaned, and Alex sighed again.

"I'm not trying to embarrass you."

"Yes, you are!" I moaned. "You're mean!"

"Listen," he said, slapping me on the back, "you can do this. Just go in there and talk to her."

"What possible difference will it make if I do?"

"Well, you never know," he said. "She's on Tessa's volleyball team, and Tessa said she hasn't had a boyfriend, like, ever. Chances are she's totally desperate enough to go out with you."

"Very nice."

"I'm serious!"

"I know!" I yelled. "That's the problem! You're constantly insulting me, and half the time you don't even know you're doing it! Do you have some kind of weird hockey-related brain damage I'm not aware of?"

He must have been in a good mood, because he let that one slide.

"Just go in and buy something," he said. "Pay her a compliment. Tell her she has a great smile

181

or that you like what she's wearing or whatever. Make her feel good. Girls tend to like that."

Thank god it was a slow day. Nobody was there but Claudia. She was sitting in the window reading a book with the sun behind her lighting up her blonde hair like a halo. When the bell on the door tinkled, she looked up and smiled at us, and I went into thermonuclear meltdown right there on the spot.

"Hello," she said, putting down her book.

I couldn't speak. I could only give her a weak wave.

"Move!" Alex whispered. He pushed me forward, and then he stuffed his hands in his pockets and ambled over to the other side of the room.

It took every ounce of energy I had to put one foot in front of the other, so even though there was only about five feet between me and the counter, it felt like it took ages to get there. I stared at the floor as I walked, and it wasn't until I lifted my head that I noticed Claudia had gotten up from her window seat and was waiting for me at the register.

"Can I get you something?" She had a smudge of what looked like frosting on her cheek, up by her ear. Call me a perv, but I totally wanted to lick it off.

"Uh, sure," I said, trying to smile.

She smiled back, waiting.

"Um," I said. It felt like the Sahara Desert had blown into my mouth. When I swallowed, it actually made a weird clicking sound. "I'll take a dozen kobliha?"

She nodded and lifted a box from the stack on the counter behind her.

"Vhat kind?"

"Uh," I said. I looked into the case. They could have been filled with leftovers from an alien autopsy for all I cared. "Any kind. You pick."

"You vant me to pick?" she said, frowning.

"You're the expert," I said.

She smiled again, bigger this time, and ducked her head.

Was I flirting? *Did I just flirt?*

She filled the box and tied it with string, and then she brought it to the cash register.

"Wheel that be oll?"

"Uh," I said. I looked around desperately and grabbed a loaf of rye bread off the shelf in front of me. "No. This too."

"Okay," she said. "This is day old. If you vant fresh, I cut for you."

"No, no," I said quickly. "No cut. That's fine."

She smiled and rang it up. "Anything else?"

I looked around again. "What's this here?" I asked, holding up a yellow tube from a stack near the register.

She looked at me and raised an eyebrow. "That's marzipan," she said. "Almond paste. Is for baking."

"I'll take three," I said. She gave me another strange look and put them into the bag. I could hear Alex clearing his throat across the room, so I handed her the twenty he'd given me in the car. She put it into the big, old-fashioned cash register, and then she counted out the difference under her breath.

"Two seventy-five is change," she said. She dropped it into my hand, which was shaking slightly.

"Thanks," I said. I smiled at her, and Alex cleared his throat again.

This was it. This was the moment. It was now or never.

I took a deep breath. "Uh," I started, "I just wanted to tell you that I really like your—"

Here's where it got weird. Alex had told me to pay her a compliment, so what I'd planned to say was, "I really like the necklace you're wearing." Unfortunately, at the same time I was about to say that, some evil and weirdly perverse part of my brain kept whispering, *Breasts! You like her breasts. Say it. Say breasts. Breasts, breasts, breasts, breasts—*

"I really like your—"

Now it was like a legion of perverse trolls had hijacked my brain, and they were all singing in their manly troll voices, *Breasts! Breasts! Breasts! Breasts! Breasty, breasty, breasts, breasts!* It was like being caught in the middle of an X-rated Disney movie.

"Aaah!" I said, practically strangling. My head felt like it was going to explode from the effort I was making to say the right thing, and to make matters worse, my nose started running. I swiped it with my finger.

"I really like your—" I tried one more time.

Suddenly she gave me an alarmed look. "Nose," she said.

"Yes," I said, confused, "I do like your nose, but I was actually talking abo—"

"No," she said, covering her own nose with her hand. "Your nose, I think, is bleeding."

I looked down at my fingers, and they were slick with blood.

"Oh my god!" I shouted, clapping my hands over my face. It was too late, though. My nose was a bloody geyser that was spattering all over the counter and the wrapped bread on the shelf in front of me.

"I'm so sorry!" I yelled. I staggered backward blindly and ran into a rack of buns. It swayed and threatened to pitch over onto the floor, but Alex caught it before it had a chance. I turned on my heel, slipped on a bag of onion rolls, and came crashing down, leaving another splatter of blood as well as two big, gory handprints on the floor.

Then I pulled myself to my feet and raced out the door.

CHAPTER TWENTY-THREE

When Alex got to the car, he put the box of kobliha on the console between us and threw the bag at me.

"Here's your marzipan," he said with disgust. "Doing some baking, are you?"

"This is your fault!" I shouted. I was still pinching my nose, so my voice sounded high and whiny. "I told you I wasn't ready to do it!"

"I will never understand," he muttered, as we tore away from the curb, "how you can take the simplest task and turn it into something so painful. You went into a bakery to talk to a girl, and by the time you left, it looked like a freaking crime scene. It just makes no sense to me."

"Well, I'm sorry I'm not perfect like you!"

He glared at me.

"It's true, though! You do exactly what you want, whenever you want, and somehow it always works out for you! You're like the king of the freaking world!"

"Yeah, I do whatever I want." He laughed sarcastically. "That's hilarious."

"You do!"

"Well, if that's true, maybe you can explain to me why I've been stuck living in the ass-end of nowhere for the last four months."

"You know what?" I said, turning in my seat to face him. "That's a good question. Why *are* you here, anyway?"

He glanced over at me but didn't say anything. He just clamped his lips together and tightened his grip on the steering wheel.

"Come on, Alex," I said. "Spill it. I'm dying to know, and no one around here ever talks about it."

"Good. They shouldn't."

"Why?"

"Because it's *my* business. Maybe I don't want anyone to know."

"Why? Did you do something bad? Did Mr. Perfect screw up somehow?"

He turned to me, but he looked more hurt than angry.

"Yeah, actually. I did," he said.

"Really?" I was so shocked, for a second I forgot about being mad. "What did you do? Did you, like, kill someone?"

"Yeah," he said dryly. "A twerpy little ballroom dancer who never shut his trap. Reminded me a lot of you, actually."

"Very funny," I said. "Come on. What was it? Were you, like, abusing alcohol or something?"

"No."

"*Drugs?*"

"God, no." He rolled his eyes. "Look, it's not important. Can't we just drop it?"

"Definitely not."

He glanced over at me and sighed again.

"Fine," he said. "Have it your way."

He cleared his throat and rubbed at the stubble on his cheek. Then he tapped on the steering wheel and cleared his throat again. Just when I thought he was never going to open his mouth, he said, "So last year, I got drafted to the major juniors—"

"You were in the major juniors?"

"Yes." He sighed.

"Wow!" I said. "That's a big deal!"

"Do you want to hear this story or not?"

"Totally."

"Then shut up and let me talk."

He glanced over at me warily and took a deep breath.

"I was drafted to the major juniors, and they put me in a new school where I got into fights every time I had the chance. Finally I sent a guy to the hospital, so I got kicked out, and the headmaster threatened to press charges if my parents tried to enroll me in another private school."

"Wow."

"Yeah, wow. Then in the locker room after my last game, I punched my coach and broke his jaw, and the team released me for the rest of the season to deal with my anger issues."

We turned into the driveway, and Alex shut off the car. He stared out the windshield and kept his hands on the steering wheel.

"Rather than dump me in a public school in the city, my parents forced me to come here. I guess they figured it was better than nothing, although they didn't have much of a choice."

He let go of the wheel and turned to face me.

"And that's it," he said miserably. "I was mean and violent, and I hurt people. I almost got arrested for assault. Still think I'm king of the world?"

I sat there for a moment, shaking my head.

"I don't get it," I said finally.

"What?" he said impatiently. "What don't you get, Will?"

"You've been here for months, Alex, and you haven't fought with anyone. Except for Artie and Wayne, and they had it coming. You didn't even fight Duke after he suicide-passed you, and I thought you would have killed him for that."

"What's your point?" He had a serious edge in his voice, and I knew I'd have to tread carefully.

"It's just—you were in the *juniors*. That's the big time. Everybody knows if you do well in the juniors you get drafted to the NHL, like, the second you turn eighteen. I just don't understand why you'd make so much trouble for yourself."

Even as I said those words, an idea took shape in my mind that was so ridiculous it was hard to even speak it aloud. I looked at Alex. He had his head down and was staring at his lap, like somehow he already knew what I was going to say.

"Do you even *want* to play hockey anymore?"

I thought he'd get mad and say, "Of course I do, you idiot," but instead he just sat back in his seat and stared dully out the window. When he spoke, his voice was hollow.

"I don't know," he said.

My mind was officially blown.

"What do you mean, you don't know?" I said. "You're so talented! You could be the next Sidney Crosby!"

Alex was rubbing his face with both hands, but when I said that, he stopped and looked at me. "God, kid, do you have any idea what it takes to get that far? The time it takes? It's, like, nonstop hockey, day after day. It's constant practicing and training."

"So?"

"So maybe I want to do something else for once."

"Like what?"

He sat there, shaking his head. He was looking at me like he just couldn't wrap his brain around how colossally stupid I was.

"You don't get it, do you," he said finally. "Until I got kicked off my team last year, do you know how long I went without practicing or playing a game?"

"No."

"Four days." He spit the words at me and shook his head again. "Four days in fourteen years was the longest I ever went without playing hockey. And that was when my grandmother died, and we had to travel to Florida to go to the funeral. For god's sake, last year my parents even rented out the rink on Christmas day and paid a coach triple-time so I could power skate and shoot drills for two hours."

He leaned back in his seat. His mouth was an angry line.

"When I play hockey—serious hockey—there's no time for anything else. No time for going out, no time for a girlfriend, no time to even play a different sport like baseball or soc—"

"Oh, come on," I interrupted. "Are you trying to tell me you'd give up a career in the NHL just to join a bowling league? Give me a break."

He glared at me and gripped the steering wheel with one white-knuckled fist, like it was taking everything he had not to rip my face off.

"I'm telling you, you little pain in the ass, that I could kill myself day after day for the next five years and still not make it, and in the meantime, I'll miss out on a whole bunch of other stuff that might actually be a lot of fun."

"But what if you do make it?"

He turned his head to look out the window.

"Then that's it," he said, shrugging. "It's hockey forever, or at least long enough for me to miss my chance to do anything else."

"I don't understand. You don't play like you want to give up. You play like you love it."

He sighed. "I used to love it," he said. "I *remember* loving it. That was a long time ago, though. Now I'm just—*tired*."

He heaved another sigh.

"Still," I said. "You've got something you can do that people actually admire. When you play hockey, people fall all over you. Everyone cares about what you do and what you think because you're a big star."

"So what?"

"So, you've got a chance to impress people. To make them like you."

"For god's sake, Will. If you spend the rest of your life worrying about things like that, you're going to be a very unhappy little person."

I couldn't let it go. "But at least your parents would be proud of you. Isn't that worth it?"

At the mention of his parents, his lip curled.

"My parents? Are you kidding me?" He shook his head. "My parents aren't like your parents, Will. All they do is work. Practically the only time I ever saw them was at my games, and then they spent most of their time banging on the glass, screaming and swearing like a couple of jackasses. Do you have any idea what it's like trying to play hockey when that's going on right next to you?"

"No," I said. Obviously my mom had never acted like that at my games. My dad never behaved that way either. It wasn't his style.

Alex shook his head. "Man, I've had a better

time playing hockey these last few months than I ever have, knowing my father isn't going to tear me apart on the car ride home for the twenty things he thought I did wrong during the game."

"Come on," I said. "There's no way he could be that hard on you. You're too good."

"You think so, huh?" He laughed bitterly. "The last time I even spoke with my father was the day I left for Evanston. He told me I was a loser and a screw-up and the biggest disappointment of his life. And it wasn't the first time he'd said something like that. Not by a long shot."

Holy crap on a cracker, I thought. *What kind of dude says that to his kid?*

"What's funny is, when my parents sent me here, they thought they were punishing me, but this is the first time in my life I've actually felt happy. It's the first time I've felt like I had a home and was part of a family that, like, cared about *me* and not just about how many goals I could score in a game."

He rubbed at his eyes with the heels of his hands and sighed again.

"At least here," he said, "I've managed to get some peace."

I didn't know what to say. I sat there next to him, listening to the sound of the engine cooling, trying to think of something to tell him that might make him feel better. Then it occurred to me.

"You know, Alex," I said, "if you don't want to

go back to the juniors, you could just play really badly, and then they wouldn't want you."

Alex raised his head slowly and looked at me, his mouth lifted in a half smile. "What?"

"No, seriously," I said, getting excited. It seemed to me like the perfect plan. I twisted around in my seat so I was facing him. "You could slow down a little, mess up a few plays, miss a few shots."

Alex's face crinkled up.

"*Miss* a few *shots*?"

"Yeah!"

He snorted. "Please," he said. "As if I would *ever* do that. Now get out. I've got to pick Tessa up."

I reached for the door handle, but instead of leaving, I held back for a second.

"Alex," I said, "they'll probably call you back sooner or later. What'll you do then?"

He sighed. "I don't know," he said.

He smiled at me sadly, and it was the first time since I met him that he actually looked like a seventeen-year-old kid.

CHAPTER TWENTY-FOUR

The fair was only a month away. I had circled it on my calendar in black Sharpie, and every time I saw it, I could hear funeral bells chiming. That didn't stop me from working on the routine, though. If there was one thing I'd learned from Jesús, it was that commitment is everything. Even the prospect of one's own imminent death is no excuse for being a bad partner.

Tessa and I decided on the tango because out of all the dances, it was our favorite.

I had my own personal reasons for preferring it, the main one being that, according to Jesús, it could only be danced by the manliest of men.

I was five-foot-nothing. I had a pigeon chest and thighs like baby arms. I couldn't play hockey to save my life.

But I was very, very good at dancing the tango. So that meant something.

"There's a handful of people from the studio who can't make it to the show," Tessa said as we lay on our backs and did our after-practice stretches. "So Jesús is planning a milonga for the end of June."

A milonga is basically what you call it when people get together to dance the tango, except with food. This was good news because it meant Rita would bring her buffalo chicken wing dip, which, next to kissing Claudia Valenta, I'm pretty sure was about as close to heaven on earth as I was ever going to get.

"Will you be around? Jesús wants us to do our routine."

"I'll be there," I said.

She was wearing tights with just a little flimsy skirt tied around her waist. I could barely even look in her direction.

"I'm going to ask Alex to come," she said.

"To dance or to watch?"

"To dance."

I sat up and barked out a laugh. "You're insane."

"Why?"

"Because there's no way he'll ever do that. Not in a million years."

"Come on."

"Seriously," I said. "Alex is a *real man*." I made air quotes with my fingers. "And *real men* don't dance."

"God, Will," she said, rolling her eyes. "I'm so tired of hearing this."

"I'm tired of saying it, but I don't make the rules."

Tessa pulled herself into a sitting position and brushed her hair away from her face angrily.

"What rules?" she said.

"The rule that says there's certain things that real men don't do, and dancing is, like, at the top of the list."

"But what about Jesús? And PJ? And Mike? They're *real men*." She made air quotes, too, only hers were super sarcastic. "What about my dad? He ballroom danced for years. He was the first person to teach me. And he was a *real man*."

I would have argued with her, but once someone brings a dead father into the conversation, there's not a lot a person can say.

So instead I sighed.

She sighed too. "It just seems like you've got a pretty narrow definition of what it means to be a man, Will. I mean, shouldn't it have less to do with what someone does with his time, and more to do with the kind of person he is?"

"I don't know," I said doubtfully.

"Think about it," she said. "If someone is a good husband, or a good dad, or a good friend, and is kind, and honest, and brave, and has integrity— doesn't that say more about what kind of man he is than whether or not he knows how to do a foxtrot?"

It made perfect sense when Tessa put it that way. But the sad fact was, there were a bunch of people in my life who most certainly didn't think the way Tessa did. Like Artie. Like Evan and Kole and their friends. Like my dad. And that was a big problem.

Alex showed up just before practice was over, and we hung around the reception desk after everyone left and waited for Tessa to change for work. Jesús came out of his office holding a cup of espresso that he placed carefully in front of Alex.

"Here you go," Jesús said, giving Alex a pat on the shoulder. "It's a double."

"You're a lifesaver, Jesús," Alex said, and he knocked back the espresso in one gulp.

Despite the fact that the two of them were as different as two people could possibly be, Alex and Jesús got along quite well. Alex didn't seem to mind Jesús's quirks or that he was always trying to get him to take dance lessons, and Jesús was always marveling at Alex's size. He called him "El Grande."

"And for you, Jefe," Jesús said, nodding at me solemnly, "I've got something special."

He reached under the reception desk and pulled out a garment bag.

"This here I made for you. For the big show." He gave the bag a shake. "And it is my masterpiece."

I could feel myself starting to panic. His *masterpiece*? What the heck did that mean?

"I made this because I'm so proud of you. You are my best dancer and a good boy," he said. "And you are gonna love it!"

He laid it gently across my arms, as if it were a baby or something super delicate, and then he took me by the shoulders. There were actual tears in his eyes.

"Wear this and make me proud. Okay?"

"Okay?" I said, glancing fearfully at Alex.

"Now go," Jesús said, flapping his hands at us. "I'm too emotional. Just go."

I thanked him, and when he went back to his office, I turned to Alex.

"What did he mean by his *masterpiece*?" I whispered.

He shrugged. "I guess you'll see soon enough."

We dropped Tessa off at the library, and the minute we got home, I flew up the stairs to my room and laid the bag across my bed. I stood there staring at it for a moment, and then in one swift movement, I unzipped it and pulled out what was inside.

I was a dead man.

The plan was that Tessa was going to wear a red dress, and I was going to wear a simple black suit with a red tie to match. Unfortunately Jesús's idea of simple was to outfit me in a sparkly bullfighter's costume, complete with a ruffly pirate's shirt, a cape, and a tricorne hat.

"Are you trying it on?" Alex called from the kitchen.

"Uh," I called back. "This isn't exactly what I had in mind!"

"Just put it on and let's see!"

It took me about ten minutes just to get the pants on, because they had a button fly and went up practically to my nipples. They were also so tight you could almost see the outline of my package, which basically looked like a shrink-wrapped peanut.

I put on the hat and walked into the kitchen, where Alex was stuffing a sandwich into his face. I spread my arms out so the cape flared a little.

"Olé?" I said weakly, trying to smile.

Alex swallowed what he was chewing and stared up at me with his mouth half-open.

"What. The hell."

"So what do you think?" I asked him, cringing.

He took another bite of his sandwich. "It's sparkly," he said over his mouthful.

"Yes," I said, looking down at myself. "I think maybe Jesús went a little overboard with the bedazzling."

"No," Alex breathed. "Not at all. Are those epaulettes?"

"I think that's what you call them," I said, looking at the gold braided doodads on my shoulders that made me look like a reject from some kind of Las Vegas army brigade.

"Turn around," he said. "Let's see you from the back."

I rotated slowly, holding up my arms.

"Wait. Is that—Elvis—on your cape?"

"Yeah."

That's when he started to laugh. "Oh my god, kid."

I turned back around. "Is it that bad?"

"It's so bad," he said. "I think if you showed up in a dress, you'd still have less chance of being beaten up in the parking lot."

"Come on. Be serious."

Alex took another bite. "I swear to god, I have never been more serious in my life."

"Okay, I know it's a little outrageous," I said. I'm not sure who I was trying to convince, him or me. "But this *is* the kind of thing people wear when they do ballroom dancing."

"I don't care if it's the kind of thing people wear when they do open-heart surgery. You still look like an idiot."

That's when it really hit me.

"Oh my god, Alex!" I yelled. "What am I going to do? I can't show up at the Spencerville Fair in this! But if I don't wear it, it'll kill Jesús. You heard him! He said it was his masterpiece!" I was practically crying.

Of course, that was the moment my parents chose to walk into the kitchen. And as luck would have it, Poppy was with them.

When he and my dad saw me, their mouths fell open in unison. In any other situation, it might have been funny, but it wasn't this time. This time it was freaking terrifying. In fact, I was so scared I thought I was going to pee my bedazzled pants right there.

The silence seemed to stretch on for hours, until finally Mom said, "My goodness, what is this, Will?

Are you in a play that you forgot to tell us about?"

She was smiling, but Dad and Poppy were staring at me like they'd both had a stroke.

I couldn't speak. I just stood there looking at everyone, and that's when Alex stepped up beside me. He put his hand on my shoulder and cleared his throat.

"So, yeah, uh, Will's been taking dance lessons?" he said like it was a question. It was obvious he was trying to be super casual about it, but his voice cracked. "And, uh, he's gotten really good at it? So, uh, that's what's going on."

"Is this true, Will?" Mom asked. She was beaming.

I still couldn't speak. And I had pretty much sweated through my pirate shirt.

Alex cleared his throat again. "Yeah, uh, and, like, he's so good, he's been asked to perform in the big dance show at the Spencerville Fair. With Tessa. Which is, you know, like, a really big honor and everything."

He smiled down at me nervously and gave my shoulder a shake. That's when Poppy snorted.

"A dance show!" he shouted in a voice loud enough to wake the dead. "My grandson's in a dance show? What are you, some kind of PANSY or something?"

If I could have hired someone to kill me right there on the spot, I would have done it. And I wouldn't have cared what kind of heinous death it was as long as I could have been off the earth at that moment.

Mom turned to Poppy in outrage. "James!" she said. "That's enough!"

But Poppy wasn't done.

"Jesus H. Christ!" he yelled again. "The boy's got rhinestones on his pants! What the hell kind of house are you running, Paul?"

So far, Dad hadn't said anything. He just looked me over while he rubbed his mouth with his hand. But when Poppy said that, Dad glanced at him sharply and then turned and pointed a finger at me.

"Get up to your room and take that off," he said quietly. Then without looking at Poppy, he said, "I think it's time for you to go home now, Dad."

I didn't even wait to see Poppy's reaction, although I could hear him complaining as I sprinted to my room. I ripped off the costume and shoved it in the back of my closet.

A moment later, I heard Poppy grumble out the front door and the sound of someone coming up the stairs. I was pulling my T-shirt over my head when Dad stepped into my room and shut the door.

"I'd like to talk to you," he said.

"Dad, before you say anything, you should know that costume was totally not my idea. Jesús, my instructor, made it for me, and I think it's completely ridiculous—"

Dad nodded and held up his hand.

"But you gotta know," I pleaded, "the outfit I have in mind is really quite conservative. Just a black suit, with a tie—"

"Will," he said, "this isn't about the costume."

"Okay." I crossed my arms over my chest, the way Alex did, in an effort to look more manly, but my heart was beating, like, a thousand times a minute. I had to purse my lips to keep my chin from trembling.

Dad sighed as he pulled the chair out from my desk and sat down wearily.

"I got a call yesterday from the parents of one of my students," he said. "Mike Safi. How well do you know him?"

"Safi?" I said. "I know Safi. Is he all right?"

Dad paused for a minute, like he wasn't sure he should tell me.

"He's quite sick," he said. "Turns out he hasn't been eating or sleeping much in the last couple of months."

Oh man. I had no idea. I mean, I had *some* idea. He hadn't looked great for a while. But I had no idea it was that bad.

"Apparently he's had some trouble fitting in this year," Dad said. "His parents think maybe he's being bullied at school."

That would be putting it mildly. Torture would have been a better description of what Safi'd put up with all year.

"Would you know anything about it?" he asked, eyeing me carefully.

"No," I mumbled.

"It's a tricky situation," Dad continued. "On

one hand, if someone's picking on—Safi—I want to know about it so I can stop it. But on the other hand—" He paused. "Safi is a bit of an odd boy. You know, the cowboy costumes and all that."

My heart began to pick up speed. "What are you saying? Are you saying Safi deserves to be bullied?"

"No," Dad said, and his eyes were serious. "No one deserves to be picked on. Not ever."

Inwardly I breathed a sigh of relief.

"But I also think," he added, as my heart began to sink again, "that if you want to get along with people, sometimes *you* have to make the effort to fit in."

I didn't know what to say. I mean, obviously he knew nothing about Safi or he would've known Safi tried harder than anyone to be a part of things. He just couldn't seem to get it right, somehow.

"And now you're taking—dance lessons," he said, sighing.

"Yes." It was the most I could choke out.

"And this show at the fair? Was this your idea?"

"No," I said quickly. "Not at all. I totally got roped into it."

"So you can get out of it?"

A piece of my heart tore off in my chest.

"Well, not really," I said. "I'm kind of obligated now."

"Are there going to be any other boys your age in the show?"

I shook my head. "No," I said.

He nodded and rubbed his hands together while he gazed at the floor.

"I think—" he said. Then he stopped and sighed again. "It just seems to me that maybe this dancing thing is not the best idea for you right now."

"Do you mean the show or dancing in general?"

He cleared his throat and then shrugged a little as if to ask, What's the difference?

"But how would you know?" I asked him, trying very hard not to sound whiny. "You've never even seen me do it!"

"I don't have to see you do it to know that it might create obstacles for you that maybe you're not even aware of."

"So are you telling me to stop?"

"It's your decision, Will," he said. "I just think maybe you'd be happier in the long run if you focused your energy on other activities."

I had to fight to keep from crying. The last thing I wanted to do was to burst into tears in front of him, so I balled my hands up into fists and bit the inside of my cheek. I think he was expecting me to say something, but I couldn't since there was only one clear thought bouncing through my mind: *shame shame shame shame shame shame shame shame shame shame shame.*

Shame on him, shame on me, shame on the whole big, stupid world.

Dad stood up and patted me on the shoulder.

"Think about it," he said. "Okay, Will?"

I nodded. He shoved his hands into his pockets and stood there for a second like he was going to say something else. Then he shuffled to the door.

"Mom'll have dinner ready soon," he said.

Then he left.

The discussion was over.

CHAPTER TWENTY-FIVE

Except it wasn't.

I waited until I heard Dad go into the kitchen, and then I tiptoed into the hall and leaned over the banister. I could hear snatches of my mom and dad's conversation, which was heating up fast.

"... let him be ... be fine ..."

"... seen what can happen ..."

"... worry too much, Paul ..."

"... have no idea ..."

"... a mistake ... up to him!"

"Goddammit, enough is enough, Marion!"

I couldn't bear to listen to them fighting about me, so I did what any self-respecting teenager would do.

I bolted.

I made it about seven blocks before Alex pulled up beside me. The window was down, and he had one arm draped over the steering wheel while he leaned across the seat.

"Hey!" he called to me.

I ignored him and kept walking.

"You all right?"

"I'm fine," I said, still walking.

He kept pace with me a little farther, and then he spoke up again. "Are you coming home or what?"

"Not right now, thanks."

I passed a couple of people on the sidewalk, and they shot the two of us quizzical glances. Once they were out of earshot, Alex leaned over again.

"Don't listen to Poppy, Will. He's a deeply warped individual."

"I couldn't care less about Poppy," I said, and I glared at him so he knew I meant it.

Alex nodded. He sat back in his seat and watched the road for a moment. Then he leaned over again. "Okay, so your dad was pissed," he said. "But he'll get over it. He just needs some time to get used to the idea."

"Sure thing," I said.

He sighed. "Why don't you get in the car, and we'll talk about it."

"No."

"Will, just get in the car."

"No!"

Even at a glance, I could tell he was starting to get mad, because his muscles were bulging from how hard he was gripping the wheel.

"Get in the car, you idiot. I'm not fooling around."

"Bite me!"

When I said that, he called me "a little shit" and swung the car over to the side of the road. I started to run when I heard the door slam. Then the sound of Alex's feet pounding on the pavement behind me.

By the time I'd turned through the gates of Shady Hill Cemetery, I'd outpaced Alex by at least fifty yards. Of course, that might have had something to do with the fact that the whole time he was running he was cursing at me and yelling for me to stop, which I doubt helped his performance.

I ran down the paths and up the hill to the willow tree and stood there next to Gordie's grave. Alex finally made it to where I was standing, and he bent over with his hands on his knees, practically gasping for breath.

"What are we doing here?" he panted.

"This is where my brother is buried," I said.

It took a minute for it to register with him. Then he stood up and wiped the sweat away from his forehead with his arm.

"I didn't know you had a brother," he said.

I nodded. "I did. Before I was born."

Alex walked over to where I was standing and looked at the tombstone, which was ginormous. It had the face of an angel carved into the top and my brother's name and the dates of his birth and death in the middle, with an inscription underneath that read: *In the weeping of the rain. At the shrinking of the tide.* They were lines from a poem by Edna St. Vincent Millay called "Time Does Not Bring Relief." I know because I looked it up. It's about this woman who can't get over this person she loves who died, and how she sees his face everywhere no matter how much time passes or how she tries to forget him. It pretty much suited my parents' situation to a T.

"Paul Gordon Stone," Alex said. "He was named after your dad."

"Yeah," I said, "but they called him Gordie. My dad named him after Gordie Howe, the hockey player."

"I know who Gordie Howe is."

"Of course you do," I said. I nudged a tuft of grass with my shoe. "He was my dad's favorite hockey player and everything."

"Who'd they name you after?"

I shrugged. "No one I know of."

Alex didn't say anything. He just nodded.

"He died when he was six months old. My brother, I mean. Not Gordie Howe."

"Well, duh," Alex said quietly. We were both practically whispering even though there was no one but the two of us in the cemetery. The two of us and about a thousand dead people.

Alex cleared his throat. "How did he die?"

"Crib death."

"Isn't that when they die in their sleep?"

"Yep."

He gave a low whistle. "Man, that's tough."

He took a step back and looked at the grave again.

"Why are your parents' names here?"

"I guess they want to be buried on either side of him, you know, when they die."

"That's creepier than hell."

"Not really. A lot of people buy their plots ahead of time," I said. "It's not out of the ordinary."

"No," he said. "I mean it's creepy to see your parents' names on a tombstone when they're not even dead yet. That's got to mess with their minds a little."

"I doubt it bothers them," I said. "I'm sure they're relieved to know that when they die, they'll finally be with my brother again."

I sighed.

That's when Alex turned to look at me. His head was tilted a little to one side.

"Come on, kid," he said, in the kind of gentle voice I'd only ever heard him use with Tessa. "You can't seriously feel left out over this."

I shrugged and sat down on the bench. It didn't seem ridiculous to feel a little insulted my parents hadn't planned for my death in any way. What if I died tomorrow? What if I died a year from now and there was no place for me next to them? I'd probably be stuck in some plot on the other side of the cemetery, next to the dude whose actual name was Hardin Long—no joke—while my parents enjoyed eternity next to my brother. One happy little family.

But I didn't say any of that. Instead I turned to Alex. "Did you know my dad was the one who found my brother when he died?"

Alex sat down next to me and shook his head,

looking almost embarrassed. "Obviously that's not something I could really know—"

"When the ambulance guys got there," I said, cutting him off, "my dad wouldn't let go of him. It took them an hour before they could talk him into handing my brother over."

"God, who told you that?"

"Poppy."

Alex rolled his eyes. "That figures," he said.

"I'm glad he told me. It's better that I know how much Dad loved Gordie."

"He loves you too, Will."

"Not like Gordie."

"Did he tell you that?"

"No, but come on. Gordie was his firstborn. Dad gave him his name and the name of his biggest idol. I mean, it's obvious."

"Will—" Alex started.

"And if he'd lived, I bet my brother would have been a really awesome person. A big guy and strong. A great hockey player. The kind of son my dad could have really been proud of." My voice had gotten all wobbly.

"Come on, Will. Don't do this to yourself."

I looked up at Alex and swiped at my nose with the back of my hand. "I bet he'd have been an amazing person. Probably a lot like you."

Alex sighed. "Oh man," he whispered.

I took a deep breath and tried to compose myself, but it was hard.

"Instead my dad's got me."

"What's wrong with you?"

"Where do I start? I'm scrawny. I can't play hockey. I don't fit in. I don't do anything anyone could be proud of. I'm an embarrassment."

"Stop," Alex said, looking mad. "You are not."

"Yes, I am. He's ashamed of me. I bet he wishes I was never born. Or maybe that I was the one lying in this grave, instead of my brother."

It was all the worst things I'd ever thought about myself but had never said out loud. When I was done saying them, I put my head in my hands and started to cry. After a moment, I felt Alex's arm around my shoulder, and then I leaned into his chest and really wailed. He sat there with me until I'd calmed down enough to just hiccup.

"You all right?" he asked quietly.

I shrugged.

"You should wipe your nose."

I wiped it.

"Not on my shirt! Gross!"

"Sorry," I said. I sat up straight and rubbed at my eyes.

"My dad wants me to quit dance class."

"Oh," Alex said. He sounded disappointed. "So what are you going to do?"

"Quit, I guess." Just saying the words made me want to cry again. "He said that"—I lowered my voice to imitate my dad—"dancing might create problems for me I hadn't even considered."

Alex rubbed at the stubble on his cheek and seemed to think about it for a moment.

"Does it matter?" he asked finally.

"What do you mean?"

"I mean, even if you took a lot of heat for it, wouldn't you still want to do it anyway?"

"Maybe," I said. "But I can't go against what my dad says."

"Why not?"

"Because he's my dad!" I half laughed. "And I have to do what he tells me!"

"But why?" he asked. "I mean, it's your life. You should do what's right for you, no matter what anyone else thinks about it, including your dad."

"Easier said than done, Alex," I said. "You of all people know how it goes, or you wouldn't be so worried about getting called back to the juniors."

"Actually," he said, "I'm *not* worried about that anymore. Because I'm not going back."

"What?"

He shrugged as if what he was saying was a no-brainer. "I'm not going back. I'm going to stay here another year and play junior A, and then I'm going to Queen's University. They've already offered me a scholarship."

"But what about the NHL?"

"What about it?" he asked. "I can still play hockey after university. This way, I'll get to stay in school."

"And that's a *plus* for you?"

"Yeah," he said. "I love school."

I was on the verge of laughing and calling him a loser, but when I looked at him, he had a funny little smile on his face, like he hadn't really meant to tell me how he felt and was kind of embarrassed but was trying to be cool about it anyway.

"Have you told your parents yet? Or my dad?" I asked him.

"No," he said. "Not yet."

"They won't be happy."

"I know," he said, and then he sighed. "They'll get over it." The way he was looking at me, though, with sad, anxious eyes, told me he wasn't so sure. He straightened himself up and clapped his hand down on my shoulder.

"And your dad will get over the dancing thing too. That's if you decide you've got the stones to tell him you're going to do what you want to do," he said.

We stood up and surveyed the rows of graves that surrounded us.

"It just seems like life is way too short to let someone else live it for you," he said, shrugging. Then he shoved his hands in his pockets and looked down at me. "Now can we get out of here? This place gives me the creeps."

"Okay," I said. "Just wait a second."

Like always, I brushed the leaves and grass clippings away from Gordie's tombstone, and I gave it a little pat and stood up.

"See you later, Gordie," I said.

Alex slung his arm around my shoulder.

"Listen, kid," he said as we walked to the gate. "I'm not going to pretend to understand why you've got your nuts in such a twist over your brother. Honestly, there's no way of knowing if he would have been some kind of superstar. For all you know, he might have grown up to be a total loser. God rest his soul and everything," he added.

"Okay," I said, not feeling better.

"But one thing I *do* know is that he would have been lucky to have you for a little brother. That's the truth."

I glanced up at him to see if he was serious, but he was looking away. His face was red.

"Do you really think so?"

"Of course I do, you moron," he said, looking down at me. "I wouldn't have said it if I didn't mean it."

He shifted around and put me in a headlock, and then he dragged me out of the cemetery.

CHAPTER TWENTY-SIX

A week later I still hadn't talked to my dad. I had talked to my mom, who was very excited and made me tell her every detail about dance class and the fair performance. Which made it obvious to me that as far as the Stone parental unit was concerned, there was clearly not a whole lot of communication going on vis-à-vis the status of my dancing career.

The only answer was to avoid both of them. Unfortunately, between doing that and sneaking out to dance class, I was experiencing record levels of stress.

Then there was Safi. He missed an entire week of school, and even though I tried calling him once or twice, I always got his sister, who said he didn't feel like talking. Since he lived out in the country, it wasn't like I could just take a walk to his house, so finally I asked Mom to drive me.

Even though he'd asked me over a bunch of times, I'd never actually been to Safi's farm—I'd never even seen it. For some weird reason, though, I'd always imagined it would be some kind of run-down clapboard house with a shacky barn in a field, like something out of that book *Of Mice and Men* we had to read for English.

But Safi's place was a sprawling homestead with, like, a huge stone house and all kinds of freshly painted barns and buildings. The driveway was fine-crushed gravel, and the lawn was manicured with bushes and flower beds.

"Holy cow," I said. "This place is ginormous!"

"Oh yes," Mom said. "Your dad told me the Safis are major milk suppliers to all the big companies in Canada. They have been for eight generations."

Maybe that was why Safi was so amped to be a farmer. It was basically in his DNA.

Safi's mom met me in the driveway. She was wearing a flannel jacket and jeans and big gummy boots that went up to her knees.

"Oh my goodness, Will!" she said, waving to my mom as she drove off. "It's so nice of you to come for a visit! Mike's grooming Susie in the barn. I'll show you the way."

Susie was Safi's horse, and I knew all about her, because the year before she'd won two blue ribbons at the Spencerville Fair, and Safi was so proud that he transferred a photo of her face onto a T-shirt he wore twice weekly. That is until Artie drew a picture of a penis on the back of it with black Sharpie.

Mrs. Safi and I walked together up the hill and into one of the smaller barns, where Susie was tethered in a stall. She was monstrously big, with a reddish-colored coat and a white stripe down her nose. Safi was so busy brushing her, he didn't even look up when we walked in.

"Mike, look who's here!" Safi's mom said, beyond enthusiastically. "Will!"

Safi looked at me, and he put his head down and continued brushing.

"Hey," he said dully.

"Hey," I said.

I hadn't realized until that moment how thin he'd gotten. He was practically drowning in his plaid work shirt. His neck was scrawny, and it looked like his skin was stretched too tightly across his face. He was also pale and had those same black circles under his eyes. Honestly, he looked as bad as I'd ever seen him.

"Should I bring out some refreshments?" Safi's mom said. "Maybe Will would like some lemonade and cookies?"

Safi stopped brushing and looked at me. "Do you want lemonade and cookies?" he asked in a tired voice.

"I'm okay," I said.

Safi looked at his mom. "We're okay," he said, and he started brushing again.

"That's fine," Safi's mom said, nodding vigorously. "But maybe when you're done here, you boys could come in the house and play some video games. If you want. Lena and I can handle your chores. Maybe Dad could order pizza from Gigi's."

She was trying to smile but was mostly just wringing her hands while she looked anxiously back and forth between the two of us.

"I can get my own chores done, Mom," he said, but his tone was sad rather than sarcastic.

Safi's mom looked at me and kind of shrugged helplessly.

"Well," she said, "I guess I'll leave you boys alone. Let me know if you need anything." When Safi said nothing, she nodded at me and left.

I took a couple of tentative steps into the stall while still keeping as far away from Safi's horse as humanly possible.

"Hey," I said.

"Hey," he said.

"How's it going?" I said.

He shrugged.

Even though most of the time Safi's constant nervous yammering made me want to rip my ears off, his silence was a somewhat disconcerting.

I stepped a little farther into the stall.

"Listen, Safi—" I said, and right at that moment, Susie swung her big butt around and practically walloped me with it. I yelped and skittered into a corner.

"Whoa, girl," Safi murmured while he stroked her neck. Then he looked at me and made a sound that was probably supposed to be a laugh but sounded more like he was clearing his throat.

"Are you afraid of horses or something?"

"No, no," I lied. "They're fine."

"You sure?" he asked, as I flattened myself against the wall and tried to inch my way toward the door.

"Of course," I said. "It's just, at my old school, I knew this girl named Charlotte who got kicked in the face by a horse, and she had to go through like twelve hours of surgery to reconstruct her cheekbone, and even after it was over, her left eye stayed bloodred for six months. She looked like an extra from *Night of the Living Dead*."

Safi laughed again—a dry, hard chuckle—and shook his head.

"Susie won't hurt you," he said. "Just don't stand behind her."

I have to admit, I was seeing a whole different side of Safi. He was just so *quiet*. And, obviously, part of that was because he was sad. But even underneath the sadness, he seemed relaxed, almost Zen, like those bald monk dudes who live in the mountains of Tibet and meditate eight hours a day under a vow of silence. Safi moved patiently around his horse, brushing her coat and picking up her hoofs and inspecting them like it was no big deal, as if he weren't at risk of being kicked or maimed or crushed by a thousand pounds of animal flesh. And when the horse started doing little skippy jumps that sent me running from the stall, Safi murmured "Whoa, whoa, whoa" and "It's okay, girl" into her neck in this low voice that managed to sound reassuring but also commanding, and absolutely not like Safi at all.

And, like, sure he was wearing all the same cowboy gear he wore to school—the jeans, the plaid jacket, the boots, the John Deere baseball cap—but for some reason he didn't look dorky. In fact, he actually looked kind of cool, like he belonged in a commercial for Stetson cologne. My English teacher would have called it a lesson in context.

"So how are you feeling, anyway?"

Safi pulled a bigger brush out of a bucket by his feet and sighed. "I don't know what everybody's worried about. I just passed out for a second at 4-H, and before I knew it, my parents were driving me to the doctor, and everybody started freaking out about my weight."

"You *passed out*?"

"For a *second*," he said. "It's not a big deal. They're just overreacting."

"Are you coming back to school?"

Safi shrugged glumly. "I don't know. Lena heard from one of her friends' little sisters that I was getting picked on, and she told my parents, so now it's become this big thing. Mom wants to put me in another school, but Dad says I need to stick it out. Lena just keeps saying, 'Everywhere you go, there you'll be,' which I guess is her way of telling me I'll be a mess wherever I end up."

"You're not a mess," I said with what I hoped was a voice of confidence.

Safi sighed again and shook his head. "I wish I could just stay here."

"I'm with you on that one," I said. "I'd *love* to be homeschooled."

"No," he said. "I mean, I wish I could stay in this barn. Live here for the rest of my life and forget about everything else."

Somebody else might have told him he was being silly, but I understood what he meant. Mostly because I felt exactly that way about the dance studio. Like, if I had the option of living forever in the ballroom, with its purple walls and people who liked me and didn't feel compelled to hold me down so they could fart on my head, I would have gladly taken it.

Safi sighed and stroked Susie's mane while she nibbled a little on his collar.

"Here in this place, everything makes sense," he said. "I know what to do *here*. But at school it's like there's a whole set of rules, and I don't know what they are. Everything I do is wrong. Everything I say is wrong. *I'm* all wrong."

"That's not true," I said.

"It is, though," he said, letting out a shaky breath. "At school I can't be the person I am, but I don't know how to be the person they want me to be either."

He looked up at me and tried to smile, but his eyes were wet and his mouth was all jittery, like it was taking everything for him not to burst into tears.

"I guess I'm stuck," he said.

After all these months of listening to Safi drone on and on about cows and horses and tillage equipment, I never dreamed the two of us had anything truly in common—other than being outcasts, that is.

Turns out we were more alike than I realized.

CHAPTER TWENTY-SEVEN

I stayed at Safi's place for a couple of hours. We ate pizza and played Halo, and by the time I left, he'd managed to cheer up a little.

I felt like crap, though. His mom kept thanking me for coming over, and at one point when I came upstairs from the basement to go to the bathroom, she stopped me in the kitchen. She was smiling, but she actually kind of had tears in her eyes.

She said, "Will, you've been such a good friend to Mike. A good, true friend. And I just want you to know how much I appreciate that."

She was talking to me like I was a hero or something, but deep down I knew I hadn't really made that much of an effort to be a good friend to Safi. I mean, he was always inviting me for sleepovers or to hang at his house after school, but I always made up excuses for why I couldn't come. It was like I couldn't commit to being in a real friendship with him or something. Deep down, a part of me suspected that I probably wouldn't have even *been* friends with Safi—cattle-obsessed, cowboy-hat-wearing Safi—if I'd had any kind of choice. Then it occurred to me that maybe if I'd been a better friend, he wouldn't have felt so sad.

And that made me feel like the biggest turd in the universe.

Mom picked me up at Safi's and dropped me at home on the way to her book club, but even though the rest of the night was wide open, I was too bummed to even think about doing anything productive. So I sat on the porch and watched Alex play hockey by himself in the driveway, which was mind-numbingly boring enough to keep my mind off my troubles.

I watched as he took a shot. Then he walked over and dug the ball out of the net, bounced it on his stick a couple of times just to show off, and made another shot. He did that over and over, until finally he called to me.

"Come play, Will!"

"Sure," I said. "I've always wondered how it would feel to be squashed aggressively into a driveway by a six-foot-three stick-wielding monster."

Alex snorted a little. "I'm six-four," he said. "And besides, you don't have to play against me. Just stand in the net."

"And have your balls flying in my face? No, thanks."

Alex started to laugh, and I realized what I'd said.

"You know what I meant!" I shouted.

"Oh, come on, grandma," he said. "I've got a

glove and a stick here for you. And there's an old helmet in the garage I can get if you're so worried about it."

"Yeah, no thanks."

Alex walked over to where I was sitting and poked me with his stick.

"Come on," he said. "Quit being such a wuss and stand in the net."

"I don't feel like it."

"Come on, Skidmark," he said, grinning and poking me again.

"No!" I said. "And those glasses make you look like a dork, by the way."

He raised his eyebrows and looked at me for a second, and then he threw down his stick and grabbed me. I tried to get away, but he pulled me off the step and had me in a headlock before I even knew what was happening.

"You are such a jerk!" I hollered as he wrestled me over to the driveway. I tried hitting him in the butt with my fist a couple of times, but it was like punching a boulder, and all it did was make him laugh and noogie me harder.

Then he got a hold of the waistband of my underwear and tugged.

"Don't do it!" I hollered.

"Say you'll play!"

"No!"

Alex tightened his grip on my underwear, and I let out a small yip.

"Say you'll play or I'll give you a dangler!" he said.

"There's no such thing as a dangler, you loser!"

He jerked me up by my underwear until my feet were dangling off the ground, and I squealed like a baby pig.

"All right, all right!" I shouted. "I'll play."

"Good," he said. He let me go, but not before he messed up my hair one last time. Then he tossed me the glove. "Now quit whining and get ready."

I glared at him while I attempted to extract what felt like yards of fabric from my butt crack. Then I walked over to the net and slumped in front of it. I didn't even bother to hold up the glove.

"Don't you want to take a stance or something?" Alex asked. "Maybe crouch down a little and, like, actually defend the net?"

"Just take the shot."

Alex shrugged. "Suit yourself."

I swear he purposely aimed the ball right for my nuts. When I deflected it, it was going so fast it bounced almost to the street.

"That was a pretty decent save," Alex said, nodding. "You've got good reflexes."

I was actually kind of impressed myself, although to be honest, the only reason I moved so quickly was because I was afraid if I didn't, I might lose my ability to have children someday. But I played it cool anyway and shrugged.

"It was all right," I said. "I mean, it was kind of a floater anyway."

Alex smiled to himself as he gathered the rebound, and before I knew what was happening, he flicked his wrist and the ball flew at me, glove side high.

He might have tucked it in the top right corner of the net, except miracle of all miracles, I managed to save it again.

"Ha, ha!" I shouted, throwing it back to him. "No goal for you, sucka!" Then I did a little merengue inside the net.

Alex rolled his eyes. "All right, cool it, Carey Price. Let's see what else you got."

I got into position, and Alex took a pretty hard wrist shot, which I caught. Then he snapped for the corner, and I kicked it away. He got a couple in on my blocker side, but for the most part, I managed to keep up with him.

"Well, well," he said, grinning at me. "Look at you."

"What?" I said, batting away another shot.

"If I didn't know any better, I'd think you were actually enjoying yourself."

"It's all right," I said, shrugging.

But he was right. It was kind of fun. At least until he wound up for a big, old-fashioned Bobby Hull slap shot. I lunged to the other end of the net and deflected it, which wouldn't have been a problem except for the fact that he shot at lightning speed, and even though it was only a tennis ball, it was like getting hit with a big, fuzzy bullet.

I dropped my stick and danced around again, this time in pain.

"Gaaaaah!" I hollered. "What's the matter with you?!"

"What?"

"Did you have to shoot it *that* hard?!"

"Don't be such a wuss!"

"I think you broke my arm!"

"Just rub it a little," he said, disgusted. "God, you're such a baby!"

Suddenly someone spoke up behind us. "Why don't you put on some gear?"

It was Dad. He was standing there with a blocker and some shin pads. I assumed he got them from the garage since we had enough old equipment to open up our own used sporting goods store.

I stopped rubbing my arm and blinked at him. "Oh, thanks," I said. "But we were just messing around."

"I noticed," he said. Then he threw the pads at me. "Go on. Gear up!"

The pads were so heavy, when I caught them I nearly tipped over backward. Dad didn't say anything, though. He just retreated into the garage while Alex walked over and stood beside me.

"What's going on?" I whispered. "Where did he go?"

"I don't know."

"What am I supposed to do with these?"

"You're supposed to put them on, doofus."

"But I don't even want to play anymore. I've got class in a while, and plus, you really hurt my arm."

"So tell him," he said.

"Tell him what?"

"Tell him what you told me at the cemetery. That you want to stick with dance class, and you don't want to play hockey. Now's the perfect time."

"Yeah, right," I said, fumbling with a buckle on one of the pads. "Can you imagine what would happen if I said that? If I was like, 'Hey, Dad. Thanks for the goalie pads. I can't use them right now, though, because I'm late for the girly dance class you don't want me to take anymore.' I'm sure he'd be super impressed."

"That's backward," Alex said.

"Of course it's backward. My whole life is backward."

"No, you idiot," he said. "Your pad."

I looked down at my leg.

"How?"

"The outer roll has to be facing the outside," he said. "And you've got the buckles all messed up. For god's sake, what's wrong with you?"

"How am I supposed to know how to put these things on? I've never worn goalie pads in my life!"

"You're hopeless!" he said, and then while I stood there like a moron, Alex knelt down and started undoing the buckles.

"You know, if you just talked to your dad and told him the truth," he muttered, as he fit the correct pad on the correct leg, "you wouldn't have to go through all this."

"Oh, please tell me more, Alex," I said. He was jerking my leg around as he did up the straps, and I was having trouble staying on my feet. "And when you're done, you can get on the phone and tell *your* dad that you're not going back to the major juniors, because as I recall, you haven't had *that* conversation yet."

Alex glared up at me and yanked one of the straps so hard I yelped a little, but he didn't say anything. Then he finished buckling up the second pad, and Dad came out of the garage with a hockey stick, a goalie helmet, and a bucket of tennis balls.

"This ought to fit," he said, tossing the helmet to me.

"I don't . . . understand . . . what's happening," I said.

"Well, I saw you playing out here with your cousin," Dad said, nodding at me. "Looks to me like you've got some talent as a goalie, son!"

A goalie? Oh, sweet lord, no.

Dad put his hands on his hips and pressed his lips together like he could barely contain his joy. Then he beamed at Alex.

"Wouldn't you say so, Alex?"

Alex smiled weakly. "Yeah, sure," he said.

"First things first," Dad said. "Let's see what kind of moves you've got. Can you butterfly?"

Butterfly? It sounded familiar, but I had no clue

what he was talking about. But they were both waiting for me to do something, so I lifted my arms slowly and fluttered them like wings.

Alex closed his eyes and smacked himself in the forehead. Dad shook his head at me.

"No, son," he said gravely, "that's not right. Can you show him, Alex?"

Alex sighed and got into a goalie position. He fell down to his knees and got back up again, slowly and kind of wincing.

"Oh," I said. "I know what *that* is. I just didn't know what it was called."

"Do you think you can do it?" Dad asked.

"Sure." I shrugged.

Of course I could. It was one of the moves in the Russian Cossack dance Jesús taught us for fun one afternoon. It was totally easy.

I bounced down to my knees and back up again.

Dad glanced at Alex. "That's good," he said. "Can you do it a bunch of times?"

I bounced up and down seven or eight more times in a row. Dad and Alex exchanged looks.

"Hmm," Dad said. "Can you do the splits?"

"Front or side?"

"Either."

I did one of each, and then I looked up at Dad and Alex.

"Is that good?"

Dad and Alex looked at each other again, and then Dad looked down at me.

"It's excellent," he said.

Then he smiled at me. It was the kind of smile I hadn't seen since I was a kid, way back before he gave up on me completely.

For the next hour, Dad taught me pretty much everything he knew about how to be a goalie. It was a lot of boring technical stuff I tried really hard to remember, which was tough because I didn't entirely know what he was talking about. Stuff like how to move laterally and stay square to the puck and cover my angles. About controlling rebounds and playing the puck behind the net.

Then he handed the bucket of tennis balls to Alex and said, "Feed him some one-timers."

I had to put the helmet on, which stunk like a combination of sweat, bad breath, and cat pee. Then Dad started taking shots. He got the first few in easy, probably because I was nervous.

"Keep your stick down," he said. "Make sure to cover your five-hole."

"I beg your pardon?"

"The gap between your feet."

"Oh. Right."

The next few shots were high and to the right, and I caught all of them.

"Way to flash the leather, Will," Dad said, grinning.

He shot a few more, saying stuff like, "Keep your eye on the puck" and "Be big! Cut down on your angles!" I tried to be as brave as possible even though his shots were probably faster than Alex's, and some of them whooshed a little too close to my man parts.

After a while, Alex stopped passing balls to Dad and cleared his throat.

"Sorry, Uncle Paul," he said, "but I've got to pick up Tessa. I'm taking her to dance class."

When he said "dance class," he gave me a look, and when I didn't say anything, he cleared his throat again.

"Do you want to come along, Will?" he asked.

Maybe it was my imagination, but it seemed as though things suddenly got very quiet. Like, deserted-street-in-an-old-Western-right-before-a-gunfight quiet. Alex was standing there, looking at me, and I could see Dad watching me out of the corner of my eye.

This was it. This was my moment. I didn't have to be stuck anymore, like Safi. All I had to do was open my mouth and say, *As a matter of fact, I would like to come with you, Alex. I'm sorry, Dad, but dancing is very important to me. Way more important than hockey. And I can't give it up.*

Instead I swallowed. "Why would I want to come along?" I asked, in a voice that was a lot higher than usual. "I'm having a lot of fun playing hockey with my dad."

Alex glared at me, shook his head in disgust, and turned to walk down the driveway.

I watched him as he got into his car and

squealed away from the curb, and Dad put his arm around my shoulder.

"Come on, son," he said. "I want to teach you how to poke-check."

"Sure thing," I said.

We played for another half an hour before we stopped.

"You catch on quick, Will!" Dad said, as he gathered up the tennis balls and put them back into the bucket. The smile he gave me was so genuine that I could literally feel my heart ballooning to three times its normal size. I was like the Grinch, except I hadn't stolen anyone's toys or tried to ruin Christmas or anything.

"Well, I've always been a fast learner," I said.

Dad laughed and rubbed my head.

"Listen," he said, "your mom and Alex are out for the night. I say we go in and order a pizza. You up for it?"

"You bet!" I said.

As we made our way into the house, I literally could not remember the last time I felt so happy.

Too bad it didn't last.

CHAPTER TWENTY-EIGHT

Two days later, we were in the middle of dinner when Dad dropped the bomb.

"So I spoke to Bob Howard yesterday," he said.

No one responded, not even my mom, who was dumping spoonfuls of potato salad I didn't ask for on my plate.

"He mentioned maybe Will would like to attend the Johnny Bower goalie camp this year."

Mom, Alex, and I all raised our heads at once. I can't speak for myself, but the expressions on my mom's and Alex's faces were pretty comical. They were looking at my dad like they'd suddenly caught him wearing his underwear on the outside of his pants.

Our combined gazes must have made him a little uncomfortable, because for a moment he didn't seem to know what to do with himself. He adjusted the salt and pepper shakers until they were perfectly aligned, and then he picked up his fork and held it without eating.

"It's a sleepaway camp," he said finally. "It runs for three days at the end of May."

"Don't you think Will gets enough hockey during the regular season?" Mom said, glancing quickly at me.

"I wouldn't say that," Dad said. "Besides, if he's looking to try out for a goalie position next year, he's going to need to get working right away."

Ugh. Next season. I couldn't even bear to think about it.

"What do you say, Will?" Dad asked, leaning forward in his seat. "Do you think you might like to give it a go?"

I could see the hope in his eyes, and as much as I wanted to say no, I couldn't kill the moment.

"Sure," I said. "I'll definitely think about it."

Alex, who'd been watching us, blinked as if something had suddenly occurred to him.

I held my breath.

"Three days at the end of May," he said. "Is that Victoria Day weekend?"

Dad nodded.

"The Spencerville Fair's that weekend," Alex said. "Will is supposed to dance in the show."

"That's right," Mom said, nodding at Alex. "And I, for one, am looking forward to it."

She reached over and squeezed my hand. Dad looked at his plate and pressed his lips together until they were white around the edges.

"Will and I have discussed the situation, Marion," he said in a low voice. "Will decided it might be best if he took a break from . . . that . . .

for a while." He gestured with his hand, as if the word *dancing* was so bad he couldn't even say it.

Mom looked at me. Her eyebrows were all scrunched together.

"Is that true, Will?"

I stuttered out an answer. Something along the lines of, "Well, like, you know," and then I coughed a few times into my fist.

I guess Mom took that as a yes, because she took a deep breath and shot a look at my dad. Then she said "I see" in a clipped voice and cut her pork chop hard enough to saw through the table.

Dad didn't seem to notice. He just gave me a hopeful look.

"So what do you think, champ? Do you want to give goalie camp a try?"

Man. It had been so long since he'd called me that. And even though the thought of dumping dancing felt like my heart was being ripped out and replaced by a flaming bag of dog turds, another part of me was like, *Do it, Will. Say yes. Say yes, and things will be okay. It's just that easy.*

So I choked down a piece of pork chop and smiled as widely as I could.

"Sounds great," I said. "Sign me up."

Mom's cutlery clattered to her plate. She glared at my dad without saying anything, and then she got up from the table and went into the kitchen. I heard the cupboard door bang open and the sound of her scraping her plate loudly into the compost bin.

I looked over at Alex, who was shaking his head at me. He sat back in his chair.

"May I be excused, sir?" he asked my dad. It's funny—in some ways Alex could be the biggest slob I'd ever met, but when he wanted, he had impeccable table manners.

Dad nodded at him. Alex picked up his plate and walked around the table into the kitchen, scowling at me all the way. Then it was just me and my dad sitting alone together.

Awkward was not the word for it. I could actually feel my pulse speeding up with the stress of trying to think of something to say.

Finally Dad looked up at me from his plate.

"So I guess we'll have to get you some proper equipment."

"I guess so," I said.

He smiled at me a little and nodded.

"It could be a lot of fun," he said, his voice cracking. He cleared his throat. "You could make some new friends."

"Yes," I said quickly. "That would be great. To make some new friends, I mean. I would try really hard to do that."

His smile faded. He put down his knife and fork and rubbed at his stubble, which I noticed had a lot more gray in it than ever before. His eyes, too, seemed red and tired. The fact is, I'd never seen him look so old and worn out, and for a second it felt like a big rock was pressing on my chest. This is embarrassing to admit, but at that moment all I wanted to do was wrap my arms around his neck and hug him tight like I did when I was a little kid.

"I think—" he said. "I think I'm done here."

I glanced at his half-eaten meal and then at my own, which I had hardly touched.

"I think I am too."

We stood up from the table, and I followed him into the kitchen. We scraped our plates into the compost bin, and he took mine from me and bent down to put them both into the dishwasher.

We looked at each other.

"It's garbage night," he said quietly. "Don't forget."

"I won't," I said.

"Tell your mom I went out to work in the garage."

"Okay," I said.

He was almost through the door before I got the nerve to speak.

"Need any help?" I asked him.

"No," he said, shrugging. "I'm just fixing the lawnmower. It's no big deal."

"Okay," I said again.

I went up to my room with my insides aching because I wanted my dad to need me for something, and it didn't seem like he ever would.

CHAPTER TWENTY-NINE

Tessa did not take the news well.

Oh, no. She did not.

At first she was sort of reasonable. When I told her I had to quit dancing, she was all sympathetic and understanding, and she tried really hard to change my mind. Once she realized she couldn't, and that I was also backing out of the show, she totally freaked. She yelled a bunch of stuff at me about how hard we'd worked and about me being selfish, which I heard perfectly even though I was holding the phone a foot away from my head. And then she hung up on me. Since then, she'd totally been giving me the silent treatment.

"She's being completely unreasonable," I told Alex as we drove home from the arena, where he'd spent the afternoon trying to get me ready for hockey camp. And by trying, I mean making me run laps and do like a thousand burpees until I was ready to barf, and that was all before I even had my skates on. After that he made me strap on pads and do stops-and-starts and post-to-posts and then skate around little traffic cones he set up all over the ice. Every moment was a horror show.

"You ditched her at the last minute," he said. "Without warning, too, just so you could spend four days getting your ass handed to you at hockey camp. If anyone's being unreasonable here, I think it's you."

"Maybe I'll do okay at hockey camp," I said half-heartedly. "It's entirely possible I've got a career as a goalie in my future."

"I don't think the NHL is holding its breath, kid," Alex mumbled.

We had just turned the corner onto our street when Alex leaned forward suddenly to squint through the windshield. Then he dropped a massive f-bomb.

"What is it?" I asked.

His shoulders sank, and he turned to me.

"My father's here."

Even though I couldn't remember meeting Uncle Eric, there's no way I could have mistaken him for anyone else since he looked almost exactly like my dad. Well, not exactly. I mean, they were the identical height and build and had the same dark hair and brown eyes. But unlike my dad, who was wearing jeans and an old Metallica T-shirt, my uncle was decked out in a sleek gray suit. His hair was coiffed and perfect with not a strand out of place, and he was wearing a pretty expensive-looking gold watch, as well as several rings on his fingers. Plus I can't be entirely sure about this, but I'm almost positive he had clear polish on his fingernails.

It was like coming face-to-face with the millionaire Ken-doll version of my dad. For some reason it creeped the mighty bejeezus out of me.

I didn't have much of a chance to think about it, though, because the minute Alex and I came through the door, Uncle Eric greeted me with a slap on the back that practically sent me flying across the room. Then he turned to Alex, but instead of hugging him like I expected he would, he reached out and shook Alex's hand like they were business associates.

"How are you, Alex?" he asked, flashing a wide smile. His teeth were so perfectly white, I kept expecting a little cartoon star to twinkle on one of them.

"I'm fine," Alex said, although he couldn't have looked less fine. He was suddenly very pale, and after Uncle Eric released his hand, Alex sat on the couch next to my dad, about as far away from his dad as he could possibly get.

"It seems like you've been getting along well here," Uncle Eric said, taking a seat in Dad's favorite chair.

Instead of saying anything, Alex just shrugged a little.

"Oh yes, Alex has done very well this year," my mom said, as she handed a glass of lemonade to each of us. "He made the honor roll at school and was named MVP of his hockey team. And he's such a good boy. Such a nice young man."

Mom looked at Alex with so much pride you'd have sworn he was her own son, but for once I didn't feel jealous about it. I was too busy feeling sorry for Alex, who looked like someone had dropped his nuts in a vise and was slowly cranking the handle.

"Alex has always done very well academically," my uncle said. "But I'm glad to hear he hasn't made a nuisance of himself. That is certainly a surprise."

Uncle Eric chuckled a little, but no one else did. Alex smiled faintly, like it was the kind of remark he expected to hear, while my mom looked at my uncle like he'd just taken a dump on the living room rug. My dad sat there rubbing a random paint stain on his leg as if he could somehow get it to disappear.

Alex spoke up. "Where's Mom?" he asked.

"Oh, you know your mother," Uncle Eric said, still smiling. "Always busy with one thing or another."

"That's too bad," Alex said, "considering I haven't seen or talked to her in almost five months."

Uncle Eric's eyes narrowed, but his smile remained. "Now don't start, Alex," he said. "I'm not here to fight with you."

Alex sighed. "Why are you here?" he asked.

Uncle Eric didn't seem bothered by the question or by the sadness in Alex's voice.

"Don't be silly," he said, chuckling again. "I'm here to see you, of course."

Alex waited. The rest of us did too.

"*And* I'm here to tell you the good news." He leaned forward in his seat a little, like he was letting us in on a secret.

"After months of phone calls and emails, I finally worked things out, Alex," he said. "You've been officially invited back to the major juniors. They want to meet with you tomorrow to talk about the conditions of your return. So you need to pack up. We're going home."

It was like all the air had been sucked out of the room. My mom shot my dad a panicked look, but he didn't seem to notice.

"Good for you," Dad said, giving Alex a pat on the shoulder. "I told you it would all work out."

Alex nodded and tried to smile, but his face was grim. When he didn't say anything after a moment, his father turned to him.

"What's wrong with you, Alex?" he boomed. "This is good news! You're finally coming home!"

"Home," Alex murmured. Then he sighed again.

Despite the tension in the air, I was feeling pretty excited. Any minute now, I knew Alex was going to open his mouth and tell everyone he had no intention of returning to the juniors. He was going to stand up to his dad and tell him that from now on he was going to make his own decisions and live his own life. He was going to strike a blow for all us little guys who didn't have the stones to stand up for ourselves.

I was ready.

I was waiting.

But the seconds ticked by, and for some reason all Alex did was sit there. Chewing on his lip and staring gloomily into his lemonade, like all the secrets of the universe were somehow at the bottom of his glass.

He didn't say a word.

Dad and Uncle Eric started discussing the logistics of Alex's return, and I had to physically restrain myself from standing up and yelling, *What's wrong with you? Tell him you don't want to go, for god's sake!* I forced myself to stay calm, however, by picking up my glass of lemonade and taking a sip.

Maybe the intense anxiety in the room caused my throat to constrict or something, but the lemonade did not go down smoothly, and I started to choke. I did my best to hold it in at first because I didn't want to make a scene, but once I realized I was breathing lemonade instead of oxygen, panic set in. I started coughing and hacking and waving my hands around frantically while I gasped for air. I was also spitting lemonade everywhere, all over myself and all over my mom, who was pounding on my back in alarm.

To make matters worse, once I finally got my breath a little, I let out this deep, involuntary belch that was so loud, if we'd been in a cartoon everybody's hair would have blown back from their face. But even though I apologized like a kajillion times, it didn't stop my uncle from looking at me like I was a skeevy old Band-Aid he had pulled out of his crème brûlée.

As I sat there still hacking and being patted down by my mom with giant swaths of paper towels, I finally managed to catch Alex's eye.

"Life's. Too short," I managed to croak, before I launched into another coughing fit.

When I said that, Alex seemed to wake up a little. He watched me gravely while I got a hold of myself, and then he sat up taller and took a deep breath.

"Yeah, that's just the thing," he said, turning to face his dad. "I heard from Queen's University too. It's conditional, but they basically promised me a hockey scholarship when I graduate from high school."

Uncle Eric's eyebrows rose, and Alex swallowed.

"So I've decided to stay in Evanston for another year and not go back to the juniors." His hands were shaking slightly, and he tucked them under his arms.

Uncle Eric's smile faded and his face turned hard.

"Did you know about this, Paul?" he asked.

Dad cleared his throat as his eyes darted in Alex's direction.

"Alex mentioned it was an option he was exploring, but he was never definite about it."

Uncle Eric turned to Alex. "Now, Alex," he said,

like he was talking to a three-year-old, "you know that university hockey was never part of our plan. We decided you'd move up to the juniors at sixteen and sign at eighteen. That's *always* been the plan."

"That was *your* plan," Alex said. "No one ever asked me what *I* wanted."

"You think you're going to get drafted out of university?"

"It happens."

"You're kidding yourself. The scouts aren't going to look at you after you play four years of pansy college hockey. They want someone who's making a solid commitment, not someone who looks like he's keeping his options open."

"Maybe I'd like some options," Alex said. "For once in my life."

Uncle Eric laughed bitterly. "You want options," he said. "Do you have any idea how lucky you are? Can you even fathom how much money has been spent on your career—for equipment, coaches, training camps, rink time, and the hundreds of other things necessary to get you to where you are right now?"

"I don't know," Alex said. "I'd probably guess tens of thousands, at least."

"That's right. And now you sit here and spout this garbage at me about not going back to the juniors?"

He looked like he wanted to lunge over the coffee table and take a swing at Alex. Instead Uncle Eric sat forward in his seat a little and pointed at him.

Every word he said came out like a bullet.

"You need to quit acting like a spoiled brat, Alex," he said. "You were raised to be a winner, and now you've got a chance to achieve something great. Your uncle had that chance too, and I bet if you asked him, he'd tell you playing in the NHL was the greatest thing he's ever done in his life. Am I right, Paul?"

We all turned to my dad. Especially Alex, who looked at him with eyes that were fearful and hopeful at the same time.

Dad did not look happy. He glanced up at Uncle Eric, but instead of answering his question, he turned to Alex.

"It's a great opportunity, Alex," he said. "I think you'd be a fool to pass on it."

I sighed. Although I wasn't surprised, it definitely wasn't what I hoped he'd say. Mom must have felt the same way, because she looked like she was ready to burst into tears.

"But Paul," she said, "Alex made it clear he wants to stay here with us."

Dad gave Uncle Eric another glance, and he shook his head.

"This isn't Alex's home," he said gently. "A lot of people have worked really hard to get him where he is, and I think he's got a responsibility to see it through."

When Dad said that, Alex's face fell and he sank back into the couch, deflated. Mom opened her mouth to say something, but before she could, Dad turned to Alex.

"In the end, it's your decision," he said. "What do you think?"

Alex looked at his father and then at mine. They were both leaning forward in their seats, faces tense, like a couple of vultures about to descend on a heap of roadkill. It was obvious that Alex didn't stand a chance.

"I guess you're right," Alex said finally. "I guess it makes the most sense."

Uncle Eric sat back smiling and looking almost relieved.

"Of course it does," he said. "Hockey was what you were born to do, Alex, and someday you'll thank me and your uncle for not letting you throw your life away."

From the look on Alex's face, I knew Uncle Eric couldn't be more wrong.

CHAPTER THIRTY

After that things moved pretty quickly. Uncle Eric had a meeting and couldn't wait for Alex to get his stuff together, so he left. My mom cried and hugged Alex for what seemed like an eternity. Then she left the house to go for a long walk, but not before she and my dad had another quiet but pretty heated argument in the kitchen. I couldn't make out what they were saying, but when they were done, she stormed out the front door, while my dad watched, pale and grim faced, from the hallway. Once she was gone, he called up to Alex that he was going to the rink to fetch the rest of his hockey equipment.

I couldn't bear to help Alex pack, but it didn't matter anyway. He locked himself in his room, and the only time he spoke to me was when he asked if I could bring his things downstairs for him while he drove over to Tessa's to say goodbye.

I had just hauled the last of his suitcases to the driveway when he pulled up in his car.

"How'd she take it?" I asked him, as he got out and slammed the door.

He was doing his best to avoid my gaze, but it was obvious he'd been crying, because his eyes were red.

"Not well," he said. "Maybe you can go and check on her later. See if she's okay."

"I doubt she'd be interested in listening to anything I have to say."

"Oh yeah," he said. "I forgot."

"I guess everything's a mess," I said, kicking dejectedly at a tire.

"Guess so."

I watched him silently as he loaded his things into his car, and then I just couldn't bear it.

"God, Alex," I burst out, "why didn't you say something?"

He sighed. "What did you want me to say, Will?"

"I don't know. You could have tried harder to make them listen to you. You barely put up a fight!"

He shook his head. "It wouldn't have made a difference. It never does."

"But you gave up so easy!"

"Well," he said tiredly, "so did you."

"What's that supposed to mean?"

He ran his hand through his hair until it stood up in sweaty spikes.

"You had a thousand chances to tell your dad you're done with hockey, and you wimped out."

"It's not the same thing."

He threw the last bag into the trunk. "It is *exactly* the same thing."

He was wrong, though. There was a world of difference between me and Alex. Alex was smart, good looking, and a god on the ice. In other words, the exact opposite of me. The idea that he and I might have the same problem was ludicrous.

Wasn't it?

"Look," he said. "We both caved. So stop trying to make me feel worse about it than I already do."

"But what about Tessa?" I tried again. "How can you leave her?"

Alex sighed miserably. "Trust me," he said. "She's better off anyway."

"What are you talking about?"

He came around the side of the car to where I was standing.

"I'm talking about the fact that every time Tessa and I get together, she gives me this look, like, I don't know." He stopped and searched for words. "Like I'm the best person she's ever seen."

He was right. She lit up whenever she saw him. Like, every time.

"So?" I said. "What's the problem with that?"

"The problem is, my dad's right. All I've ever done is disappoint people. And one of these days, I know I'm going to screw up somehow, the same way I always do, and then I'll never see that look on her face again."

He slammed the trunk closed. "I'd rather leave now."

"But that's crazy," I said. "Everybody messes

up sometimes. You don't just give up on someone because they make a mistake."

"Oh, no?" he asked.

I didn't know what to say. I thought about why Alex was in Evanston to begin with. He'd made a bunch of mistakes—bad ones—but instead of dealing with it, his parents sent him away to our house. They never visited, never called to say hi or to tell him they missed him. I realized that as far as Alex knew, mistakes were colossal and second chances were rare.

He leaned against his car and crossed his arms, gazing past me at the house.

"Your dad's right, kid," he said. "This isn't my home, and it's time for me to go. The longer I stay, the harder it'll be to leave."

He opened the car door and tossed his coat on the seat.

"So what do I do now?" I asked him.

"What do you mean?"

I put my head down and kicked a rock across the driveway with as much manly force as I could. Tears were threatening, though, and I swiped at my eyes with my hand.

"You're, like, the best friend I ever had," I said. I kicked at another stone.

Alex shut the door and came over to where I was standing. He gave me a nudge with his elbow, and when I didn't look up at him, he cleared his throat and reached into his back pocket.

"Here," he said, handing me a piece of folded paper.

"What's this?"

I opened the paper. It was a check made out to me for a thousand dollars. A *thousand* dollars.

I looked up at him. "This is a thousand dollars. You can't be serious."

He shrugged. "It's for dance lessons," he said. "I know you're going to get back to them one of these days. When you do, this'll cover you for a while."

It was literally the nicest thing anyone had ever done for me. I was so stunned, I couldn't even move. I just stood there with my mouth open, looking like a statue of the world's biggest idiot.

Alex cleared his throat again and gave me an awkward pat on the shoulder. That's when I threw my arms around him and hugged him so hard I nearly knocked him off his feet.

"Thank you," I mumbled into his sweatshirt.

"Just don't spend it on booze and women," he said, as he squeezed me back.

In the distance, I could hear the minivan coming down the street.

"That's your dad," Alex said.

"I know," I said, letting go of him and wiping at my face. "Let's just say goodbye now. I don't want him seeing me like this. He already thinks I'm a loser."

"Okay," Alex said.

We tried to do one of those multistep hand-shakes, but I got confused and messed it up. Alex called me a jackass and put me in a headlock and gave me a noogie.

It was a fitting goodbye.

Then my dad pulled in the driveway, and I retreated toward the house.

I was almost to the door when I stopped and turned around, rubbing my sore head.

"Alex," I called.

"Yeah?"

"You can believe all those bad things your dad told you, but I've—I've seen who you really are." I stopped and took a shaky breath. "You're the best person I know."

Alex didn't say anything. His jaw tightened, and he nodded slightly.

"Thanks, kid," he said in a husky voice.

My dad got out of the car, so I beat it into the house.

Ten minutes later, Alex was gone.

I was alone again. Completely and totally alone, like I was before Alex came to stay with us, only this time it was worse because things were a bigger mess now than they had ever been, and I'd lost the only person I could talk to about it who would understand.

As I wandered around the house, which felt super empty now that all of Alex's crap was gone, it was like a switch flipped inside me. For the first time ever, instead of feeling sad or guilty, I felt really angry at the whole big stupid mess my life had become and at the one person who, it seemed to me, was responsible for making it that way.

Dad.

It was his fault Alex left.

It was his fault Mom was a mess.

It was his fault I quit dancing and Tessa wouldn't speak to me and I couldn't show my face at the dance studio.

Each one of us—me, Mom, Alex—had trusted my dad to call the plays. But he called them wrong, and we were all losing because of it.

CHAPTER THIRTY-ONE

Three weeks passed and before I knew it, it was the first day of hockey camp and the night of the big show I was no longer a part of.

Dad and I drove to the arena in silence. I hadn't spoken to him since Alex left, except to say yes, no, and I don't feel well, which was the excuse I used when he suggested we practice shooting pucks in the driveway. It was the best I could do, since I really wanted to tell him that he could roll his hockey stick up tight and cram it.

It was obvious he knew I was mad at him, because when we pulled up to the arena, he turned to me.

"Look, Will," he said, "I know things haven't been great at home." His seat creaked as he shifted around. "Your mom's still mad about your cousin leaving, and I know you miss him."

That was an understatement. Between quitting dancing and Alex leaving, everything in my life was a disaster. But things between my parents weren't much better. Mom stayed out a lot—at school or at her book club—and when she was home and spoke to my dad, she was pretty frosty. More than once I caught him watching her with sad, worried eyes, but when it came right down to it, he didn't have much to say to her either.

To be honest, the cold-war tension was starting to wear me down. Maybe I was overreacting, but for the first time in my life, the word *divorce* began to seem like an actual possibility, which was a thought that made me gnaw on my fingernails until they were practically down to the stumps, like Safi's.

I might have talked to Alex about it, but he never called. Part of me knew from the start that he wouldn't—that the minute he went back to Montreal, he'd be gone for good. And even though my mom told me I could call him whenever I felt like it, I didn't. Somehow I was afraid our conversation would be awkward or that we wouldn't have much to say to each other, and it would seem like we were strangers, and I'd get off the phone wondering if we'd ever really been friends at all.

When I didn't say anything, Dad sighed.

"Things will get back to normal soon," he said. "You'll see."

"I don't want things to go back to normal," I said, without looking at him. "Normal sucks."

I had never spoken to my dad like that in my life, and I expected he would tear a strip off me for it, but he didn't.

Instead he said, "What do you mean?"

"I mean Alex should be here at home with us where he belongs," I said. "And he would be"—I paused and turned to glare at him. "Except you and Uncle Eric bullied him into leaving."

Dad's eyes widened. "Will," he said. "We didn't *bully* him. He made a decision—a smart decision—to focus on his hockey career."

"It's not what he wanted, though. He wanted to stay here with us. But *you* told him to go. *You* told him this wasn't his home."

Dad shook his head and rubbed at his mouth with his hand.

"Will, I'm—" he started.

Before he could say more, Coach knocked on the window. Both Dad and I jumped, and then Dad smiled weakly at Coach and rolled the window down.

"You ready for training camp, Will?" Coach hollered.

"I can hardly wait, sir," I said.

"Well, let's go!" he shouted, slapping the roof of the truck. "We're about to start!"

Dad rolled up the window and turned to me.

"Look," he said, "can we talk about this later?"

"Why bother?" I said. "Alex is already gone."

I yanked open the door and jumped out, and Dad got out too. A bunch of guys milled around the bus waiting to get on board. All of them were twice my size.

"I don't recognize any of these guys," I said.

Dad took a step to the side and looked down at me.

"It's mostly ninth and tenth graders at this camp. But you'll meet up with them again this fall, when you start high school."

When I didn't move, he gave me a tight smile.

"It'll be all right, son. Go on."

I took a step forward.

Suddenly one of the guys in the crowd yelled out, "Hey, look everybody! Fresh meat!"

Before I knew what was happening, he started chanting, "Fresh meat! Fresh meat! Fresh meat!" over and over until the rest of the group joined him.

The chant got faster and faster until finally all the guys broke into a fit of snarling and growling and barking. They were like a pack of wild dogs.

It was the most terrifying moment of my life, no joke. I looked up at my dad to see if he was equally horrified, but he had his hands on his hips and was shaking his head at them as if only mildly perturbed by their antics.

"They're just ranking on you, Will," he said, speaking loudly to be heard over the noise. "Ignore them."

If *ranking on me* meant scaring me so badly I'd already thrown up in my mouth a little, then I suppose he was right. Either way, it was hard to ignore, even when the boys broke up laughing and got on the bus.

"They always do it to the new guys," Dad said.

"It's no big deal. We'll talk more when you get home."

He started walking toward the bus but turned around when he realized I wasn't beside him.

"What are you doing?" he called to me. "Let's go!"

I shook my head.

Dad glanced reluctantly over his shoulder and then trotted over to me.

"What's going on?" he asked in a low voice.

"I'm not doing this," I said.

"If this is about Alex, now is not the time—"

"It's not about Alex. It's about me, and I don't want to do this."

Dad glanced over his shoulder again, and then he crouched down so he could look at me face-to-face.

"Come on, Will," he said. "Don't tell me you're going to quit now."

I didn't tell him, but I hoped my shrug spoke for itself.

He put his hands on my shoulders. "Will, listen to me," he said fiercely, giving me a little shake. "If you don't want to play goalie this year, that's up to you. But if you don't get onto that bus right now, things are going to get a whole lot tougher for you. That I can promise."

"What do you mean?"

"I mean those guys will never let you forget it."

"So?"

"So this is your chance to prove yourself—to earn some respect."

It was hard to look him in the eye, but I did my best.

"Whose respect?" I asked him. "Theirs? Or yours?"

My dad blinked. He opened his mouth to say something, but nothing came out. I shook my head at him, and then I turned and walked back to the truck.

After a moment, Dad followed. He climbed in after me and sat silently for a minute. Then he put the key into the ignition, slammed the truck into gear, and to my relief, drove out of the parking lot.

As we made our way home, he turned to me. "I never said you had to do this," he said quietly. "You told me you thought it was a good idea."

"I thought it was," I snapped. "I thought maybe if I went to this camp that somehow everything might work out this time, and you'd be happy."

He didn't look away from the road. Instead he shook his head.

"I'd be happy?" he said incredulously. "I was doing this for you, Will. All I've ever wanted was what's best for you."

"You don't have a clue what's best for me," I muttered.

I knew I was pushing it talking to my dad that way, and I didn't care. All the feelings that had been simmering inside of me had finally boiled to the surface.

"I know you're angry," he said in a hoarse voice.

"You bet I am," I said. "You sent my best friend away."

"Will, for god's sake, I did not *send* him away."

"Yes, you did. He was waiting for you to tell him he could stay, and you knew it, and you told him to go anyway because, just like his dad, you've got this stupid idea about him being in the NHL."

"Now, you listen here—"

But I wasn't listening.

"You know," I said, "I used to feel bad whenever Poppy gave you a hard time about not playing hockey. It used to make me so mad the way he'd bully you about it and yell at you for ruining your life. But I realized something. You're just like him."

Dad's eyes were all pain, but in that moment, I didn't care.

"Will," he said in a strangled voice.

"It's true," I said. "You don't care what happens to Alex as long as he gets to the NHL and stays there. You don't care how he feels. You don't care how *I* feel either. You're too busy trying to turn me into some kind of jock when that's not who I am. And then you take the one thing in my life that I'm really good at and that makes me happy, and you tell me to quit. Worse, you turn it into something I feel like I should be ashamed of."

"I never told you you had to—"

"Quit? No, it was only a *suggestion*. You never tell me anything. You tell Mom stuff, and Alex, but when it comes to me, you spend all your time hiding away in the garage or at school or at the rink. Practically the only time you speak to me is when you ask me to pass the butter or remind me to take out the garbage. It's like you can't stand to be around me."

We pulled into the driveway, and I flung off my seat belt and grabbed for the door.

"You don't care about me!" I said. "You don't even know me anymore, and that makes you the least-qualified person to decide what's best for me!"

I jumped out of the truck, but before I ran inside, I turned back.

"I'm dancing in that show tonight, if Jesús will let me, and I know you think it's a bad idea. But I hope you'll come and watch me anyway, because I want you there. I want you to see me do something I'm really good at, and I want you to be proud of me. For once."

I waited for him to look at me and say he'd come, but he just sat there with his hands on the steering wheel, staring out the windshield. I couldn't be sure if he even heard me or not. So I slammed the door and ran to the house.

Instead of following me in, Dad backed down the driveway with a screech and tore off down the street.

CHAPTER THIRTY-TWO

No one picked up at Tessa's when I called. Finally I ran over to her house and punched the doorbell a hundred times until Sheri opened the door.

"What do you want?" she snarled at me.

She must have just woken up, because she was wearing a very skimpy nightgown, and her blonde hair was messy like she'd been sleeping on it. Clearly she hadn't washed her makeup off the night before because it was all smeared and crusty looking around her eyes. She looked like an angry, Victoria's Secret–wearing raccoon.

"Is Tessa around?"

"She's sleeping."

"Ah, okay."

I didn't know what to say, mostly because Sheri was glaring at me like she was ready to kill me. I didn't know where to look either, because her nightie was super short and tight, and she was practically falling out of it. So I just kept my head down and stared at the floor.

"You know, you and your cousin are real pieces of work," she said, leaning against the doorframe.

"*He* promised her he was sticking around, and then surprise, surprise, he leaves with barely any warning."

"I think it's a little more complicated than that," I said.

She ignored me and took a step closer so she could hover over me with her hands on her hips. Even though she had wicked morning breath, she was still super hot, and I prayed things would behave themselves down below.

"And *you*, you little turd," she said, giving me a painful poke in the chest with her fingernail. "You tell her you're going to do the show and then break her heart by backing out at the last minute. What kind of loser are you?"

"A big one," I said with a sigh.

Suddenly Tessa appeared in the doorway. In a bathrobe, thankfully.

"I've got this, Sheri," she said, stepping in front of her sister. "Thanks."

"Are you sure, Tessa?" Sheri asked, shooting me the stink eye again. "I can totally kick his weenie ass for you if you want me to."

Oh, please do it. Please wear that nightgown and kick my weenie ass.

"No, it's fine," Tessa said. "I can handle it."

Tessa took a step onto the porch and closed the door behind her. Then she crossed her arms over her chest and sighed.

"What do you want, Will?" she asked. Then

she crinkled her nose at me. "And why are you so sweaty?"

"It doesn't matter," I said. "Look, I know you're mad at me."

"Yes, I am."

"And I know I messed up big time."

"That's putting it mildly."

"But I'm here to tell you that I'm sorry, and I'm back, and I want to do the show tonight."

She looked at me for a moment, and then she stepped back into the house and started closing the door. "Good luck with that," she said.

"Please, Tessa!" I shouted, holding the door open with my hand. "I need you!"

She sighed. "The show's *tonight*, Will. There's no way we can pull it off. It's too late."

"It's not too late," I said. "I mean, sure, we lost a couple of weeks of practice, but it's not a big deal. We know the routine!"

"A couple of weeks?" she said, glaring at me. "That's a *huge* deal, Will. And besides, we're not in the lineup!"

"Jesús will find a way to get us on. I'm sure of it."

When she didn't say anything, I swallowed and took a step closer.

"I need to do this, Tessa," I said quietly. "Not just for myself, but for my dad too. I want to show him, once and for all, that I'm not ashamed of who I am. And if he can't find a way to be proud of me, at least I can show him I'm proud of myself."

Tessa looked at me for a moment longer, and her eyes softened.

"You should be proud of yourself, Will," she said quietly. "You've got a lot to be proud of."

"So can we be partners again?" I asked. I pinched my lips together and held my breath.

"Fine," she said, but just as I started doing a celebratory dance, she held up her hand.

"But Will," she said gravely, "I swear to god, if you ever bail on me like that again, I will hunt you down and kick your weenie butt myself."

"I promise I never will," I said.

She held the door open for me, but I hesitated.

"Aren't you coming in?" she asked.

"Is your sister in there?"

"Yes."

"In her pajamas?"

Tessa's eyebrow went up. "Yes," she said.

"I think it would be safer if I stayed out here."

Tessa called Jesús and worked things out, and the two of us spent almost the entire afternoon practicing in my basement. Mom brought us unending supplies of sandwiches and sports drinks. Now that Alex was gone, she definitely had a surplus of food. She never said anything about hockey camp, or about Dad, who by five o'clock still hadn't come home.

I couldn't worry about that at the moment, though. I still had to think about how I was going to explain myself to Jesús. I mean, I quit on him, and I didn't even have the nerve to tell him myself. I was totally prepared for him to call me a loser in Spanish and maybe even fake spit on me a little.

But when we arrived at the fair, and Jesús caught sight of me, he came running over and kissed me right in the middle of the forehead.

"Jefe!" he said, his eyes filling up with tears. "I'm so happy to see you!"

I was so ashamed I could barely look at him. "I'm sorry I let you down, Jesús."

He put his hands on my shoulders.

"Oh, Jefe," he said, shaking his head gravely. "You don't have to say you're sorry, okay? What matters is you are here. You found your courage, and that is beautiful to me."

He smiled widely at me and gave my shoulders a shake. "You are a superstar, okay? Very, very especial."

He hugged me tight, and then he let me go and wiped tears from his eyes.

"Now come," he said. "Meet my friends."

He took us into a small tent just next to the stage that was filled with the most beautiful people I'd ever seen. Tall women in glittery dresses who looked like supermodels and tanned men in suits with slicked-back hair who were freaking ripped with muscles. They were honest-to-god professional dancers who looked like they'd be more at home sipping champagne on a yacht off the coast of France than standing around in a dusty fair tent that smelled like cow manure.

Even so, they were super friendly and excited that Tessa and I were in the show. They told us funny stories about Jesús from when they knew him in Toronto and *oohed* and *aahed* over our costumes. They didn't seem to mind at all when Tessa and I grilled them about technique.

As nice as they were, I still missed the old gang from the studio, Annie and PJ especially. But when Tessa and I climbed onstage and peeked at the audience from the wings, there they all were—almost the entire dance school gang—in the front row. Seeing PJ sitting there with his fez and Annie in her shiny purple pants and sweatshirt that said DANCING QUEEN on it in glittery letters made a wave of relief wash over me.

Unfortunately, a second later that good feeling went up in flames.

"Oh my god!" I groaned.

Tessa looked at me, alarmed. "What is it?"

"In the third row," I said. "It's Evan and Kole."

But it wasn't only Evan and Kole. It was the starting line of the triple-A team—Caleb and Mason and Kyle and Ethan and Dave. Berger was with them too, only this time instead of Cheetos, he had a fully loaded chili dog. They were all just sitting there waiting for the show to begin.

"Oh my god," I whispered. "What could they possibly be doing here?"

"You know what people in Evanston are like," Tessa said. "They'll come out to watch just about anything. I mean, how else do you explain the popularity of tractor pulls?"

"But dancing?"

Tessa shrugged. "A show's a show," she said.

That did not make me feel better. Before I could say anything, she nudged me.

"Look. There's your mom."

She was just taking her seat in the second row. Alone.

"My dad's not here," I said in a flat voice. My stomach started doing sick flips.

"Are you sure?" Tessa said, scanning the crowd. "There's a lot of people out there."

"I don't think he's coming."

Tessa took a deep breath. "He'll come," she said, nodding. "He's probably just late. But he'll be here, Will. I know it."

She didn't look like she really believed it, though. She put her arm around me and gave me a sympathetic squeeze while I groaned a little and clutched my stomach.

Then the show started, and we stood together in the wings and watched while one by one, each set of dancers took the stage. Jesús danced too, with a beautiful Russian woman named Maria who had big brown eyes and legs up to her earlobes. It wasn't often we got a chance to watch him doing his thing with a real professional, and it reminded me what an incredible dancer he was. His timing, like his footwork, was always perfect, and even though he wasn't a particularly tall guy, his posture was so good it made him look like a giant on the dance floor. Plus, talk about an athlete. The dude was all muscle. He was so strong he could lift his partner up over his head like she weighed nothing and set her back down just as easily, and she was almost as tall as he was. In fact, watching Jesús dance was like watching Alex play hockey—both of them were so strong and confident, every move seemed effortless.

Unfortunately it was tough to concentrate on the stage when all I could think about was the audience, which was full of people who were waiting to watch me make a fool of myself. And of course there was that sad, empty seat next to my mom, and all the things it meant. None of that was doing anything to help the volcano of explosive diarrhea that threatened to erupt at any second.

Little by little, the Disney trolls crept back into my brain, only this time instead of chanting *Breasts!* they were saying things like *This is a mistake!* and *Save yourself!* and *What are you waiting for, you pathetic loser? Run!*

I never got the chance. The emcee called our names, and before I even knew what was happening, Tessa put her arm in mine, and the two of us walked onstage.

The lights blinded me, and I wished for the kajillionth time that I was wearing a suit rather than

Jesús's incredibly tight, practically spandex costume. For one thing, I wouldn't have worried about popping some random panic boner I couldn't hide. Plus regular pants would have mostly camouflaged my shaking legs. It was too late to do anything about it, though. Tessa and I took our position in the center of the stage, and the music began.

The routine Jesús had choreographed for us was pretty complicated. There were a lot of intricate movements, plus a couple of small lifts, and even though we'd done fine during practice, I'd be lying if I said I wasn't more than a little doubtful we'd manage to pull it off.

Sure enough, in the first fifteen seconds of the song, I was supposed to catch Tessa in a neck drop, but I lost my balance and almost let her fall to the stage. I caught her at the last minute, but that didn't stop the crowd from letting out a collective gasp. When I pulled her back into my arms, she still had a smile plastered on her face, but her eyes were shooting me a look like she was ready to kill me.

It got worse before it got better. I stepped on her foot during the ocho cortado, and I must have hurt her, because I could see the tears in her eyes as we moved into the salida. I don't know if she was retaliating or what, but she was like a millimeter away from kicking me in the crotch during the gancho. She was so close to ground zero, in fact, that my nuts started throbbing, and I wondered if we were going to get through the dance together, or if we were just going to spend the rest of the song beating the bejeezus out of each other.

As it turned out, though, I didn't need to worry. After we managed the first lift successfully, we both relaxed, and everything else fell away. I stopped thinking so much about the steps or that Tessa was going smash my nuts into oblivion. Tessa loosened up and quit back-leading, and before we knew it, everything felt as natural and as easy as breathing.

It helped too that the audience was totally into it. Even the hockey guys, which was amazing. Like, midway through the dance, for example, Tessa lifted her leg to my shoulder, and I caught it and held it there, pressing her against me so she was basically doing the splits standing up. All the guys started hooting like a gang of chimps, and I heard Berger yell out, "Way to go, Stone!"

It was awesome.

When the song ended, everyone clapped and whistled. In fact, the crowd was so stoked, they were, like, inches away from tossing roses at our feet.

In my best dreams, I could never have imagined things turning out that way. And it was great. Really, it was. But the whole time we were taking our bows, my eyes kept coming back to that chair beside Mom. It was still empty.

Dad never showed up.

CHAPTER THIRTY-THREE

Tessa and I stood onstage hugging each other long after the curtain came down. When she pulled away from me, she dabbed at her eye makeup, which was smudged because she was crying a little. I think I was crying a little too. From happiness but also from sadness.

"Will, that was *amazing*!" she said. She was still swiping at her eyes and kind of half laughing and half crying. "You were so good! And I know it sounds crazy, but it was like—it was like I could *feel* my dad looking down and watching us, you know?"

"It doesn't sound crazy at all."

It did sound ironic, though. The idea that Tessa's dead father had traveled across everlasting eternity so he could make it to the performance, while my dad couldn't manage to make the ten-minute trip in his Ford F-150 felt like a kick in the teeth.

"I wish Alex had been here!" Tessa sighed. "I mean, I know he's stuck in Montreal and everything, but I still wish he could have made it tonight. He would have been so proud of you, Will."

"Yeah." I smiled. "He'd have been proud of you too."

Tessa smiled and wiped at her eyes again, while I swallowed a hard lump in my throat.

"Do you miss him as much as I do?" I asked.

She shook her head sadly. "I miss him more than you can possibly imagine."

I nodded.

She took a deep breath and let it go, and then she shrugged and smiled at me through her tears.

"But let's not be sad now, Will!" she said. She took both of my hands in hers and bounced a little. "We did it! We danced on the same stage as international superstars! And we kicked butt!"

"I guess we did." I laughed.

We hugged again. We'd barely made it off the stage before Mom came barreling around the corner with her arms out.

"You were so good, honey!" she said, crushing me in her grip.

"Did Dad come? Is he with you?" I asked over her shoulder.

When Mom drew back, her face had fallen a little.

"I didn't see him," she said. "But that doesn't mean he's not here somewhere. Maybe he got lost trying to get to the stage."

"Maybe," I said. I doubted it, though. It was finally time to get real about the situation.

He didn't come.

That was it. He didn't come, and I'd ruined everything. Whether it was because of the dancing or the things I'd said in the truck, I'd finally succeeded in driving a wedge between me and my dad that was so big there was no way we would ever recover.

I didn't think I could feel any worse. Like, I couldn't possibly imagine things could get any suckier than they were at that particular moment.

A second later, Annie came around the corner.

And Claudia Valenta was with her.

The minute I saw her, my brain literally stopped functioning. Seriously, if it had been hooked up to one of those hospital machines, all it would show would be a straight line with no *boops* in between.

"Hey!" Annie called as she pulled Claudia along. When she got close, she threw her arms around me and Tessa and gave us a hug. Tessa hugged her back, while I stood there frozen.

"You did so well! I'm so proud of the both of you!" she exclaimed.

I stole a quick glance at Claudia, who was waiting patiently off to the side. She was wearing some kind of jean-skirt thing, and her legs were long and tanned. She was also wearing another one of those tank tops like she'd been wearing at the Dairy Queen, and her breasts were just, like, *magnificent.*

Annie patted my face a couple of times, and then she reached for Claudia's hand and pulled her closer.

"This is my friend from church I told you about," she said, winking obviously at me. "This is Claudia."

"Hello!" Claudia said, giving me a small wave.

Instead of saying hi, I made a sound like *guuuuuhhhh.*

"Claudia is thinking about coming to the studio for dance lessons, Will," Annie said. "What do you think about that?"

"Guuhhh—reat!" I said, finally getting a hold of myself. "That sounds like a fantastic idea!" I gave her the thumbs-up, which was so lame that I mentally smacked myself in the head for being such a loser.

Then Claudia tilted her head like she was trying to place me and gave me an embarrassed smile.

"I think vee meet before—at bakery." She put her hand to her face. "Your nose vas bleeding."

"Yeah, that was me," I sighed. "I'm an idiot."

She laughed. "You're no idiot," she said. "You are such good dancer. I never knew a guy who can dance like you."

"Th-thanks," I stuttered, while Annie waggled her eyebrows at me.

"Well, I'll just let the two of you get to know each other," Annie said.

She and Tessa moved along to talk to Jesús, who was by the stage with the rest of the dancers.

I'm not sure where my mom had wandered off to, but all of a sudden it was just me and Claudia Valenta standing there. Alone together. It was like every daydream and every nightmare I'd ever had rolled into one.

A moment of awkward silence stretched between

us before I got up the nerve to say something.

"So—ah—you're thinking of taking dance lessons?" I asked her.

"Yes," she said, nodding.

"Have you—ah—ever ballroom danced before?"

Claudia laughed a little and dropped her head.

"No," she said. "I never dance. I have the two right feet."

Some of her hair had slipped out of her braids and wisped around her face like angel feathers. She was so beautiful I wanted to throw up.

Instead of doing that, I said, "You don't have to worry. Jesús is a great teacher."

Claudia's face fell a little. "I thought you were teacher," she said.

"Oh, well, I mean, I'm not a teacher really," I said. "But I could probably show you a few things, you know, like, on the side. If you'd like."

"I vould like," she said. She blushed and smiled at me, and it was literally the best moment of my life.

And the worst.

Because that's when Pavel showed up.

Freaking Pavel.

He was a big, tall, blond guy who might have looked like he stepped out of a Calvin Klein ad, except he had a bowl cut and was wearing a Members Only jacket. He came up behind Claudia out of nowhere and put his arm around her shoulder, and she turned around and looked up at him as if he was god's gift to all creation.

"I'm sorry, Vill," she said, turning back to me. "This is Pavel. He is, ah—" She stopped and thought for a moment. "Jak se rekne? He is, like, boy friend?" she said. "Yes. Boy friend from Czech Republic. He come for visit."

I couldn't speak.

I would never speak again.

I was going to run away, join a monastery, and spend the rest of my days in silence wearing burlap undershorts.

"Ano," Pavel said, nodding at Claudia. "Boy. Friend." Then he turned his blue-eyed, movie-star smile on me. "Boy. Friend."

Yeah, okay. Whatever. You win. Just do me a favor and stomp my brains in with your big Eastern European feet. Put me out of my misery.

I gave him a weak wave like a sick dog that can barely lift its tail to wag it, while Claudia crossed her arms over her chest.

"Is cold tonight, a little, I think," she said.

I waited for him to give her his jacket, but he was too busy staring at me with a stunned smile to even notice she was cold. I took off my cape and handed it to Claudia.

"Here," I said.

"Oh, no," she said, looking down at it. "I can't."

"Take it." I shook it at her. "Seriously. I'm always hot."

She took it from me and put it on.

"This is very beautiful," she said, admiring Jesús's handiwork. Then she looked up at me and smiled again. "Thank you for this, Vill. You are very kind."

I shrugged again. "No big deal," I said.

And I meant it. Nothing felt like a big deal anymore. Life was just a big ol' pile of crap.

"Well, I've got to get out of here," I said to them. "I've got a . . . meeting . . . on the other side of the fair grounds."

"A meeting?" Claudia said.

"Yeah, it's for science class," I babbled. "I'm doing a project about cows, so I've got to head over to the show barns. Because that's where they keep the cows. In the barns."

I honestly had no idea what I was talking about.

"Don't you vant your . . . cape . . . back?" she asked.

"Keep it for now," I said. "I'll get it some other time."

She took a step toward me.

"I work at bakery tomorrow," she said, twisting her hands into a knot. "You could swing by and pick up? I make special Czech dessert. You know, only for saying thank you."

"Don't trouble yourself," I said. "Just give it to Tessa at school on Tuesday."

"Oh, okay," she said, swallowing. She stepped back beside Pavel and nodded. "Thank you then, Vill."

I walked away and left her standing there with her big, stupid Czech man hunk. It was probably a rude thing to do, but I didn't have the heart left to care.

I didn't have the heart for anything anymore.

CHAPTER THIRTY-FOUR

As I stumbled onto the midway, everything was sort of blurry. Before I knew it, I'd managed to find my way into the farm area, which consisted of three or four domed aluminum structures that housed the animals all the 4-H'ers brought in for competition.

I made a right turn into the livestock barn and traveled down the middle aisle, looking for Safi and Susie. He'd entered her in the showmanship and in-hand trail competitions, and she was a shoo-in to win, just like last year.

Unfortunately the barn was deserted. The cows and pigs were already cleared out, and all that was left were empty stalls full of hay and mud and manure. There was literally nothing to see, so it was odd when a bunch of guys pushed past me on their way to the back of the building.

I followed along numbly to where a crowd had gathered, and it wasn't until I'd gotten quite close that I recognized some of the guys from Artie's gang. I froze in my tracks.

"What do you think you're doing, Kavanaugh?" one of them called out.

I couldn't see what was happening because they were all standing shoulder to shoulder, but I heard what sounded like the squeal of a pig, and everyone laughed.

"Just giving John Deere a bit of a trim," Artie hollered back. "Who knew he had this much hair under that stupid cowboy hat."

John Deere. Cowboy hat. There was only one person he could have been talking about. Without even thinking, I squeezed between the bodies until I found myself at the edge of the pen.

And that's when I saw him.

Artie was standing there holding a pair of professional-looking clippers that farmers used to shear sheep. Behind that turd, crouching in the corner of the pen, was Safi. He was cowering, crying, and bleeding from his nose and looked more terrified than I'd ever seen anyone look. When I saw him, I went basically supersonic with rage.

Before I could even think about what I was doing, I grabbed an old wooden rake handle leaning against the wall. I brandished it in both hands, like it was a sword.

"Stay away from him, Artie!" I yelled.

Artie didn't even blink. He looked at me dumbly and then broke out in a smile.

"Well, looky who's here," he said.

I held my ground.

When Artie stepped away from the corner and moved closer to me, Safi got to his feet and managed to scramble out the other side of the pen. Artie didn't notice, though. His sights were set on me.

"That's an interesting-looking outfit," he said, eyeing me up and down. "Even for a loser like you."

The rest of the guys started to laugh, and Artie moved closer.

"I heard your cousin skipped town," he said.

"So what?"

"So that means your bodyguard's gone," he said. "It means now I'm free to kick your ass."

The guys laughed again, but this time I laughed with them.

"Maybe so," I said. "You sure couldn't do it when my cousin was here. After he beat you up the first time, you practically peed your pants whenever he was around."

A murmur went up from the crowd, and Artie narrowed his eyes at me.

"I'm going to kill you for that," he said. He was so mad he was practically snorting steam. In fact, he looked so much like a big, stupid bull that I wished I still had my cape so I could shake it at him. Instead I took a deep breath.

"Just try, you moron," I said.

He charged at me, and I managed to evade him by jumping to the side at the last minute. As he went flying past me, I swung the handle as hard as I could with both hands and caught him right in the butt with it. He staggered across the pen and slammed into the fence. The rest of the guys laughed and a few of them called out *olé!*, which of course made Artie even madder.

Wayne was mad too, and he climbed up onto the gate.

"Kill him, Artie!" he hollered, his eyes full of hate. The dude was out for blood.

Artie turned around and came at me again, but I sidestepped him once more, and this time I caught him in the knees with the handle. He went down shrieking and grasping his legs, and I thought—not without intense happiness—that maybe I'd broken something.

That's when Wayne jumped the fence.

"Enough of this crap," he said as he came at me. I tried to swing, but he was too fast, and he pulled the handle out of my hands. Then he punched me so hard I swear I saw a thousand stars explode in front of me. I twisted around and fell in the mud. While I was lying there listening to the cymbals crashing in my head, Wayne stalked over, grabbed the front of my pirate shirt, and hauled me up to my knees. He stared down at me, like an angry, red-faced pig. From my angle, I could see right up his piggy nostrils, and he had a big green bat in his cave.

"That was for Artie," he said, as he cocked his arm back. "This one's for me."

The last thing I saw was his fist coming toward my face.

After that, everything went black.

CHAPTER THIRTY-FIVE

The next twenty minutes or so were a blur. I must have passed out, because I couldn't seem to open my eyes, but I could still hear people talking around me—random voices that kept fading in and out.

"We should find his mom. I think he's concussed," someone said.

It sounded like Tessa.

"I haven't seen anyone go down that hard since three-time Professional Rodeo Cowboy Association world bull-riding champion Dick Tuffman got kicked in the face by a rogue stallion."

That was definitely Safi.

Then a low voice spoke. "Hey, kid. Let's go. Time to wake up."

It was Alex.

Even though my eyes felt like they were weighed down with cement, I managed to get them open, and there he was, squatting in front of me, holding on to my shoulders.

"Hey!" he said. "You're alive!" He smiled and gave me a little shake. "Heard you took on the moron twins by yourself. What are you? Stupid or something?"

If we hadn't been in public, and surrounded by a kajillion people, I would have literally fallen into his arms. I was that happy to see him.

"You should have seen it, Alex," I said, grinning at him even though my face hurt like crazy. "Artie was ready to kill me, and I still managed to take him out at the knees."

Alex laughed. "I guess the sun shines on a dog's ass some days, doesn't it?"

"It does," I agreed.

I looked around. I was sitting on a bale of hay outside the building, next to the Barn of Learning and the stand where they sold lemonade and cotton candy.

"What are you doing here, anyway?" I asked him.

"What do you think?" he said, like I'd asked him a stupid question. "I came back to see your big show."

"Well, you missed it," I said. I leaned against the wall and reached up to touch my face. It felt huge and lumpy.

He shifted over and sat down next to me. "Sorry about that," he said. "It took longer than we thought to get back here, and by the time we did, it was over."

"Who's we?"

"Me and your dad. He drove up to Montreal to get me this morning. He was driving so fast to get home for your show, he blew out the truck's engine.

I had my car, but we still had to wait for a tow truck to come."

"Really?"

Alex nodded. "When we got to the stage, someone told him they saw you heading toward the barns. We showed up just as that loser knocked you out, and your dad jumped the fence, like, one-handed, and dragged him off you. I thought Uncle Paul was going to kill him. It was seriously scary."

"My *dad*?" I asked him.

"Yes, your dad," Alex said.

"That's hard to believe."

Alex's face sobered for a moment. "He wanted to be here, Will," he said. "I swear. All he kept saying was how he had to make it back on time. That he didn't want to let you down again."

Wow.

"Where is he now?" I asked, looking around.

"He's in there talking to the cops." Alex jerked a thumb over his shoulder toward the barn.

"The police?"

"Yes, the police. God, are you brain damaged or something? That cowboy kid ran and found them after you jumped in the pen and decided to be a hero."

I scrambled to get up, but before I could go anywhere, my mom came squealing around the corner with Tessa and Safi as well as Safi's parents trailing along behind her.

"Ohmigod, ohmigod, ohmigod, whathappened whathappened?" my mom practically screamed.

She was all over me and was crying so much she didn't even see Alex. When she turned and noticed him, she was all over him too.

"OhmigodAlexwhatareyoudoingherethankgod yourehere—whatsgoingon?"

Alex opened his mouth to explain when my dad came walking out of the barn with two police officers. Artie and Wayne were with them, and I noticed Artie was limping badly. I felt pretty happy about that—I'm not going to lie.

When the cops saw Safi and his parents, they called them over, and my mom leaped up and ran to my dad. After everything that had happened, I didn't know what to say to Dad, so instead of running over, I hung back with Alex and Tessa and watched.

I couldn't hear what my parents were talking about, but my mom was obviously freaking out because she kept waving her arms around. Dad, on the other hand, just looked tired. His shoulders were kind of slumped, and he had his hands stuffed in his pockets. Every once in a while he shot a worried glance in my direction.

Once he and Mom finished, Dad walked over.

"Are you all right, Will?" he asked, squatting down in front of me. He reached up and stroked my hair a little, which was something he hadn't done since I was, like, six.

"I'm all right," I said. "It probably looks worse than it feels."

"I'm sorry I missed your show," he said. "I wanted to be here for it."

"I know you tried to get here," I said. "Alex told me."

He nodded sadly and gave my shoulder a little shake. Then he glanced over to the police officers. Artie and Wayne were already sitting in the back seat of one of the cruisers.

"I have to go to the police station now," Dad said, glancing up at my mom.

"But why?" I asked, panicked. "Are you in trouble?"

"No," he said. "They need my statement, and it's going to take a while. Go on home with Mom."

He stood up and began to walk away. He was almost out of sight when I finally spoke up.

"I'll wait up for you," I called after him.

He stopped and turned around. He opened his mouth, and for a minute I thought he was going to say no like every other time.

But then he said, "That'd be fine."

CHAPTER THIRTY-SIX

The four of us—Mom, me, Alex, and Tessa—didn't hang around for long after that. Mom talked to Safi's parents for a bit, but Safi was still pretty shaken up, so he didn't have much to say. Before we left, though, he stood up and kind of threw his arms around me.

"Thanks for, you know, saving me," he said gruffly once he let go.

I put my hand on his shoulder.

"The reign of terror is over, Safi," I said, giving him a reassuring shake. "Artie and Wayne are finally going to get what's coming to them."

"Do you really think so?" Safi asked.

"Definitely," I said. "Things are going to get better. I know it."

I meant it too. Not just because Artie and Wayne had finally exposed themselves as the demented psychopaths they were, but also because if Evan and Kole and the entire starting lineup of the bantam triple-A hockey team could sit in the audience of a dance show and find reason to cheer me on, maybe there was hope for all of us.

We said our goodbyes, and as soon as we got home, Mom dragged me upstairs to the bathroom to tend to my face. Thanks to Wayne, I had a gash on my cheekbone, and my eye was about ten different shades of blue and green.

I could tell Mom was furious, but she was doing her best to hold it together. She couldn't stop muttering to herself, though. Most of it was incoherent, but when I flinched as she cleaned my cheek, she barked, "That scumbag. I hope your father *crucifies* him."

It was such an un-Mom thing to say, I actually laughed out loud.

Even though it was almost midnight, she went to the kitchen and made Alex, Tessa, and me a huge meal: eggs, bacon, sausage, toast, and home fries. She even made crepes for dessert, which were our favorite.

After that she excused herself. "I'm going to wait for your father upstairs," she said wearily. "I need to lie down."

Just as she was leaving the kitchen, though, she stopped and turned back. She smiled at us and put her hand over her heart.

"I'm just so happy to have both my boys home," she said. She dabbed at her face a little with a Kleenex, and then she went upstairs.

Alex grinned at me. "Your mom's amazing," he said.

"I know," I said.

The three of us sat down at the table, and for a while we were too busy eating to talk. Well, I was too busy. Alex and Tessa were eating too, but they couldn't stop smiling and sneaking kisses when they thought I wasn't looking. I was on the verge of telling them to get a room.

Instead I said, "I guess this means you're sticking around."

Alex tore his eyes away from Tessa long enough to cram a wad of toast in his mouth.

"Well, somebody's got to keep an eye on you," he said. "God knows what kind of shenanigans you might get into if I leave again."

"So what happened?" Tessa asked. "Will's dad just showed up and told you to come back?"

Alex stabbed his fork into his crepe and took a deep breath. He looked at me.

"Kind of," he said. "I was heading out to practice when Uncle Paul showed up. He told me how the two of you had had a big talk, and that you had got him thinking about me and hockey and my future, and then, like, out of nowhere, he grabbed me by the shoulders and said, 'It's okay to tell me what you really want, Alex. Whatever you decide, I promise I'll support you.'"

"Holy crap," I said.

"I know," Alex said. "It was the first time in my life an adult ever said anything remotely close to that. I was so shocked I almost couldn't speak."

"So what did you say?" Tessa asked.

"I told him I wanted to come home," he said over another mouthful. "And the best part was that I didn't have to tell him what home I was talking about."

Tessa and I smiled at each other.

"Then my dad came outside and the two of them got into this huge shouting match, and I thought for sure one of the neighbors was going to call the cops. They calmed down, though, and went inside, and in the end your dad managed to convince my dad I'd play better hockey if I weren't completely miserable. Although I'm sure he wouldn't have minded as long as I did what he wanted me to do," he added with a grimace.

"It doesn't matter what your dad thinks," Tessa said, closing her eyes and giving him another squeeze. "All that matters is that you're here."

Alex smiled at me sadly. I think we both knew it wasn't as easy as all that.

Still, she was mostly right. Alex was going to be okay.

He was finally home.

Alex left to take Tessa home, and Dad pulled into the driveway twenty minutes later. I was waiting for him in the living room and was almost asleep when I heard the key in the lock. I leaped up and met him at the door.

He didn't say anything at first. He just kicked

off his shoes wearily and hung up his coat. Then he looked at me and sighed.

"I need a drink," he said.

I followed him into the kitchen, where he got a beer from the fridge, but instead of taking it to the living room, he opened the back door.

"Come," he said.

We sat together on the top step of the porch. He had his elbows on his knees and his gaze fixed on his beer bottle, which he was rolling slowly back and forth between his hands.

For a while, neither of us said anything. We sat and listened to the crickets chirping. It would have been really peaceful if it hadn't felt like I had a thousand-pound weight pressing on my chest.

Finally my dad sighed. "You should know those boys who hurt you and Michael are being charged by the police."

"Will I have to testify in court?"

"I doubt it," he said. He took a swig of his beer. "There were enough witnesses who saw what was going on, including me. I'm just sorry I didn't get there in time to stop it."

He glanced over at me quickly, and then he shook his head and continued to study his beer bottle.

I knew I needed to say something to put things right, so I took a deep breath. "I want to tell you that I'm sorry about the things I said to you in the truck."

He smiled a little. A tight, bitter smile. "Don't

be," he said. He took another swig of his beer. "I deserved it."

"No, you didn't."

"Sure, I did. It seems like all I've done lately is let you down."

"That's not true," I said, although I knew it mostly was. Still, it was killing me to see him looking so sad, and I was willing to say anything if it'd make him feel better.

"The hockey is my fault, Dad," I said. "I'm the one who can't play."

"But I put you there," he said, finally turning to look at me. He took another sip of his beer and sighed. "I knew you were having a rough time at school, but I didn't know what to do to make it better. But I knew that when *I* was your age, sports saved me."

"Saved you from what?" What could a guy like my dad ever need saving from?

He shrugged and set his bottle down on the porch. "I don't know. Just trouble. I was small like you when I was a kid, and sometimes I got pushed around."

Well, that was news. I wished someone had told me sooner. The idea that I might one day be as big as my dad would have totally given me something to live for.

"And of course," he said, raising his eyebrows at me, "living with Poppy was no picnic."

I imagined he was putting that mildly.

"But," he said, "hockey gave me a place to get away from things. I'd get on the ice, and I could forget who I was for a while. I wanted you to have something like that in your life."

"I do," I said. "That's exactly how I feel about dancing."

He nodded slowly and dropped his head to look at the floor. "I know," he said quietly. "I didn't realize how much it meant to you. I'm sorry."

Sorry. My dad said he was *sorry*. It was like one of the seven signs of the apocalypse, and part of me felt like running for cover in case there was an earthquake or I was about to be attacked by a swarm of flesh-eating locusts. Instead I sat there and shook my head.

"It's my fault," I said. "I mean, I know I've been a—a disappointment. I should have spoken up and told you I didn't want to play. I guess I just wanted to be the kind of son you could be proud of. You know, the kind of son Gordie would have been."

When I said Gordie's name, Dad flinched like I'd hit him, and his eyes filled with tears. I was so terrified he was going to start crying it felt like my heart was going to explode.

"Your brother?" he said hoarsely. "How do you—"

"Poppy told me."

Dad shook his head and sighed. "But your brother—he was a baby. How could you possibly think—"

"I don't know," I said quickly. "It just always felt

like he would have done more with his life if he'd lived than I have, and I guess I was just tired of feeling like a sad replacement."

Everything in my dad's body seemed to sag. "For god's sake, Will," he said. "You were never a replacement. Or a disappointment. You were a second chance for me and your mom. You were a *miracle*."

My dad's never been prone to exaggeration, so when he called me a miracle, I was tempted to believe him. For a moment I felt so relieved and so happy it was like I was about to burst out of my own skin. But I also felt terrible because my dad was just sitting there looking like I'd ripped his heart out and stomped on it.

"And I *am* proud of you, son. You stood up to me. You stood up for your friend, even though you took a beating for it. Everyone's been on you, but you've still made your own decisions and done your own thing. You're a good man, Will."

"So are you," I said.

He shook his head. Everything about him was heavy and sad.

"I don't know," he said, staring down at his bottle. "I—I always swore I'd be a better dad than my father. I don't know how I got everything so wrong."

"You're nothing at all like Poppy," I said, and I meant it. "You're a great dad."

He smiled like he wanted to believe me but couldn't. Then he turned and told me something I hadn't heard for a long time.

"I love you, Will," he said, his voice breaking a little. "And I've *always* been proud of you. I'll be sorry until the end of my days that I ever did anything to make you believe I wasn't."

He wiped tears away from his eyes and tried to smile, but his mouth kept turning down like it had a mind of its own. So I did what I'd been dying to do for ages. I wrapped my arms around his neck and hugged him. He hugged me back so hard I thought he might crack one of my ribs.

We stayed like that for a long time, and then I kissed him on his bristly cheek. When he drew back, his eyes were wet again.

"We'll find a way," he said, sniffing and giving my head a rub. "We'll find a way to work it all out."

CHAPTER THIRTY-SEVEN

And we did. I resumed dance classes, and Jesús invited both my parents to the milonga so they could see me and Tessa dance. Alex came along, too, and they were all suitably impressed with our performance. For real. In fact, Dad was so impressed that my mom and Jesús actually managed to convince him (okay, my mom begged him) to come for a private lesson the following week.

Even though I really hoped Dad would actually enjoy himself and would want to go back for more lessons, unfortunately, that wasn't the case. I'm all right with it, though. If there's one thing I've learned in life it's that you've got to let people find their own destiny. My dad is a hockey player, not a ballroom dancer, and that's okay.

Sometimes life can surprise you, though. As soon as it was cold enough, Dad, Alex, and I made a rink in the backyard. It was for shinny only. No power skating, no drills, and no practicing allowed.

And here's the funny thing. Once all the pressure and expectations were gone, hockey became what it was supposed to be: a game. A *fun* game. I was as surprised as anyone to find myself lacing up my skates every night so I could go outside to play with my dad.

Just me and my dad and sometimes Alex. Hanging out and talking and batting a puck around. It was awesome.

The best time, though, was Christmas. After presents and endless amounts of food, we all got dressed and headed outside. Dad had rigged up a floodlight so we could skate at night, and the snow was falling softly in big, feathery flakes. Everything looked so peaceful that for a moment I felt like I was in the middle of a Tim Horton's commercial.

We made teams—Alex and Tessa against me, Dad, Mom, and Safi, who I made sure to invite. At first Mom thought it was unfair that we stacked the deck—that is, until Tessa and Alex started cleaning up. It wasn't a surprise—they made a pretty awesome team.

It wasn't long, though, before the two of them wanted to go off and do their own thing. I didn't mind. It gave me a chance to sit on the bench with Claudia.

That's right. Claudia. As in Valenta. As in the future mother of my Olympic medal–winning children.

She showed up at the studio the day after the fair with my cape and a box of this stuff called krówki—basically fudge but way better—that she'd made herself. She heard about the fight with

Artie and Wayne and was properly sympathetic about my bruises. She explained to me that her friend Pavel wanted to come along because he had kind of a crush on me, but she decided to leave him at home.

"Holy cow, Pavel is gay?" I asked her.

When she nodded, I thought I was going to cry from happiness.

"Pavel is gay!" I shouted to no one in particular.

"Yes," Claudia said, giving me a weird look. "He is very nice boy. A good friend."

"I believe you," I said, calming down a little. "And I'm flattered he likes me, but I'm pretty much into girls. Like, big time."

"Oh," Claudia said, her face breaking out into a smile. "That's good." Then she laughed a little and did that thing shy girls do where they duck their heads and look at you through their eyelashes. It just about slayed me.

Even though she was totally flirting, it still took me an eternity to figure out she was actually interested in me, and then it took a month after that to get up the nerve to ask her out.

"You idiot," Alex said, when I told him I finally did it. "I told you she liked you way back when she showed up at the studio. What took you so long?"

"I guess I didn't see it," I said.

There's a lot of stuff you can tell about a person by looking. Like, I know when Mom's about to cry or when Alex is ready to blow his top. I know when

Dad has had enough of all of us and wants to be left alone.

Love, though, is way more complicated. It's not always warm and fuzzy, like it is in movies and on TV. I mean, sure, sometimes you barely have to look for it. But sometimes it's hard to find, and when you do, it isn't nearly as spectacular as it should be. Sometimes it's everywhere—big and bold—but still impossible to recognize, especially when you think you don't deserve it.

But me and my dad—and Alex too—we didn't have that problem anymore. After everything we went through, our eyes were clear and wide open.

And the view was beautiful.

ACKNOWLEDGMENTS

This book has been a very, very long time coming, and there are so many people who helped me along the way. Too many, actually, so I'm apologizing in advance if I've forgotten someone. I promise I'll get you the next time.

To my most excellent agent, Amy Tompkins: thank you for your unfailing positivity, for believing so much in this book and finding a place for it, and for talking me down from more than one ledge.

To my amazing editor, Karen Boss: thank you for your guidance and expertise, for caring about this story and its characters as much as I do, and for being just an all-around awesome person to work with. I'm still down to hang anytime. Many thanks to eagle-eyed Jackie Dever and Emily Quill for copyediting and proofreading skills, and to Cat Schaad, designer extraordinaire.

To Mom, my champion: thank you for always making me feel like I could do anything I wanted in life. And to Dad, the OG storyteller: thank you for your humor and for teaching me what hard work and resilience really look like.

Many thanks to the amazing students, teachers, and faculty at Lower Canada College. It's hard to imagine not achieving my dreams when I have 900-plus people cheering me on! A special shout-out to my peeps in the Bowling Alley—you are a wacky group of weirdos, and I'm honored to share space with you.

To my awesome 2015–16 grade-seven class, who let me read each chapter of this book as I was writing it and gave me invaluable feedback and encouragement: I told you if I ever got published, I would thank you in the acknowledgments section, and even though you're all grown up now, a promise is a promise. So many thanks to Emma Bellerive, Kenza Bole, Manu Boucher, Sofia Fata, Kirsten Hardiman, Sebastian Jiminez, Justin Lewin, Sam Macri, William McGibbon, George Potter, Sebastian Reinhardt, Max Saulnier, Tiffany Spector, Zak Starke, Jeremy Steinberg, Emma Velan, and Harry Wiltzer.

To the hockey folks: many thanks to Kirk Llano for patiently sharing his encyclopaedic knowledge of the ins and outs of leagues, levels, and rules with me. And to Christina Papageorgakopoulos, Jack Rubin, Gianni Rossi, Ted Shaw, and Adam Starr for letting me ask them a million questions, even if it sometimes meant pulling them out of math class. (Sorry, Jack.) And to Jeff Sykes for giving me words for the action, as well as for explaining to me in vivid detail what it feels like to get kicked in the nuts.

To Mason Albert, Ethan Beaudet, Ethan Brinberg, Nicholas Deichmann, Eric Flinker, Kyle Folkerson, Ethan Gendron, and David Rosenbloom, who shared their list of their least "manly" activities with me. I basically transcribed the entire conversation word for word, and it is one of my favorite scenes in the book. Many thanks.

To the smart and beautiful Maria Makarov, who told me she loved this book before she'd even read a word of it.

I give so many thanks to all my early readers—François-Xavier Brunet, Emma Malcolm, Stephanie Moran, Matthew Safi, P.J. Tremblay, and Kathryn Vezsenyi—for plowing through what were, at times, some pretty rough drafts. Your insights were invaluable, and your enthusiasm and support buoyed me.

To Alex Mazzella and Michele Owen, my sisters from other misters: thank you for your constant love and support. You are amazing women, and your friendship means the world to me.

To James McRae, who didn't think it was crazy at all when I said I wanted to write a book about hockey boys even though I knew nothing about the sport. "Write the book," he said, "and I'll help you with the hockey stuff." Thank you, James, for your stories and insights, your feedback (always dead on), and your constant, enthusiastic support—you are my buddy for life.

To Sylvia McNicoll, my literary fairy godmother:

I'm not sure this book would have seen the light of day if it hadn't been for your incredible generosity. You are a world-class human being and a true professional, and I'm grateful to call you a friend.

To Charlie and Sam, who make me proud every day. The best job I will ever have is being your mom. Thank you for giving me a reason to do all the things I do.

And finally to Richard, my best friend and partner in crime: this book is as much yours as it is mine. Thank you for sharing your life with me and for showing our sons every day what it means to be a good man.

The author at the Barn of Learning at the actual
Spencerville Fair, one of the oldest fairs in Canada.